from

WARIS

to

HEER

from

WARIS

to

HEER

HAROON KHALID

VINTAGE

An imprint of Penguin Random House

VINTAGE

USA | Canada | UK | Ireland | Australia
New Zealand | India | South Africa | China | Singapore

Vintage is part of the Penguin Random House group of companies
whose addresses can be found at global.penguinrandomhouse.com

Published by Penguin Random House India Pvt. Ltd
4th Floor, Capital Tower 1, MG Road,
Gurugram 122 002, Haryana, India

First published in Vintage by Penguin Random House India 2024

Copyright © Haroon Khalid 2024

10 9 8 7 6 5 4 3 2 1

This project has been supported by grants from Canada Council for the
Arts and Ontario Arts Council

ISBN 9780143459101

Typeset in Bembo Std by Manipal Technologies Limited, Manipal
Printed at Replika Press Pvt. Ltd, India

www.penguin.co.in

To my nani and dadi, the personification of Punjab and its stories

Contents

Prologue

To think of Waris Shah's *Heer–Ranjha* as just a love legend is to render a great disservice to its genius. It has layers upon layers of symbolism and allusions—political, historical, spiritual and philosophical. Its hundred-odd pages are a repository of a thousand years of Punjabi literary tradition, its folk legends, religiosity, geography and its people and their sensibilities.

Written at a time when seismic changes were taking place in the political landscape of Punjab—the disintegration of the Mughal empire, the invasions of Ahmad Shah Abdali and the rise of the Sikh *misls*—the work is an eyewitness account of these major shifts. Through the *qissa* of Heer–Ranjha, Waris Shah introduces us to eighteenth-century Punjab, caught in the whirlwind of these storms.

Translated as 'story', qissa derives its origin from Arabic literature where it was used to refer to religious stories and to the biographies of prophets and spiritual figures. By the time the genre entered Punjab with the arrival of the Muslims, it had come to mean love stories. However, these love legends continued to be imbued with religious symbolism, discourse and messages, and played an important role in the vernacularization of Islam and religion in general, beyond the confines of any one religious tradition. At a time when not many people could speak Persian, Arabic or Sanskrit, and even fewer could read the Quran or the Gita, these love legends, composed in the vernacular language, and meant to be recited and performed, as opposed to being read, played an important role in the dissemination of religious messaging, creating a hybrid religiosity, a mix and mash of Islam, Hinduism, Sikhism and folk traditions. This 'hybridity' is beautifully captured in Waris Shah's *Heer–Ranjha*, reflecting the syncretic religious sensibility of pre-colonial Punjab.

In order to truly appreciate the qissa of *Heer–Ranjha,* one has to first understand the literary tradition that it derives from, a tradition that has gradually been replaced by the modern novel. A qissa is distinct from a novel in many ways. To begin with, in novels there is an emphasis on telling an original story. Waris Shah, or other qissa writers of pre-colonial Punjab were not concerned about originality. They were part of a tradition that retold stories, imbuing the characters and the story with new symbols. Thus, by the time Waris Shah was writing *Heer–Ranjha,* its story and the characters were already well known. Waris knew that and it shaped the way the qissa was written. Waris Shah's *Heer–Ranjha* assumed that the audience was aware of the characters, the plot and the symbolism. Once this assumption was made, the qissa became free from the constraints of linearity of time, a central feature of the novel. In a qissa, the characters are not bound by time and history. They are aware of their past reincarnations and know what role they play in its most recent interpretation. Furthermore, the qissa did not maintain strict boundaries between the story and the storyteller. Waris Shah's *Heer–Ranjha* is an intimate story, carrying clues about Waris's own life, of his home, his exile, spiritual and educational training, and his views—on history, politics, caste, religion, rituals, family, friends and, most importantly, gender. Gender relations and gender violence form the central axis upon which the entire world of this qissa revolves. What prompted a man from a privileged background to think about gender relations and violence? Where did he develop this sensitivity? Hints are scattered throughout the text.

The story of *Heer–Ranjha* is also the story of Waris Shah.

An important feature of qissa writing was that it was meant to be read, recited and to be heard. In a precolonial, pre-modern world, poetry was the only medium through which 'illiterate' masses engaged with religious and other intellectual discourse. Waris Shah's *Heer–Ranjha* is part of that world. Thus, even though Waris Shah put down the story on paper, he was aware of the fact that the qissa would be heard as opposed to being read. He wrote keeping that in mind, giving an orality to the words that resonated when recited and heard.

In this novel, I want to pay homage to this complex tradition of qissa writing. What happens when a book is written assuming that the readers already know the story and are aware of its past renditions? Can the boundary between the author and the story be blurred? How will the characters of a story speak when they are self-conscious, know that they are being written, and are aware of all of their past reincarnations? Can a novel make political and social commentary without that being the main focus of the story? And finally, how is writing impacted when the author writes a novel not to be read but to be heard? Periods, commas and semi-colons then acquire a new significance. The words discover their own rhythm and what emerges is a text that is located somewhere between poetry and prose.

1

The Exile

The sharp spear pierced through the thick fold of skin on Bhai Mani Singh's back. There was hardly any blood. There wasn't much to draw. Bhai Mani could barely manage to keep his eyes open. His arms tied in front, his long untrimmed hair in a bun on the top of his head, he dragged his heavy feet. His slouching shoulders carried the burden of his age.

Had he been royalty of any sort, worldly or spiritual, the date of his birth would have been meticulously recorded. His birthday would have been celebrated every year; offerings would have been presented to him, some of which he would have distributed to the needy. Hundreds would have gathered to seek the blessing of his holy presence. But none of that happened. His birthday came and went every year, unnoticed and unacknowledged. He had been told by his father that he was born the same year that Guru Har Rai became the Guru and because that had been an important year, Bhai Mani, if he wished to, could use that year to count back his age.

(His death in 1738, however, would be a different matter. That year would become a marker for history, a reference for other, less important, events.)

Bhai Mani was of an age when making any calculations about age seemed futile. An age when his body was more dead than alive. It was an age that weighed on his eyes, keeping them shut, locked, because in his lifetime they had seen far more than they should have. They had bid farewell to Guru Tegh Bahadur when he left for Delhi where he was executed. Before the Guru departed, they had beheld the Guru who had instructed Bhai Mani to look after his son—Gobind Rai, the future Guru—in his absence. They had protected the new Guru's wife, Mata Sundri, witnessed the death of the Guru's sons, the killing of the Guru himself and then the killing of his most devoted follower, Banda Singh Bahadur. His eyes had witnessed the death of five of his own sons, sacrificed in the service of the Guru. They were firmly shut now for they did not want to see the death of his remaining sons, who were marching alongside him, firmly shut until he felt the prick of the spear on his back.

Through partially open eyes, he discerned a hazy sight of red sandstone, a subdued, tamed red amidst the dull green and sandy brown. He managed to open his eyes slightly and was able to make out one of the minarets of the Badshahi Masjid in front of him. Behind the minaret, the white bulbous dome of the mosque burnt his eyes and he shut them once again. When he managed to open his eyes a second time, he could see the red stone melting in the heat of the Punjabi summer. It appeared, to Bhai Mani, like blood dripping down the structure. Closing his eyes once again, he began shaking his head and crying loudly.

'It must have been here, somewhere here that Guru Arjun was tortured,' cried Bhai Mani. 'Oh, my Guru! Oh, my Guru!'

'Be quiet and march ahead,' said the guard behind him, impassively, giving his prisoner a slight nudge with his hand.

'Burning oil was poured over your head and you didn't even flinch. Oh, my Guru! Oh, my Guru!'

'You came back to the city of your ancestors. To the Lahore of Guru Ram Das, your father, where he was born, where he had played as a child. And this is how the city repaid you.'

The guard behind him, noticing that Bhai Mani would fall if he continued, walked up to him and held him by the hand to steady his frail body. He was indifferent to Bhai Mani's laments and allowed him to continue crying, his voice muffled by the thump of the marching feet of a hundred-odd soldiers, and a handful of prisoners, in this procession.

'Oh, look at these mighty structures they have constructed with our blood. How many more sacrifices will they demand?' bemoaned Bhai Mani. The procession was marching next to the wall of the Lahore fort, a massive wall decorated with the most elaborate frescoes depicting the royal splendour of kings and queens, mounted on their elephants, hunting exotic animals. Standing on the top of this wall, his shadow lurking behind the latticed window, was Zakariya Khan, the governor of Lahore.

It was on his orders that Bhai Mani Singh, along with his surviving sons, was being marched into the city. He had been planning this execution for a long time. Bhai Mani Singh had established himself at Harmandir Sahib, Amritsar, since some time. Once he had been a warrior, standing shoulder to shoulder with Guru Gobind Singh; now he devoted his life to scholarly and religious pursuits. In Amritsar, Bhai Mani's days were spent engaging with Sikh devotees, explaining the Granth Sahib to them, preaching the message of the Guru.

Since the death of Banda Singh Bahadur, several smaller Sikh political misls had sprung up and all of them sought Bhai Mani's endorsement since he was the most prominent Sikh figure alive. However, he had resisted. He understood that the Sikhs would never be able to face the might of the Mughal army if they remained divided. He wanted a united front, much like it was under Guru Gobind Singh and Banda Singh Bahadur. That is what he said to all the competing Sikh warlords who came to him for support. Given Bhai Mani's stature in the community, as the living disciple of Guru Gobind Singh and the three Gurus before him, Zakariya Khan was not wrong in assuming that he might be able to bring these different political groups together. Keeping him alive any longer might prove costly.

'Send in our informants and make sure they rile up the crowd,' Zakariya Khan ordered his *munshi* who was standing behind him, before turning around and walking off.

For decades now, since the time of Zakariya Khan's father, who had been the Mughal-appointed governor before him, the Sikhs had been barred from entering or living in Lahore, the city where the Gurus had once preached. Lahore had been where Guru Ram Das, Guru Arjun and Guru Hargobind had once thrived. It was the city where Guru Arjun and the Muslim Sufi saint, Mian Mir, had prayed together. The city where the songs of Guru Nanak had been sung by Sufi dervishes and where Hindus and Muslims had come together to seek his blessings.

Now it was a city where it had become a crime to remember this past, a city where it had become illegal to grow one's hair and keep an untrimmed beard for even these symbols of Sikhism were deemed blasphemous. It was a city where, despite all the obvious indications and signs, it had become necessary to pretend that Sikhs and Sikhism did not exist.

But these signs and symbols continued to spring up, always accompanied by screams and painful sights. For long, residents had learned to ignore them. Decapitated heads, with long hair and long beards, stuck on the top of poles, no longer warranted attention. Traders and customers continued haggling over the prices of produce, even as the thwack of axes cutting through human flesh and bone drifted in from a neighbouring building.

It was a city where all distinctions between prison, torture cell, market, home and sacred spaces had been obliterated. Arms, legs and other chopped up body parts were dumped into any open space and the residents of the city had learned to think of them as nothing but rotting animal carcasses. Dogs, cats and crows feasted on these parts, while people nonchalantly estimated the freshness of the vegetables they wanted to buy.

Zakariya Khan ruled the city with an iron fist. While he ruled in the name of the Mughal authority, that distinction was more symbolic than real. The age-old connection between Lahore and Delhi had been severed for a while now. Lahore was no longer the provincial subservient to the regal capital. It was, in the beginning of the eighteenth century, truly coming of age, discovering its independence, its tyranny. A series of enfeebled Mughal monarchs had lost control of the empire and their governors had begun exercising their autonomy. Revenues generated from Punjab that once flowed through Lahore to Delhi were now held back in Lahore. The governor of Lahore was in fact the king of Lahore.

But even as the governor's chokehold over Lahore strengthened, the rest of Punjab began slipping away from his grasp. No longer supported by Mughal reinforcements from Delhi, Lahore began losing control over the surrounding areas. There was rebellion all around—Sikh guerilla groups, fighting for their survival, supported by other marginalized groups and communities, Muslims and Hindus alike. The circle of the governor's sway, of Lahore's control, was, in fact, getting smaller.

The more Punjab slipped away from him, the stronger he clutched Lahore and the surrounding areas. Lahore compensated for the rest of the province. Public executions of captured Sikh leaders and other rebels had become the norm. Through these executions and the display of the bodies, it had become easy to pretend that the governor was in complete control. It had become easy to believe that despotism meant authority, that Lahore meant Punjab. For Zakariya Khan himself, it had become easier to live in his own myths.

Having given his orders, he walked off towards his inner chambers, looking to rest for a little while before he heard back from his informants about the execution, the response of Bhai Mani Singh and the people of Lahore. Lying on his bed, his eyes tightly shut, he was secure in his conviction that his writ still ran large, that Punjab had been salvaged.

Bhai Mani was quiet now, his body exhausted after having been dragged around by the guards. Momentarily, he would open his eyes and catch a sight of the city, of its glorious past exemplified by its Mughal-era monuments. He would mutter a silent prayer in memory of the Sikh martyrs and the hundreds of innocent devotees who had chosen to die rather than abandon the way of the Gurus.

As the procession entered the walled city, a group of people slowly gathered around them. Suddenly, a cabbage was flung at Bhai Mani's face. The guards made no effort to find out where it had come from. It didn't hit him with much force but still, he was taken aback. His eyes sprang wide upon, startled by the surroundings and the crowds around him. 'Kafir! Kafir!' came the blood-curdling shouts from the crowd. Several faces merged into one, and one loud voice came through—'Kafir!'

Strangely, a smile arose on Bhai Mani's face. This wasn't a battle he was going to lose. The mantle of age flew off his shoulders and the fetters of weariness on his feet vanished. He renewed his pace, straightened his back and walked with determination, as if he were embracing the title of Kafir, as if he were eager to arrive at his destination, as if he couldn't wait to meet the divine. Surprised, the guards holding his arms let go of him.

A hushed silence overtook the crowd. The cries of 'Kafir' had faded away, until they had completely disappeared. Soon the silence was overtaken by whispers. 'Guru Arjun didn't cry out in pain when burning oil was poured on his head in this heat,' someone whispered. 'May Allah curse Jahangir and his progeny for the rest of eternity,' flew another whisper. 'Look at his age. What need is there to do this to him?' 'This is unacceptable.' 'If Mian Mir were alive today, what would he say?' Among the whispers were fragments of prayers, Muslim and Hindu, not Sikh, for they were always uttered silently; even the whispers of Sikh prayers were unacceptable.

Standing in the crowd, seventeen-year-old Waris whispered a silent prayer. 'May his pain be eased,' he said. He observed the old body of Bhai Mani Singh, with its wrinkles, the tanned skin and the bruises and clots of blood patterned all over. 'What kind of justice is this?' he thought to himself. Waris could not look away from Bhai Mani as he walked proudly, looking at the crowd, smiling, as if he were a royal returning to his capital.

Waris had just arrived from his village, Jandiala, about sixty kilometres from Lahore, to the big city, when he noticed the crowd, all seemingly headed in the same direction. Ever since he had been a young boy, Waris had dreamed of being a part of the magnificent universe of Lahore, where Sufi poets sang and danced on the streets, where every day was a celebration. The city of scholars, of scribes, of publishers and readers, of madrasahs, *dharmsalas* and royal patronage, where every night poets gathered, wine flowed and the young eyes of lovers inspired the impromptu composition of verses.

Just a few moments ago, his first sight of Lahore had washed away all his tiredness, the difficulties of the journey, the fear and paranoia he had felt at the sight of every stranger and the sleepless nights he had spent at the community caravanserai, hugging his *potli*, his only possession, amidst the snores of strangers, waiting only to be united with Lahore as a lover with his beloved.

Just a little while ago, he had caught his first glimpse of the tall minarets and the white dome of the Badshahi Masjid, which had reaffirmed his faith in the divine. He wondered what it would be like to offer namaz at this mosque, standing behind the emperor, all devotees following the same ritual, their uniformity of action removing all distinctions between the ruler and the ruled.

Next to the mosque, he glimpsed the tall walls of the Lahore Fort and its latticed windows behind which lay the beautiful world of the harem. This was a world forever hidden, a world he would never see. He imagined a beautiful maiden, nay, a group of them, looking in his direction as he made his way in the city. He imagined them talking about him and suddenly felt self-conscious. He felt his dried lips, his sunburned skin. He wanted these women to look away. He wanted them to stop looking at him.

The city was consumed by itself. No one gave him a second look. He wondered how many more travellers had come to Lahore that same day in search of a new life. He wondered how many of these people on the streets, who now looked so integral to its landscape, were newcomers like him.

Walking through Taxali Gate, named after the royal mint, he noticed the tall security towers at the gate, where two royal guards sat with their bows and arrows. He looked at the double- and triple-storey houses, with women at the balconies bending to catch a glimpse of the streets below. They looked back at him, their piercing stares causing his heart to sink. Could he belong to this city? Could Waris of Jandiala become Waris of Lahore?

'It's happening, it's happening.' The words reverberated through the crowd. One by one, the shops began to shut down as the aimless crowd started moving with purpose in the same direction. The women disappeared from the balconies and soon came down to the streets. Young men helped their older parents, while children ran around. Waris decided to follow the crowd. This was Lahore where there were more festivals and celebrations than days in the calendar or so he had heard. Perhaps the crowd was heading towards one such celebration. What better way could there be to acquaint himself with the city, to see the city in all its splendour? This was almost a celebration for him, a party welcoming him to the greatest city in the world.

He did not know that he was heading towards the public space where Bhai Mani Singh's execution was to take place. Sadly, this was to be his first impression of Lahore, a city whose reputation had been unrivalled in the young man's eyes up to this point. The city had been at the centre of every story or tale that he had heard.

As soon as the first finger of Bhai Mani was chopped off, Waris tore away from the crowd, pushing his way through the sea of people around him. His palm was on his mouth, fighting hard to hold inside the vomit that was forcing its way out. He found an open sewage drain in the corner of the street and emptied his insides into it. There was a line of people standing next to him, doing the same. Children who had been excited to see the spectacle just a few minutes ago were now howling in fear. Waris could hear the chopping sound coming from the centre and the sighs, the cries and screams of the crowd that arose with each chop. The only scream that he did not hear was that of Bhai Mani.

Wiping his mouth with his sleeve, Waris headed back towards the direction from which he had entered the city, going against the crowd that continued to flock towards the public execution. He took a deep breath as soon as he stepped outside Taxali Gate, as if the city's air had been polluted by the sight he had seen and now, outside, he could finally breathe freely. He sat on the ground, shaking, hugging his knees for comfort. He felt as if he hadn't just witnessed an execution but had participated in it.

They were all participants in it. Every single resident of the city. They would soon return to their homes, pick up the chores they had abandoned in their excitement. That thought gnawed at him. He had to leave this city, leave behind the execution, leave behind the culpability of all its residents, leave behind his guilt.

He had just arrived. But now he wanted to leave.

How do you describe the perfection of this country? A country whose perfection is beyond the limitations imposed by words. Do you use symbolism from the Quran, Gita or the Granth Sahib? Do you use poetry or do you use references from legends? How do you describe the beauty of the land of eternal beauty? A land of love, ruled by gallant youth, a land where each man is more beautiful than the other, where gold earrings dangle from ears, rings decorate fingers, chests are as broad as the banks of the Indus and locks of hair sway in the monsoon wind. Oh, how a hundred hearts sink as those eyelashes flutter! A land where colourful silk kurtas and lungis rule the day and music flows at night.

How do you describe the beauty of the women of this land? The beauty of their perfectly shaped upright breasts, their slim waists like the valleys of Kashmir. How do you describe the beauty of those lips, luscious red lips, bitten by lovers in the night, recalling these stories in the day as they spin yarn? How do you describe the smoothness of their skin, so perfect that it gets soiled by a mere glance, or the beauty of a single black mole on the face, a mole that makes a crazed lover, a Majnun, out of every soul? Do you compare these beauties to the *apsaras* in the court of Indra or to the *houris* in *Jannah*?

How do you describe the beauty of this land, where the shade of each tree is as cool as it can be, a land with every fruit and flower known to humans, fruits that are always ripe to be plucked, flowers whose smells never fade away? How do you describe the beauty of the birds that visit the gardens of this land, birds that bring with them tales from other lands as they congregate close to the river?

And then there is the river, the most beautiful river, a river whose soul is love, a river which is the lover and the beloved, the devotee and the divine. A river which is the poetry of Gorakhnath, Fareed Shakarganj and Guru Nanak, the heart of Punjab, the body of Sohni, the tear of Sahiban. It is the lament of Sassi, the face of Shirin, the necklace of Laila. It is the devotion of Zulekha, the piety of Sita, the sensuality of Radha. The Chenab is the laughter of Heer.

Next to the Chenab is Takht Hazara. Oh, how do you describe the beauty of Takht Hazara, my home, the land of justice, righteousness and piety? It is the centre of the world, the town that gave birth to love, a town about which Bulleh Shah once said, 'Pilgrims go to Makkah, my Kaaba is in Takht Hazara.' The town ruled by my father, Mauja. Could one ask for a chief more just than him? Stories of his wisdom and justice were even recalled in the court of Emperor Akbar. Using standards set by him, the Mughal kings measured the quality of their judgments. If there is heaven on this earth, then it is Takht Hazara and Mauja is its guardian.

But just as humanity lost paradise to be discarded to a vengeful earth; just as the peace of the tribe of Bharata was lost in the Mahabharata War; just as Prophet Yousuf was thrown into jail; just as Ravana got his Lanka burned; just as Raja Bhoj, the wise Raja Bhoj of Ujjain, known for his military and political strength, lost his respect when he became a horse for his wife at his own court, while his courtiers laughed silently, this heaven on earth at Takht Hazara was also lost, due to the manoeuvrings of these evil partners of mankind, my sisters-in-law, *bhabhis*, who sowed seeds of distrust between us brothers, brothers who once loved each other more than life itself.

It all started when my beloved father passed on to the other world. He had a total of eight sons and two daughters, of whom I, Dhido Ranjha, am the youngest. It has never been a secret that just as Prophet Yaqub loved his son Yousuf the most, so did my father love me the most out of all his children.

Like Yousuf, I too am the most beautiful of all my beautiful siblings. No woman can resist my charm, the innocence of my face, the curves of my lips, the locks of my hair. Even the *apsaras* of the court of Indra descend upon this world and dance and sway, along with the women of my village, to the tunes of my flute. I am Krishna and they are my *gopis*. If Takht Hazara is the most perfect village in this world, the centre of the universe, then it is I, Dhido, who is the most perfect being in this village, the centre of Takht Hazara.

I am Takht Hazara and Takht Hazara is me.

It is in me that West meets East; the Semitic meets the pagan; the believer meets the infidel; Yousuf meets Krishna; monotheism meets monism; the past meets the present and the poet meets the story. I am the sacred and the profane, the masculine and the feminine, the tyrant and the humble. I am Ranjha, but I am also all the lovers that have ever lived. I am Majnun, Farhad, Mirza and Punnun. I am a specific character of a particular qissa, story, legend, the protagonist of *Heer–Ranjha*, but I am also a symbol, a metaphor, of eternal truth, the symbol of divinity in Sufi poetry. It is in me that Punjab is personified, through me that Punjab can be seen, touched and felt.

Ranjha is Punjab and Punjab is Ranjha.

As a symbol of eternity and divinity, I have no origin; but I was conceived centuries ago by some obscure poet, perhaps by a yogi or *jogi* of Punjab, perhaps during the time of that ancient Punjabi poet Gorakhnath, my origins lost in the obscurity of what you might refer to as folk poetry. I donned an oral existence for centuries before I was immortalized on paper by Damodar of Jhang, the land of my lover, my beloved, Heer, who claimed to have seen Heer and me. We were, he said, real people, contemporaries of Emperor Akbar, the only Mughal ruler worth mentioning. People point towards our mausoleum, the shrine of lovers at Jhang, where we, as true lovers, are buried in the same grave, to point out the veracity of our existence.

I can only tell you what people say.

I was then given new avatars. I am Vishnu appearing in multiple forms in this world to remind people of love. All these poets blew life into me—Charagh Awan, Ahmad Gujjar and Muqbal.

Here I am now—at the mercy of Waris, or perhaps, should we say, the fictional character of Waris. Each one of these poets created and recreated me, moulded me in their own fashion, to the extent that I ceased to be Dhido Ranjha but became Muqbal or Waris.

Ranjha is Waris and Waris is Ranjha.

'Calling out the name of my beloved,
I myself have become Ranjha,
Call me Ranjha now,
As I am no longer Heer.'

These are the words of Shah Hussain, the Sufi poet from Lahore, who fell in love with a Hindu boy, Madho. Like Majnun, he roamed around the streets of Lahore, in a red *chola*, singing his songs, expressing his love for Madho. In his poetry, in his words, Madho became Ranjha and Ranjha became divine. He took a character from the qissa of *Heer–Ranjha* and made it a symbol, a metaphor. That was his contribution to me. In the mould of Mirabai's Krishna, I came into existence.

By the time Waris entered my realm, I was both a character and a metaphor, a devotee and the divine. I was the duality of Shiva. I was the ultimate Sufi symbol, the physical representation of monism, where the believer is divine, and the divine a believer. I was the Punjabi Sufi representation of Mansur al-Hajjaj's statement, 'I am the Absolute Truth.' Hajjaj, the ninth-century Persian mystic, had been executed for uttering these words. How can all distinctions between the believer and the divine cease to exist, he was questioned.

In the hands of Waris, I am human and divine, a character and a metaphor. I am part of this world and the one beyond. In his writing, I am Damodar's Ranjha as well as Shah Hussain's Madho. Waris brought the two of us together, unlike anyone before him, and here I am now, living somewhere between these two worlds, an occupant of the physical and the metaphysical, and yet belonging to neither of them. Like Waris the wanderer, exiled from his home, escaping the violence that chased after him, I too am displaced.

Our journeys, our destinies, are intertwined. Like Waris, I too was displaced over land and property. Just as in the time of Waris, when communities that had lived together for centuries turned against each other, so did my brothers, with whom I had spent my lifetime.

My bhabhis taunted me for being by myself, for playing the flute all day, for not helping them in the fields. Just as the brothers of Prophet Yousuf had succumbed to their jealousies, so did mine. With the help of the *qazi* of the village, the bane of our existence, they deprived me of my rightful share of the property and gave me a piece of land least suitable for agriculture. The entire village witnessed it and expressed words of support but no one came to my rescue. They were all culprits. I was like Prophet Yousuf, stuck in a well, where his brothers had thrown him. I was Puran Bhagat when he was left to die by his father on the false accusation of Rani Luna, his young stepmother.

Day and night, I worked on my land, trying to grow a garden where not even a cactus could stay alive. My fingers, which only knew how to pinch the waists of women or plug the holes of my flute, now ploughed through this land, blistering and bruising all the while. It was in this state that my accursed bhabhi, Sahiba, came to visit me with food. 'Oh, deceiver of mankind, the reason for our downfall, why have you done this to me? Don't you have any mercy on me? Why have you turned our little piece of heaven into hell?' I asked her.

Raging and fuming, she replied that it was not she who had destroyed our house, but rather my stubbornness. She called me a bum, a lazy ass, an arrogant prick, who could not identify my hide from my front. 'If you are so worthy,' she asked, 'why don't you go and marry the most beautiful girl in the world, a girl so beautiful that even the angels sing songs in her praise, a girl so beautiful that even the day and night pay testimony to her beauty, a girl so beautiful that even the poetry of Sheikh Fareed and Maulana Rumi cannot capture its essence? Why don't you go and marry Heer Sial of Jhang?'

'I will scale the walls of Jhang and steal the heart of Heer, just as Raja Rasalu conquered the unconquerable fort of Rani

Kokilan. Like that exiled king of Sialkot, I too will live the life of a wanderer till I fulfil this promise. I will marry Heer and bring her to Takht Hazara. Like a rani, she will rule over all of you and like maids, you will cater to all her needs,' I retorted unthinkingly.

Saying this, I decided to leave my sanctuary, my Takht Hazara, my home, my paradise. Where once prosperity had resided, now tyranny ruled. A land which was once ruled by swans was now under the mercy of crows. Just as Punjab lost its peace and Waris lost Jandiala, I lost Takht Hazara.

With a potli on my shoulder and a stick in my hand, I left my village. My brothers, realizing the folly of their actions, pleaded and begged. They fell at my feet, kissed my head and touched my chin. They begged in the name of our father, in the name of our childhood bond, in the name of the bountiful river of Chenab. They promised to return my land to me. They promised to work on it with their own hands, while my bhabhis swore they would tolerate all my taunts with patience. Nothing worked. My home was lost, its stability torn. Brothers had turned enemies.

Ranjha of Takht Hazara had become Ranjha, the wanderer.

A thick blanket of mist clung loosely to the ground. Across the horizon, light was beginning to free itself from its shackles. Like an army of invaders, it had begun to scale the walls of the night. The first pair of eyes to take stock of the situation were those of a lone soldier. The plains of Punjab were ready to surrender. In a short while, the land would be swept away, destroying everything that lay in its path.

Soon this union of the mist and the ground would come to an end. All night long, away from the prying eyes of society, they had lain in each other's embrace, making silent love. What do armies care about lovers? The mist would be crucified on the cross of the daylight, while its beloved, the ground, would be trampled underfoot.

It's not as if the lovers had not been warned. Smelling the horses of the invading forces, roosters had raised an alarm much before the head of the first soldier had appeared from behind the wall of the night. A little later had come the lamenting of the birds. Stray dogs too had woken from slumber and begun barking, even as buffaloes wagged their tails. The signs were everywhere, but such was the ecstatic pleasure of lovemaking, of arms in tight embrace, of breaths in unison, of burning chests, of the aroma of bodies, the sweet nectar of sweat, that the lovers thought they would remain in this state forever. How can the passion of youth ever be rescued from the pitfall of arrogance, the illusion of permanency, from the disdain of fear?

Deep in the darkness, on the edge of the horizon, he saw the silhouette of his mother. It was a beautiful face, wrapped in a white *chaddar*, dark complexion with big eyes. She was tall and slim, standing straight and staring back at him. Her look wrapped itself around his little body, protecting it from the cold night. He shifted his weight to get more comfortable, to adjust himself in her tight embrace. Her hand ran through his hair as she whispered his name, 'Waris.'

'Waris.'

She held his face with both of her hands and planted a kiss on his cheek.

'Waris *puttar*. Waris.'

She ran her hand through his hair and gave him another kiss. Waris opened his eyes and saw the face of his father leaning on his charpoy. Gulsher Shah smiled at his son and continued running his fingers through his hair. Despite the cold, his sleeves had been folded up to his elbow, while the hair on his arms was still wet. A little drop of water clung precariously to the edge of his beard, unsure whether to fall or keep swaying.

'Wake up, puttar,' said Gulsher. 'It's time for *fajr*. I have warmed water for you and placed it next to the *chulha*. Please do your *wuzu* and join me at the mosque. Your brothers have already left.'

Standing up, Gulsher rolled down his sleeves. He grabbed his woollen shawl hanging on a nail on the wall and a white strip of cloth from the table. As soon as he opened the door, a cold breeze quickly invaded the warm room. 'Don't be late for the *jamaat*,' he said, as he stepped over the threshold, wrapping the shawl around his chest, and tying the white strip of cloth around his head, forming his *pagri*. He closed the door as he stepped out.

Waris shut his eyes again in search of his mother. He focused, trying hard to recall her face, which was so vivid only a few moments ago. It was now just an abstraction, a figure in white. He tried chasing after the figure, but it was quickly fading away. It was gone now. Just an empty space, a void.

He turned around to see his father standing behind him. It was a clear image, the same man he had seen a few seconds ago, a man of average height, in his mid-twenties, wearing a white kurta and a lungi, with a white pagri on his head, and a brown shawl around his shoulder. He held a small *tasbih* in his hand which he was reciting, whispering silently one of the ninety-nine names of God, each name a mystery, a trait, a characteristic, possessed by God in an infinite amount.

'Al-Hakeem,' he mouthed.

'Truth exists in this world because it is one of the names, characteristics of Allah. That which is not a characteristic of God doesn't exist. So, if this was not one of the names of Allah, then Truth would not have existed. God is also Al-Kareem, the generous, so He bestows His creations with some of these traits.

We humans are given a tiny fraction of a trait that God possesses an infinite amount of. Do you know what characteristic God has shared with you, Waris?' said Gulsher, waiting for a few seconds for Waris to respond. When Waris didn't reply, Gulsher said, 'Al-Hakeem, the wise. You are the wisest of my sons.'

Gulsher Shah had had this conversation with Waris a few days earlier, after Waris had returned from his Quran class from the madrasah. As part of their lesson, the students had to learn the ninety-nine names of Allah. One of the sharpest children in the class, Waris was the first pupil to learn and recite the names to the Qari. He had rushed home while his older brothers were still struggling.

'Why does Allah have so many names? Why does he need ninety-nine of them?' he had questioned his father.

Upon hearing Gulsher's explanation, the ten-year-old Waris had replied, 'In that case, God shares the trait of Al-Wadood, the loving one, with you.'

Waris and his brothers stood in one line, a jamaat behind their father. The village mosque was partially full, with fajr attracting the least number of devotees. Perhaps it was due to the partial emptiness of the mosque that Waris enjoyed offering fajr the most; he loved the echo of the *maulvi*'s voice, reciting the prayer in a melodic tone within the empty courtyard to the accompaniment of the cock-a-doodle-doo of the village rooster.

From further ahead, came the sounds of the tabla accompanying the kirtan being sung in the village gurdwara. As Waris continued reciting the namaz, his young mind wandered off to the gurdwara. What food would they be cooking at the langar today? He could hear his stomach growl.

His thoughts were distracted by the song of the village mendicant, an old man who refused to reveal his name to anyone, nor where he came from, nor his religion. All Waris knew about him was that he had been living in Jandiala since before Waris's birth but that he didn't hail from this village. The man used to wear green clothes patched with scraps of cloth of different colours. He wore several bangles and thick earrings made out of stone. There were two huge holes in his ears caused by the weight of the earrings. Waris hated the sight of his disfigured ears. Everyone in the village called him *kankatta jogi.*

Every morning, the mendicant, who slept under the banyan tree, unafraid of the djinns and *churails* that lived in its branches, woke up to the cries of the rooster and competed with it with his songs. He began singing before the call for prayers came from the mosque, or the kirtan began at the gurdwara, or the *bhajan* at the temple, all located around the banyan tree in the centre of the village. Carrying his begging bowl, he walked around the village, singing songs of loss, like Radha expressing her desire for Krishna or Heer expressing her fidelity to Ranjha.

Down on the ground, with his head and nose on the floor, facing the *mihrab* in a state of *sajda,* Waris tried hard to hear the song the mendicant was singing. He wanted to know with which poet the mendicant had begun the day. Was he singing in the name of Heer for her Ranjha, in the words of Shah Hussain and Bulleh Shah, or was he singing as Radha in the words of Mirabai? Perhaps he had become Kabir today expressing his love for Ram, or maybe he was humming the words of Sheikh Fareed, expressing a wife's longing for her husband, as a devotee longed for the divine.

Waris did this every day, listening carefully to the song the mendicant sang as he offered his fajr prayer. He would then sing the song all day. His mind humming it as he sat at the madrasah to learn the Quran, or as he learned Sanskrit from the pandit in the afternoon. He was one of a few Muslim children to whom the pandit had agreed to impart this ancient knowledge, at the insistence of Waris's father. There were a few of Gulsher's friends who had objected to his decision to teach Waris Sanskrit, but Gulsher was adamant. He realized that the times were changing and his son would be in a much better situation to adapt to the changing political landscape if he knew Sanskrit, along with Arabic and Persian.

He would hum the song when he was at the gurdwara eating langar, without the knowledge of his father or the teacher at the madrasah, accompanied by a few friends, as the kirtan played on in the background, or when he sometimes visited his father's shop and learned Unani medicine, and took lessons in Persian.

He would only stop humming in the night, when his father would sit on his charpoy and tell all the children tales of Guru Nanak's travels, as he went to Benares and Makkah, embarrassing fake religious leaders, while preaching through his songs. Waris would imagine Guru Nanak as the village mendicant. Gulsher would tell the children of the exploits of Raja Rasalu, as he abandoned his throne and journeyed from one kingdom to another, living a life of permanent exile, rescuing princesses and fighting demons. Sometimes he would recall the tales of Ibn-e-Batuta, the Moroccan scholar, who travelled all over the Muslim world trying to see how Islam was practised in different parts of the world.

On other occasions, he would tell the children about Prince Siddharth, who abandoned his kingdom and began travelling in search of Truth. He would tell the children how the search for Truth had made him the Buddha. Then there were stories of Prophet Khizr, the mysterious Prophet who could travel through space and time. He would tell them that Prophet Khizr was still alive and appeared often to help the pious and the righteous anywhere in the world. Gulsher often recalled the story of the Prophet's journey of the *mihraj*, when he travelled thousands of kilometres in the blink of an eye.

Waris's favourite story was that of Muhammad Al-Makki, his distant ancestor, a warrior, who travelled from Arabia to reach Sindh, fighting the enemies of Islam on the way, similar to how Raja Rasalu had fought demons. It was through him, Waris was told, that the descendants of the Prophet of Islam, the Syeds, made their way to Sindh and then Punjab. Sitting in the comfort of their homes in Jandiala, the father and children lived various lives, fought several demons and traversed hundreds of miles.

Sometimes Gulsher would tell the children about the Mughals, the story of a young king, Babur, who lost his kingdom in Ferghana and found it in Hindustan, stories about how an army gathered around him in his journey from Ferghana to Delhi. He would tell them about Humayun, the son, who lost his empire to an Afghan general and then fought back to get what was rightfully his. Most of the stories, however, were of Emperor Akbar, and his Navaratnas, the nine jewels, his extraordinary courtiers, each one possessing a unique skill. Out of all the jewels, Waris loved Raja Birbal the most, the wise minister who had a solution to every problem. Gulsher used to tell the children that Akbar was the greatest of the Mughal kings, loved by all, but that he was not the only great king of Hindustan. Before Akbar, there had been Vikramaditya, the model king who set a standard for all the kings after him, including Akbar.

'After Akbar, however, his children lived a luxurious life and did not care about the people,' Gulsher would often say. He would recall how Jahangir was an opium and alcohol addict who left the running of his kingdom to his wife, Nur Jahan.

He was particularly harsh towards Shahjahan, the killer of his brothers and nephews. 'The apple doesn't fall far from the tree,' he would say, when talking about Aurangzeb. 'By killing his brothers and nephews, he was following the standards set by his father.'

Despite being critical of Aurangzeb, his father and grandfather, Gulsher still believed that as long as they lived and ruled, there was stability in Hindustan and Punjab. 'They might have been brother killers, opium or alcohol addicts, but they provided stability to the land. Look at what has happened after the death of Aurangzeb. There is chaos everywhere. In Punjab, the followers of Guru Gobind Singh have wreaked havoc. They raid cities, towns and villages and deprive ordinary people like us of our hard-earned income. They take away our harvest and destroy our mosques and shrines. They did not dare raise their heads as long as Emperor Aurangzeb was alive but look at them now. To make matters worse, they don't engage in a fair fight, the righteous fight. They hide in the day and attack at night. These peasants, these Jatts, who were nobodies only a little while ago, are now trying to become our rulers. They are trying to replace the glorious Mughal empire.'

Gulsher was old enough to remember the last few years of Emperor Aurangzeb's reign. He had vague memories of the Mughal administrative structure, of the *mansabdars,* faujdar, *bakshi* and, most importantly, the *Nizam,* the governor. In theory, the administrative structure was still intact but due to the increasing number of attacks by the Sikh guerillas, they had lost their power since vast tracts of the country were now beyond Mughal control. In the past few years, the situation had worsened so much that the Mughal authorities did not even dare collect tax from Jandiala, despite it being close to Lahore. The tax was now collected by local Sikh guerilla forces. Lack of cooperation was severely dealt with; the guerilla forces were eager to inflict violence to claim legitimacy. Jandiala was still affiliated with the Mughal court in Lahore, but in reality, it was ruled by the Sikh guerillas.

For Gulsher, it was the death of Emperor Aurangzeb, the father figure, whose death had made them all orphans, that marked this transition from stability to chaos, from justice to tyranny, from heaven to hell.

Sometimes when his father had finished his stories and it was time to sleep, Waris would ask his father about the songs he had heard the mendicant sing. He would ask him the meanings of certain words or the significance of certain lines. Using lessons from the Quran, Gulsher would explain to his son the meaning of the mystic poetry. Waris loved hearing these stories and the explanations of the meaning, in his father's words, at their home, late at night when everyone had gone to sleep, and it was just him and his father. Now, in Waris's head, there was a vast repository of devotional poetry and songs that he had picked up every morning from the village mendicant.

As the congregation stood up after the sajda to perform the second *ruku* of the namaz, Waris finally figured out the song the mendicant had chosen today. It was a song he had sung several times before. It was a song by Bhagat Kabir of Benares.

'Just as a seed contains oil,
Fire's in flintstone,
Divinity lies within you,
If only you realize.'

In the state of sajda, Waris's thoughts wandered off to the conversation he had with his father about the ninety-nine names of God. 'If all of us have a tiny fraction of certain traits of God, then don't all of us have a tiny fraction of divinity within us?

Is this what Bhagat Kabir meant when he said that divinity lies within you?' he wondered, as he sat up from the sajda and then bent down again for a second time.

Perhaps it was due to the songs of the mendicant that Waris enjoyed the morning prayers.

But most of all, he loved fajr prayers because of his father. This was the only namaz of the day that they offered together. He loved the way his father woke him up every morning, kissing him, running his fingers through his hair. He loved how in the winters his father warmed water for his wuzu. He loved how his father sometimes shared his shawl with him when they returned to the house from the masjid after namaz to eat their morning meal. He loved how his father loved offering namaz in the masjid.

For young Waris, if namaz had a face and a body, it would be his father's, a beautiful face with a thin beard, spotless skin, loving eyes, a pagri on the head and a perpetual smile. Waris could not distinguish between his father and prayers, the two woven together in some of his earliest memories. He remembered climbing his father's shoulders as a child, when he was in the sajda, or observing and copying the act.

Waris was with his father every time he checked his feet, stated his intention to say the prayers and tied his hands around his waist after saying, 'Allah-u-Akbar.' His father would stand next to him in ruku, for the rest of Waris's life, long after Gulsher had gone to heaven. He could smell the skin of his father, every time he bent for sajda. His father's face appeared in front of his eyes every time he raised the index finger of his right hand to give testimony to the oneness of God. He prayed because he believed in God and wanted to follow His command, but he also prayed to remind himself of his father's face, the feel of his touch, and the softness of his kisses. As an adult, Waris never missed a prayer. He never missed an opportunity to be with his father.

Waris had never seen his mother, except in his dreams, for she had passed away when he was a baby, before his infant mind could form any concrete memory of her, but that did not mean Waris did not know love. He knew his father, Al-Wadood, the loving one.

Gulsher passed away, unexpectedly, without any prior signs of illness, when Waris was fifteen years old. The older man had spent his entire life diagnosing other people's diseases and giving them relief, but he had failed to do so for himself. He bequeathed his children his Unani medical practice and a little piece of land.

Waris, too young to remember the death of his mother, felt keenly his first experience of loss. For him, it was not just the loss of one person, but rather the loss of life as he knew it. The sights and sounds that had enchanted him, held his heart together and filled it with love were all lost. He would wake up for fajr with a heavy realization that the sound of the muezzin would echo through the mosque, its emptiness heightened by the absence of his father. His mind would no longer be swept away by the songs of the mendicant. He would no longer go to the gurdwara, the rebelliousness of the act losing its significance without the overarching figure of Gulsher. He continued his education in the madrasah but the sensation of the burning questions that the lessons should have sparked had died.

He cried a little the day his father passed away but not much after. The tears somewhere inside him, at the edge of his throat, refusing to rise or sink. Refusing to allow anything to pass, neither food nor water, nor an uninterrupted breath of air. He didn't think about his father a lot, yet grief lingered over him, its presence casting a dense shadow, weighing him down at all times, his shoulders slouching under the pressure, his eyes drooping. He never smiled. He forgot that there was a time when he smiled easily. He tried to force himself to smile sometimes to remind himself of the sensation but his body refused to comply. It seemed as if he had lost the capacity to love.

He found some comfort in his father's medical practice. The shop, the books and the medicines around him reminded him of his father's presence. He would hold the books in his hands, feel them as if he were holding the palm of his father. He would open them and read them as if his father was teaching him about new diseases and new ways of treating them, how to mix Unani medicine with Ayurveda and jogi magic with the *taveez* of Sufis. Waris learned quickly. In a different era, he would have been immensely successful, perhaps known to posterity for his knowledge of medicines. Maybe he would have written a treatise on the subject, or come up with a new theory or medicine. Perhaps he would have continued living at Jandiala, eventually recovering from the irrecoverable loss of his father's death. Had that been the case, the world would have been deprived of the literary masterpiece that Waris was destined to write. What would Punjab have been without Waris's *Heer–Ranjha*? It is through him that Punjab, as we know it, emerges. It was Punjab that gained from Waris's loss.

It was almost as if taking a cue from Gulsher Shah's death, the political situation in Punjab deteriorated. The once mighty Mughal empire had completely folded as anarchy spread all around. With no centralized state, and all taxes being received by Sikh guerilla forces, the rates were determined randomly.

This had not been the situation during the times of the Mughals when the yearly tax was determined by looking at the past average yield of the land. Now the taxes changed every year according to the whim of the person demanding the tax.

An inability to pay the taxes meant a raid on the village and confiscation of the yield. Everyone suffered due to the failure of one landholder. Waris's brothers, who had taken up the responsibility of the land bequeathed to them by their father, were finding it impossible to cope with the situation.

Things weren't much better for Waris. His medical practice depended on his ability to travel to neighbouring towns for the purchase of supplies. However, now with the disappearance of the royal highway patrol, travel was becoming increasingly expensive and difficult, particularly for traders. Even paying heavily for security did not necessarily mean that one was protected from raids. Waris had experienced one such raid on his latest trading trip when he had travelled to the city of Sheikhupura. On the way back, the caravan with which Waris was travelling was looted. In one fell swoop, Waris had lost a year's worth of supplies. His practice simply could not recover from this loss.

It was in these circumstances that Waris decided to leave Jandiala, a home that he had already lost after the death of his father. It helped that he was young and not bound by the ties of marriage, unlike his older brothers. He wasn't sure what he was going to do. Perhaps he would settle in Lahore and set up shop there. Perhaps he would join a madrasah there and pursue higher education, or maybe he would find royal patronage and become a poet.

While Waris went through this process of imagining various possibilities, the world around him was undergoing a transformation. The prospect of a new life altered the way he saw his current one. He began enjoying the songs of the mendicant, the chirping of the birds, the giggling of the children, his nieces and nephews. Memories of his father, that he had consciously buried deep in his subconscious, began coming back. They came back as the stories of Siddharth, Raja Rasalu, Prophet Yousuf, Babur, Guru Nanak, Ibn-e-Batuta and Ranjha. They came back in the form of prayer, in the sound of the azaan and in the echoes of the recitation of the Quran in an empty mosque in the morning.

His brothers, unaware of the storm brewing inside him, argued against his decision to travel. 'Have you forgotten how dangerous the roads have become? Have you forgotten what happened to you the last time you went to Sheikhupura?'

'What place is safe any more? Is our village safer than the roads outside?' Waris argued back. 'Besides, you are unsafe as long as you have something to lose. I had possessions the last time I left the safety of this village. I had a year's worth of wealth on me. What could happen to me if I travelled with nothing but the clothes on my back? Who would want to attack a mendicant like me?'

'What about the memories of our father and those of our ancestors? What about their graves? How can you abandon the land of our ancestors?' they asked.

'I am not abandoning this land or the memories of our ancestors. My father, my Jandiala, resides in my heart. He is next to me every time I bow my head down for sajda. I can smell the earth of Jandiala, feel its wind in my hair every time I close my eyes. I am not abandoning Jandiala but taking it with me. I would lose that Jandiala if I continue to stay here; its memories would fade away if I didn't leave the village.'

While Waris put up a brave front when convincing his brothers, it did not mean that anxiety did not reside in his heart. He travelled, nonetheless, battling against his fears, finding comfort in his uncertainty. He decided to travel with the love of his father and his home in his heart. He decided to travel under the protection of God. He decided to travel to learn, to experience, to love. He decided to travel to become one with Siddharth, Rasalu, Prophet Yousuf, Guru Nanak. He decided to travel as Ranjha. He decided to travel to Lahore, the greatest city in the world.

2

The Journey

The veil of slumber lifted from my eyes. I put on my clothes, a white sari and red blouse with a golden border. From my cupboard, I took out red and white bangles and a pearl necklace. I pinned up the hair on the top of my head to prevent it from falling on my face and left the rest of my long, black hair loose, allowing it to spread across my back. I dabbed some powder on my neck and pinched my cheeks for redness. I put on lipstick and a red bindi. I wore anklets and placed the tiara on the top of my head. At midnight, I left my abode with a swan as my ride.

I escaped through the tiny holes of the flute and fled into the night. With the day exhausted by the weight of expectations and responsibilities, it was now my turn to soothe these wounds, to whisper songs of love into its ears, as I caressed its hair, its head resting on my lap. It was now my turn to revive its soul, to prepare it to rise again, put on its shield and face the world.

If not for me and my consoling words, the day would not dawn. If it wasn't for me, the night would become an inescapable prison, with insurmountable walls, guarded by the demons of darkness, monsters that lurk in the hearts and souls of humans, monsters that feast on human slumber, their strength growing with every hour of the night. It is I who fight these demons, who raze the walls of this prison, who absorb chaos and churn order. It is I who keep the night from merging into the day, who prevent heroes from transforming into demons, who secure the comfort of the night from becoming a catastrophe that has no end.

I left the confines of the mosque, a beautiful mosque, a mosque that reminded me of the holiest one in the world, the mosque of the Prophet in Medina. I had seen that as well, performed several prayers there, bowing my head in acknowledgment of the divine. Here I was now, in a village without a name, a day's walk from Takht Hazara, calling on everyone to gather in this mosque.

Walking all day, under the scorching sun, without a morsel of food in his belly, my Ranjha, my Krishna, my beloved, had found the house of the divine, a house where all were welcome, a house where the divine shared its divinity with its creation. Curling up in a beautiful corner of this beautiful mosque, my Ranjha sent out his call for love, his call to prayer. As a divine being, he blew his spirit into his flute, giving birth to me. I carry within me the soul of Ranjha. It was not I who flowed through the streets of this village but the breath of Krishna.

I knocked on every door to tell the people about the presence of Ranjha, of the presence of the divine in their village. I seeped in through open spaces from under the doors and corners of the windows. I kissed someone on the neck, held the faces of others in my hands and put their ears on my chest. Both of us were now breathing in unison; our two separate hearts were beating together as if they were one.

Just a moment ago, all these souls were busy in their daily chores, treating the banality of their lives as a sacred duty. How absurd these duties looked now with my presence in their midst!

They abandoned their activities and followed me, hypnotized, as I walked through the streets, heading back to where Ranjha was summoning us all.

The entire village gathered in the courtyard of the mosque, looking at Ranjha, as he sat in a corner playing the flute with his eyes closed. Men, women and children all stood together in a line facing him. It is I who had brought all these believers together, who had reminded them of their religious obligation.

But not all those who had gathered were devotees. There were some with evil in their hearts, but piety on their faces. There were those among the crowd whom the holy book terms *munafiq*, hypocrites. People whose hearts had been sealed, who could not recognize the truth, the divine, even if it stared them in the face. Those who knew the truth within the depths of their hearts, that God resides in the heart, but refused to listen. Those who wanted to continue living the life of the infidel when they could have partaken in the blessed life of the believer. Those who fantasized about the hips of a maiden even when they stood, hands bowed, in front of the divine.

If it was up to me, I would have let them remain within the confines of their ignorance. I would never have knocked on their doors, kissed their lips and brought them to our Ranjha. But that is not my nature. Like divinity, my blessing is for everyone. It doesn't differentiate between a devotee and a hypocrite. They try to keep their hearts shut to me, turn their heads in the opposite direction when they see me, without realizing that I am everywhere. They reject me, even when they know that there is a part within their heart, tucked away deep within its recesses, that beats at my command. In the beating of that heart, that carries within it the rhythm of the eternal divine music, Om, there is no distinction between a believer and a hypocrite, a Muslim or an infidel, a woman or a man. It is in that sound that God resides, all of us constantly paying homage to His divinity with every breath. It is in that breath that I reside, and in my breath, my Ranjha.

You can imagine then the pain I feel when the hypocrite ignores the beating of his heart, when a hypocrite holds his hands on his ears to keep away that eternal sound; when a hypocrite conjures up a disgusted face at the sight of my body and then lusts for me as he adorns an expression of piety on his face. My heart tore away when I heard the sound of one such hypocrite, chastising our Ranjha.

'This is a place of worship. This is the house of God,' the qazi shouted. 'How dare you pollute it with your music? This is where we say our prayers and now you have defiled it with the sound of your flute.'

'Who are you to teach me purity and impurity?' Ranjha asked mockingly. 'You think by chanting the names of God, with a rosary in your hand and with a mark on your forehead, you can fool anyone? God is on your lips, but the devil resides in your heart. There is piety on your face but lust in your mind. No woman, child or animal is safe from your lecherousness.

'Who are you to teach me about prayers when you are not even familiar with the aleph of this ritual?' Ranjha continued, his pitch rising. 'You only recite the words but refuse to surrender. Your prayer is no different from the worship of the false idols that were shattered by Prophet Ibrahim, Moses and our beloved Prophet. You claim to be worshipping God in your prayers, but you are in fact worshipping the gods of your own ego. You claim to be bowing to God, but you know nothing about the humility it requires. How dare you teach me about prayers? Do you even know who I am? I am a lover. I am perpetually in a state of prayer. What do you think I was doing before you disturbed my prayer?'

'I know you and your kind very well,' said the qazi in disgust. 'Who do you think you are? Mansur al-Hajjaj? Have you forgotten the fate that befell that godforsaken poet who roamed the streets of Baghdad proclaiming that God resides within him and that he is, God forbid, God himself?' There was sarcasm in his tone. 'Have you forgotten how he was dealt with? His body was flayed until the blasphemy was stripped off him, and then he was beheaded. Do you want a similar fate for yourself?'

'You make light of my worship,' the qazi railed, his face red, his tone stern. 'It is my prayer that will save me from the fires of hell and bless me with the eternal happiness of paradise. On the day of judgement, it is my prayer that will help me cross Pul Sirat, the bridge of salvation, a bridge as thin and sharp as a sword, a bridge that only the believers who have offered their prayers will be able to pass while infidels like you will be cut into two and fall into the depths of hell.'

'How can I forget Mansur al-Hajjaj, my brother?' retorted Ranjha, as if al-Hajjaj was in front of his eyes. 'There will come a day when I will claim his blood money from the likes of you. How can you understand the depths of his belief, his devotion to the divine, his love for the One? You think he was mad, a blasphemer, but it is you who commit blasphemy every day and pretend that you are worshipping the One True God. Your idea of God is nothing but your image of yourself. You are so in love with your image, your idol, that you no longer realize it is not God you are worshipping but yourself. Your God gets angry when you are angry and jealous when you are jealous. Instead of borrowing divine traits and celebrating His divinity, you strip divinity of divine traits and impose on it human characteristics. It is not I or Mansur al-Hajjaj who associates another being with the One, but rather you.'

'Stop committing blasphemy in the house of God,' shouted the qazi. He was no longer composed. 'Stop fooling these innocent people with the power of your tongue. Who are you and where do you come from? Why are your treating the house of God as your own dwelling? Do you even know how you should conduct yourself here? Your lungi should be above your ankles and you should dress simply; look at those silk clothes you are wearing. You have oil in your hair and kohl in your eyes and you preach to us about religion. You seem like a thug, who has come here to seduce our women with your charms. Get up immediately and leave this holy place. Find refuge somewhere else for there is no place for you in the House of God.'

'Is this how you treat travellers in your village? Do you deny sanctuary to orphans, and to those who have been oppressed by the world?' Ranjha allowed his pause to linger in the air. 'You tell me that it is I who am treating the mosque as his home, but it is you who disrespect it every day, bringing your bad breath of onions into this holy place. Who are you to eject me from the House of God? Are you the proprietor of this property? Or a deputy assigned to God?'

'Oh, how you twist words and cast a spell with your charm!' The qazi was finding it hard to articulate his views, and was mixing his words and sentences. 'All these people can be fooled by your beautiful, innocent face and your tongue, but I know your truth. Fine, you can spend the night here but make sure that you are out of this mosque and this village first thing in the morning. I don't want to see you or hear from you any more.'

As Ranjha slept in that mosque, I sat beside him, staring at his beautiful face. He dreamt of Heer, while I dreamt of him. In the morning, I left the mosque and flew into the open space. I sang with the birds as they woke up with the first light. I blew with the wind, as it swept through the rustling leaves. I danced on the floor with the droplets that fell from the hair of the woman who had lain in the arms of her husband through the night and rushed to have a bath first thing in the morning. I sang along as she hummed, glowing in the memory of the night. I marched in the footsteps of Ranjha who, leaving the mosque, took determined steps in the direction of Heer. The day, it seemed, had recovered and was ready to love again, while the night had been conquered.

The bells within the *ghunghroo* were crying for help. He was stomping his feet passionately, as if he wanted to break the ground into two. There was a fierceness in his eyes, a determination, a will to conquer the world, a world that he had long rejected, a world that was also all too eager to disassociate with him. The ground under his feet began to crumble as the buildings around him began to swirl, even as his bare, bleeding feet continued their stomping.

Waris could see the blisters on the sides of his feet and a thick layer of dried blood on the soles. He had seen the *dhamaal* of a Sufi several times before—the unrestrained, uncoordinated dance. The submission of the mind and the soul to the will of the body. The ultimate expression of materiality, a submission of the world of ideas to the brute force of matter.

But he had never experienced this energy before. The energy of a man in his mid-fifties, his long, white beard clinging to his chin, long, sweaty hair dancing on his shoulders. A man who possessed all the energy of the world, drawing life's vitality towards him as he whirled, the only body that moved as the world around him came to a halt.

This was not the dhamaal of Bulleh Shah but rather that of Shiva himself who had temporarily found abode in the body of this mystic and was now performing the *tandava,* the dance of destruction, a dance which, if not stopped, would bring about an end to this world. This was Shams of Tabriz, the first Sufi mystic to ever harness the power of the universe through this rotation, the teacher of Maulana Rumi, reincarnated as Bulleh Shah.

However, it was not just a swirling of the body, an unchoreographed movement. There were parts of it that were rehearsed, learned, memorized and practised, till the point that its memory now resided in every muscle of the body. For twelve years, Bulleh Shah, a Syed, a direct descendant of the Prophet of Islam, like Waris, had lived in the house of a courtesan, a *kanjri,* learning her craft, a craft that was appreciated in the respectable circles of society, but reserved for the lowliest of the low, a craft whose masters were derided and ridiculed, even as the craft was celebrated. And here it was now, this craft being performed by the highest of the highs, a Syed, a caste above which there was no other caste.

Waris's initial reaction at seeing the dhamaal was embarrassment, embarrassment on behalf of a Syed making such a spectacle of himself on the streets of Kasur. Syeds are meant to be revered, approached for their wisdom and treated with the utmost respect. It was an honour to be a Syed. A Syed was blessed with special characteristics. A Syed could heal a person by his prayer or by the power of his touch. A Syed personified dignity and religiosity. A Syed was a teacher. A Syed was a king, a Shah. A Syed blessed the nobility and courtesans alike, but a Syed didn't approach a courtesan requesting her to be his teacher. A Syed didn't dance like a madman on the streets of the city.

'I ceased to be a Syed, when I fell in love with my Shah Inayat Qadri,' Bulleh Shah had said when this accusation was hurled at him earlier.

The dhamaal had ended, the world had been destroyed and now it had come back into existence, Shiva and Brahma working hand in hand. The crowd had dispersed, while Bulleh Shah, snapping out of his ecstatic state, had found a place to sit at the corner of the street, next to the mosque. He often sat there, passing sarcastic comments on visitors entering and leaving the mosque, but didn't step inside. He had stopped going to the mosque a long time ago.

Waris sat on the floor next to him, unsure of himself, still mesmerized by his performance, observing Bulleh Shah as he gently massaged his own feet. Waris wanted to offer to do that for him. He wanted to wipe the blood on the feet with the hem of his tunic, but he was too scared. Bulleh Shah's body still exuded passion, like a tandoor that continues to give off heat long after the coals have burned out. Its density overpowered Waris, exerted pressure on his being. He was afraid that if he spoke to Bulleh Shah, he would not respond with words but with fire, a fire that would consume him.

He recalled all the poems of Bulleh Shah, verses sharper than a sword, hotter than the sun, prettier than the most beautiful miniatures. These words took on wings and flew around Waris, lifting him up and taking him to his childhood, standing in the mosque with his father, while Bulleh Shah's words were sung by the village mendicant outside. Bulleh Shah was famous all over Punjab and beyond. His words, sung by dervishes, travelled from one village to another, conjuring up images of a man not afraid of anything. Here was this man, so far only known through this image, now real, alive, breathing, sitting on the street like a fakir.

Bulleh Shah seemed unaware of Waris's presence next to him. With his saffron chola drenched, sweat dripping down his forehead, he sat, inspecting his feet, signs of pain visible in his passionate eyes, the materiality of his existence catching up with him. This was not the first time he had danced on the streets of the city nor would it be the last. He had told a few of his friends who had braved the disapproval of society to associate with him, that he wanted them to perform dhamaal as part of his funeral rites. He wanted his death to be celebrated as the ultimate union between the devotee, himself, and the beloved, the divine.

He lived for another twenty years, capturing his pain in his poetry, which he would sing out loud and then, enraptured by the beauty of his own words, break out into a dhamaal. His songs would travel through the alleys of the city, finding a space even in the most restrictive of places, sometimes in the hearts of the very people who were determined to reject him and his sacrilegious words. No one was safe from his diatribe, not the pandit, nor the mullah, nor the king or his nobles, nor the pilgrims who went to Makkah nor those who bathed in the Ganga.

He had heard it all. He had been called a kafir, a dissenter, an atheist, the devil. He had accepted all these titles. 'They call you kafir, you say, yes, indeed.' On other occasions, he rejected all his identities, even that of his personage, his own name. 'I am not a believer, nor a disbeliever, I am not pure, nor impure. Bulla, what do I know who I am.' Out of all of Bulleh Shah's poems, Waris struggled with this one the most. How could all identities disappear? How can the distinction between evil and good disappear? How can the difference between a demon and God disappear? What would Waris be, if not a Syed, a resident of Jandiala and the son of Gulsher Shah? Would Waris even be Waris if he didn't have these identities? Would he even exist?

As a young man, Bulleh Shah was seen as a threat to the stability of the city by the religious and political establishment, both intertwined together. This was not a random person criticizing religious scholars and the establishment, but an intellectual himself. This was a man adept in Arabic, Persian, Sanskrit and several other languages. A man who understood the secrets of the Quran, the Sunnah and the Hadith, along with the Upanishads and Greek philosophy, a man who could quote the poetry of Bhagat Kabir, Baba Fareed, Guru Nanak, Shah Hussain, Guru Arjun and Guru Gobind Singh. A man who could converse with any religious scholar on any issue but instead conversed with the masses in their language, Punjabi. Having abandoned the security of his ivory tower, he was now on the streets. This was not Bulleh Shah but Socrates corrupting the minds of the youth.

Fearing for his life, he had gone to Lahore, before that city had descended into chaos. It was in Lahore that Bulleh Shah discovered his spiritual master, Shah Inayat Qadri. It was a bond of marriage, a bond of love. It was a bond between a *mureed* and his *murshad*. It was a bond that existed between Amir Khusrau and Nizam-ud-din Auliya. Guru Nanak and Bhai Mardana. It was a bond that held together Shah Hussain and Madho Lal, the bond between Radha and Krishna. Heer and Ranjha. Picking up the thread of Sufi poetry where it had been left by Shah Hussain, Bulleh Shah became Heer, while Shah Inayat became Ranjha.

'Calling out the name of my Ranjha,
I myself have become Ranjha,
Call me Ranjha,
As I am no longer Heer.'

It was an all-consuming love, a love where the lover, like a moth, burnt on the flame of love. It was a love with no room for the self. A love requiring self-sacrifice and existing only in the reflection of the beloved. A love that demanded a repudiation of his Syed identity, this last marker of hierarchy separating him from his beloved, Shah Inayat of the Arain caste, an agricultural caste that did not have the same stature.

'Those who call me Syed
Are destined to burn in hell,
The swings of heaven are destined for those,
Who call me Arain.'

Bulleh Shah entered the house of a courtesan to learn dance for this love. For some reason, his spiritual master, his beloved, had turned his face away from him, and the only way Bulleh Shah thought he could win back his affection was by learning to dance. Learning this dance and then performing it on the streets of the city was yet another way for him to kill his ego.

After years of displacement, Bulleh Shah, following the death of Shah Inayat, had finally returned to Kasur. The political and religious establishment that had once threatened his life were still there, but Bulleh Shah, as an older man, a man consumed by the love of his master, a man who would speak more in poetry than in prose, was seen as a lesser threat. He was allowed to roam the streets, recite his sharp verses and occasionally criticize the religious leaders.

God was not found in religious rituals, nor in a celestial palace. God did not exist in a mosque nor a temple. Neither in Kaaba nor Benares. God resided within was the essence of his philosophy. 'I am the Absolute Truth,' as Mansur al-Hajjaj had said before him. Monism, a thread that connected Bulleh Shah with mystic poets before him and would connect him with those that came after him, including Waris.

People enjoyed listening to him, but the sharpness of his tone also alienated several people who were otherwise sympathetic. Bulleh Shah did not care. He was not in it for popularity. His words were an expression of a man slowly losing himself, his sanity, in the infinite wisdom of the divine.

Another reason why he was allowed to stay this time round was because of the changed priorities of the political and religious establishment of the city. There was a storm brewing all around them, uprooting the stability of Punjab, destroying several villages and urban centres in its wake. The storm so far had bypassed Kasur. It helped that Kasur, unlike Lahore, was not an important political or economic centre. The city did not lie on the all-important route that connected Lahore to Delhi. Kasur was close enough to Lahore to draw from the city's political and economic growth but also far enough to be able to retreat into its shell when the latter was in trouble.

The Muslim Pathan families that had dominated Kasur for generations were now emerging out of the hold of the Mughal reign and were eager to maintain their stronghold over the city. They realized that the demise of Lahore could mean the rise of Kasur. In this time of uncertainty, Kasur had to provide a sense of continuity. It was projected as the last hub of Muslim culture in Punjab, a city that was safe from the Sikh guerilla forces, the Mughal armies, the Marathas in the south, and the Afghans in the west. Many scholars, traders, courtesans, artists, performers and all sorts of people, escaping the violence of rural areas and other cities, had started converging on Kasur.

It was also this image of serenity that had brought Waris there. Having witnessed the skewering of the Lahore of his imagination, he had decided to travel further east to the next largest urban centre, Kasur, the twin city of Lahore. Mythology held that these cities had been founded by Luv and Kush, the twin sons of Ram and Sita; cities that were now destined to become the last sanctuary of Muslim culture in Punjab. Having found the protection of a trading caravan that was travelling from Lahore to Kasur, Waris had convinced the kotwal of the caravan to take him along. Once in Kasur, he didn't have much trouble finding accommodation.

Every day he would walk through the narrow alleys of the city, slowly familiarizing himself with all its curves, every nook and corner, the voices of the various mendicants, the cries of the street vendors, the wooden patterns on the *jharokhas* of the havelis of the Pathan rulers. He explored the different mosques and marvelled at the carvings on the ancient temples.

On other occasions, he would travel outside the city and walk along the river Sutlej, observing the cranes sitting on its banks and the boatmen negotiating fares with travellers looking to cross the river. Further behind the city and the river, he would fix his gaze on the ancient mounds that surrounded the city, some that hid within them secrets of ancient civilizations and others formed by the currents of the river, as it whimsically changed course, a unique geographical pattern that had come to mark the rivers of Punjab. He observed little structures and huts on the top of these mounds, abodes of Sufi dervishes and jogis, philosophers who, far removed from the everyday demands of society, contemplated the challenges facing society.

A part of Waris wanted to join these circles, to isolate himself from all troubles. Sitting on a rock next to the river, staring at these huts, he would imagine life as a dervish, as a jogi. A life with but one responsibility, remembering the name of God. A life spent in intimacy with the divine, obliterating all signs of the self, of becoming the Absolute Truth. A life as a mendicant, dependent on the charity of the people, roaming about from house to house, street to street and city to city, singing songs of the divinity. A life with nothing to lose, and everything to gain. A life in which Zakariya Khan or Sikh guerilla forces were irrelevant. A life that demanded respect across political, religious, sectarian and caste divides.

However, another part of Waris wanted the exact opposite. That was the part that was in love with the hubbub of society. The part that loved the smell of street food, the bright colours of dyed clothes, the sight of a kite string coated with glass. He loved catching the eye of young, beautiful girls, the slight curve on their lips as they sought to hide a smile and the struggle of catching a glimpse and then looking away. He loved walking through crowded streets, conversing with strangers, lamenting the loss of Punjab.

This was the heart of a young man torn by contradictions. Every day he engaged with these battles, struggling to choose one of these two divergent paths. He could settle in Kasur and fulfil the dreams that he had lost in Lahore. He could set up a shop here and become a hakim. He could become a permanent member of this society, a resident of the city, a settled man.

It was on one of these sojourns, when he usually engaged with these internal debates, that he had come across Bulleh Shah, in the middle of a busy street, surrounded by dozens of people. He knew of Bulleh Shah but didn't know that he was back in Kasur. Around him, he heard the whispered mentions of his name. He heard him being called the pride of Kasur, the man whose sacred presence in the city would one day make Kasur a holy city, a major pilgrim attraction, similar to Pakpattan of Baba Fareed. The whirling dervish pulled his anxieties out of him and crushed them under his feet.

Waris realized that it was fate that had put Bulleh Shah in front of him, that he was the answer to all his questions. Much more than any other poet, Waris, as a child, had established an association with Bulleh Shah. There were several words in the poetry of Bhagat Kabir, Guru Nanak and Shah Hussain whose meaning evaded him, whereas Bulleh Shah was the most accessible. The Punjabi that Bulleh Shah used was the same dialect spoken in his village. Most importantly for Waris, Bulleh Shah was a Syed. Waris felt a certain familial connection with him, something he hadn't felt for any other poet.

Watching him perform his ecstatic dance, Waris reflected that here was a dervish, a Sufi, a jogi, who had abandoned society but was still deeply entrenched in it. Here was a man who had annihilated his self in the love of the divine, yet his name was on the lips of every man, woman and child. Here was a man who existed in both these worlds, a man whose popularity in society increased, even though he tried distancing himself from it. He could not believe that he was watching the performance of a man who was already a legend, a man who would one day, like Ranjha, become the symbol of Punjab. Perhaps Waris too could have it both.

'You can travel the entire world, from the country of the *faranghis* to China, but you would have achieved nothing, learned nothing, if you don't get yourself a master,' said Bulleh Shah to Waris. 'Without a master, we are like a boat, stuck in the middle of a river without a boatman. We are like cattle without a cowherd, a lover without a beloved. Find yourself a master, a beloved. Devote your life to him, kiss his feet and he will raise you by the hand and take you through the treacherous waters of spirituality. You can jump into the world of spirituality without a master, but your fate would be no different from Sohni, stuck in between the waves without anything to hold onto, with her Mahiwal, her beloved, on the other side of the river. Your fate, without a master, is to drown like Sohni. This was the message of Baba Fareed, the central theme of Guru Nanak's philosophy and this is my lesson to you.'

'I would not be able to find a better master than you even if I walked around the entire world, holding the sun in my right hand,' pleaded Waris. 'Please accept me, accept my humble devotion. Take me on this path of spirituality. Be my boatman, my shepherd, help me cross these treacherous waves.'

Bulleh Shah chuckled as he heard Waris say this. He was still holding his foot on his lap, pressing it lightly. Waris had finally managed to offer to massage them, but Bulleh Shah had only returned a powerful look, saying nothing.

'How can I be your master? How can I take your boat across the river when I myself am drowning in this river of love? My Shah Inayat, my beloved, died before he could see me through. What you see in front of you is not Bulleh Shah. This is a man drowning.' Bulleh Shah was speaking like a man full of grief, a man who was still mourning the death of his master, mourning his own death. 'What you saw a few moments ago was a man gasping for breath, emerging occasionally from the water. I am only alive in those moments, barely holding onto my breath. I am destined to fail, destined to drown. How can a man fighting for his own life be your boat, your shepherd, your guide?' He was out of breath, as if he were actually drowning.

'However, there is one man in Kasur who can see you through this difficult journey.' The thought had just dawned upon him, bringing with it a glimmer of optimism. Waris, eager not to miss anything, listened with rapt attention.

'His name is Makhdum Hafiz Ghulam Murtaza. He was my first spiritual master before I had to leave for Lahore. He is a truly learned scholar, not the kind of hypocrite you see all around you, who can recall entire books out of memory but don't understand even the first letter, aleph, of these books. He is a rare beacon of hope in a catastrophic world. Your life will be made if he chooses to be your master. You will be able to

cross the Chenab if he becomes your boatman. Go to him and
fall at his feet.' He spoke desperately, enacting this imaginary
conversation that would happen between Waris and Maulvi
Ghulam Murtaza through his actions and his body. 'Beg him.
Ask him to have mercy on your soul. Tell him that you will not
leave his abode until he takes you under his wing.'

Squashed between the day and the night, the sun began to
melt. Its golden juice spread all over the horizon. I was sitting
here on the banks of the Chenab, my boat hopping on the
bubbly waves of the water trying to conquer the land. My
two beautiful wives were next to me, both slender and thin,
in contrast to my fat body described as a leather bag full of
honey by our poet, Waris. How else would he describe the
body of a businessman? How else would he describe the greed
of society? My body is not just a sheath of my soul but rather
a metaphor, a symbol of the avarice of an honest man who just
wants to earn an honest living.

Men like Waris, born into the religious elite, the chosen
ones, cannot understand the lives of men like us. To them,
born into privilege, we who are born into poverty, without
the support of any ancestral wealth or the inheritance of a
title, will always be a caricature. Just look at how he describes
Mauja, his sons, and of course Ranjha, and compare it to
how he crafts me. Mauja, a landed aristocrat, the head of his
village, a beneficiary of a feudal system where he and his sons
get everything without lifting a finger, is not a symbol of
greed, but rather of beauty, benevolence? But someone like
me, who only has this rickety boat, who gets up before the
night has been completely defeated by the day, and works till

after the last squeeze of light has been extracted out of the sun, becomes a symbol of greed?

Mauja and his sons sit in their havelis, while their servants tire under the sun on their fields. They eat due to the labour of their peasants and then become chivalrous guardians of the so-called paradise when they allow these hard-working peasants a few morsels from their own hard labour. I, on the other hand, work with my own bare hands. I sit here on the banks of the river, deprived of shade on the hottest days, and without shelter on the coldest nights, charging a little fee to help passengers cross the river on my boat and it is I who am a symbol of greed. My only crime is my enterprise, my lack of dependency on people like Mauja. My crime is that I don't beg for a living but rather earn it.

To top it all, Waris had to give me two wives. What is he trying to show? That my work is thriving? That I can support not just one but two households? Or that I am a licentious character, a sex-crazed individual who cannot be satisfied by one woman? Is my lecherousness supposed to be an extension of my greed? In a qissa, a story that hides its sexuality behind metaphysical language, gets sanction for it from divinity, it is I, poor Luddan, who am a symbol of lecherousness.

O, Waris, strange are your ways.

Do you know that in many villages of Punjab it is forbidden to recall Waris's story of *Heer–Ranjha*? Even in Jhang, the city of Heer, they take great offence when someone mentions it. At their shrine, the caretakers physically beat up any singer or musician who tries to sing this poem, of which I am but a minor character. Why do you think, oh, dear reader, that is the case? Is it because of my greed or lasciviousness? Don't be mistaken. Don't be fooled by the poet's charm.

This man, who accuses me of greed, picked up a simple tale bequeathed by Damodar and Muqbil and made it sexual, justified it as divinely sanctioned. A man who claimed piety for himself spoke in a language that embarrasses even those who cannot be easily embarrassed. Don't be fooled by his spiritual language, his use of metaphors and symbols. How does a man who never married, who spent his entire life only studying the sacred word, know so much about the erection of nipples, the blushing of the skin when in the act of sexual intercourse, or the gentle biting that lovers sometimes engage in?

Don't get me wrong. I have nothing against greed or sexuality. I am a man of this world, its quintessential specimen, who loves everything the world has to offer. Don't mistake my complaints against Waris for my hatred for him. I do love him; he is my creator after all. But hasn't our creator bestowed us with free will? Allow me to exert some of that boon then. Allow me to digress a little from the path that Waris set out for me.

I do love my creator, but my love for him is also not a self-loathing, all-encompassing love as that of Heer for Ranjha. My love for him is that of this world, love that doesn't blind me to his shortcomings. I am as much a child of Waris as Ranjha or Mauja, but as you can clearly see, his love for me doesn't compare to his love for them.

My complaints to him are the complaints of a neglected child. My complaints to him are that of a devotee who the divine bestows with evil in his heart and then punishes for having that evil. Waris made me how I am. How can he then be critical of the characteristics that he gave me? Have no doubt that if I have these characteristics, if I am indeed greedy, then there is a part within Waris that is also greedy. If Ranjha is Waris and Waris is Ranjha then Luddan is Waris and Waris Luddan.

If that is a characteristic I am supposed to fulfil in this story, then I will do so with devotion. It is my dharma after all. When Ranjha approached me on that dying day, begging me to take

him across the Chenab, to meet his beloved, in the name of
Ram, Rahim, in the name of God, I could not care less for
his exhortation. A man of this world, my only God is money,
wealth. 'Show me the coins, pay me the fees. I will take you
across, to the city of your beloved. There you can lie in her
arms, fulfil your divine destiny.' But he did not have a penny,
not a single coin.

Imagine the son of Mauja, the chief of Takht Hazara, a man
who could, if he desired, have all the happiness in the world in
his home, now reduced to poverty. His clothes had begun to
fall apart, his bones had begun to show, yet his face remained
radiant. He was still as beautiful as Prophet Yousuf, as beautiful
as when he had left his home. O Waris, is ageing, the burning
of the skin, the facial personification of poverty, only reserved
for mortals like us?

I could have taken him along. What would one seat have
cost me when there were several passengers ready to pay? But
why should I? I do not owe Ranjha anything. Like a dervish, a
Sufi or jogi, he had left his home of his own accord in search of
his divinity. Snapping all his familial ties, he had decided to tie
his cord with the divine. Running away from the daily chores
of life, he now travelled from one place to another, begging for
food, choosing an easy life over a life of toil and a life of chores.
Let me remind you here that while you might be aware of his
true intentions, of his reasons for abandoning his home, I do
not. I only see him as a jogi and I am distrustful of all of them.
How could I have known that he was an actual dervish and
not a thug who, using the garb of a mendicant, found ways to
inspect the bodies of unsuspecting woman, or using sleight of
hand stole people's money bags? How could I have known that
my two beautiful wives, the pride of my greed, were safe from
his lecherous eyes?

I turned him away, preferring to save a spot for someone
who would pay. Dejected, he went away, took out his flute and
played a sad song. It was as if the world was overtaken by magic.
As if it was not his flute but rather Saraswati who was singing
through him. You, dear reader, would have already read about
the magic of his flute a few pages ago, for it is improbable that
you have directly jumped onto this page, skipping everything in
the middle. In that rare circumstance, if that is the case, I would
request you to go to the beginning of the chapter and read about
how the goddess of music speaks through Ranjha's flute.

You have to keep in mind that this is not Ranjha's flute
but Krishna's. It is in that mould that our Waris has created this
character, borrowing the legacy of gods, goddesses, prophets
and saints, while I, poor Luddan, have been given the attributes
of a mere mortal, an ordinary everyman. However, even though
I am only a brief part of this narrative, in my own humble
opinion, even if I may say so myself, my character is essential.
For it is in contrast to my humanity, that the divinity of our
protagonist, Ranjha, is established.

If that is the legacy of our Ranjha, then how could my poor
wives who, like me, are also human, resist his charm? They
rushed to him, hearing his tales of woe through his flute, as did
all my passengers who wanted to cross the Chenab on my boat.
They cried with his flute, shared in his misery with him. At that
moment, all of them were orphans, cheated by their brothers. In
that moment, it seemed as if there were only two people on the
banks of the Chenab, Ranjha and I, for everyone else had been
transformed by his spell.

Why didn't I fall for his charm while everyone else did,
you ask? How can I answer that question? That question should
be directed towards our creator, our Waris. But for the sake
of conversation, if I am to take a shot at it, I would say that's

because I am a representative of the material world, for whom reality, truth, is shaped as material reality. I am not a philosopher, an idealist, for whom the world is one big illusion, and the truth lies somewhere in the world of ideas. As a representative of the material world, the truth for me is that which can be felt materially, by the touch of my hands. Music doesn't occupy that space. My character simply doesn't have the capacity to engage with anything that is not part of the material world.

Oh, how can I be so aware, yet unaware at the same time? How can a character be a participant and an observer? In order to understand this, you'll have to understand the nature of this world, starkly different from yours. Here we are not bound by the rules of chronology. We exist in the past, the present and the future at the same time, as if time were a conquerable, tameable entity. All that is supposed to happen in this qissa, Ranjha meeting Heer, them falling in love, so on and so forth, has already happened. We were all participants in this act. We were all witnesses to it. But it is still to happen in this particular qissa. So we know what is happening, even though we don't know what is going to happen. It is a different kind of relationship with time that we enjoy.

You didn't see this coming, did you? Engaging in a philosophical discourse with an ordinary boatman. It is an inaccurate depiction of reality, you might complain. A strange manner of storytelling. That's probably because you expect stories to unfold in a particular manner, with a clear beginning, a plot and an end, a story that is unknown before it comes into existence. But how do you tell a story that is already known, that has been told for centuries? This story doesn't unfold in linearity, but rather follows the circular nature of time.

Determined to cross the river to reach his destiny, to be one with Heer, Ranjha put his potli on his head, held his shoes

in his hands and rushed towards the river. He was going to
walk through the river to the other side. Life on this side of
the bank was not worth living. He preferred drowning to this
contemptible existence. For Ranjha, it was better to become a
martyr in the search for truth, divinity, than live a life which was
unexamined. Had he chosen to walk on, his fate would have
been sealed. He would have, like Sohni, drowned in the river,
with her Mahiwal, his Heer, on the other side.

A man of this world, I was, of course, undeterred by this
irrational behavior of our protagonist. Life scores over death as
far as I am concerned. If he had chosen death for himself, then
so be it, but then my wives came rushing to me. They pleaded
with me to give him a ride, to help him reach his destiny. In
this, they were joined by others. They took Ranjha by the hand
and brought him to my boat. They seated him and ordered me
to take him across, without realizing that they had put him on
the couch of the daughter of the chief of Jhang. They had put
him on the couch of Heer, not the metaphor I have been using
previously, but rather Heer, the character, whom our Ranjha
has still not met. For, like our Ranjha, Heer too occupies both
these spaces.

While some massaged his legs, and others his arms, my own
wives fanned him as he sat on this all-important couch. What
option did I have at that moment but to accede to the demand
of people? Don't be mistaken, I was still not won over. I still
doubted his intentions and his claim to spirituality, but I had no
other option but to be his boatman.

What kind of a metaphor am I when I am a boatman, taking
our Ranjha across these treacherous waters to be one with the
divine? Am I a Sufi master holding a young disciple by the
hand and helping him cross the dangerous river of spirituality?
Or am I a symbol of Prophet Khizr, the immortal saint who

controls all water? Perhaps I am a metaphor for Jhulelal, the god who controls the mighty river Indus, into which the Chenab merges. I play multiple roles, multiple symbols appropriated from different religious traditions as they melt on the canvas of Punjab, while our Waris, our creator, marvels at the beauty of his creation.

3

The Transformation

It was the night of nights, the night of destiny. It was a night when gods, demons and humans alike, those who were still trapped in the travails of this life, those who burned in the eternity of hell and those who sipped the nectar of immortality in the heavens, all became one and set their sights on Jhang. In their maddening rage, the apsaras of the court of Indra kicked around the mattresses and the pillows, trying so very hard to regain the attention of the court, of Indra himself.

The houris of Jannah were not faring that well either. Just a moment ago, they had been playing the *daf*, drinking from golden goblets and singing heavenly songs. And now those seats had been abandoned, the juice from the golden goblets spilt on the floor, as all of heaven cast its eyes upon the Earth.

Responding to the cries and laments, the monsoon wind rose like an army of soldiers from the Bay of Bengal. With lightning speed, as if it were the army of Hulagu Khan that had in time immemorial decapitated thousands of heads in Punjab and lit a bonfire of the heads to warm itself, it reached Jhang. Here these mercenary soldiers impregnated the clouds which blocked the view between heaven and earth, between its occupants and me.

They unleashed a flurry of tears, crying on behalf of the apsaras and houris, crying that a more beautiful creature now existed on earth, in Jhang.

The Chenab was fuming with rage. As if intoxicated, she swirled like a bull in heat. She had to see for herself, make sure that the rumours were true. Daughter of the great Himalayas, the home of Shiva, the ascetic, the ultimate jogi, she had been hearing stories through her long arduous journey, in search of her lover, whom she had promised to meet at the Sindh coast.

She raced in the direction of Jhang. Oblivious to the pain of separation that her lover experienced in her absence, she headed off now in a different direction. Trapped in the hills of the Himalayas, she had counted the minutes and days to the time when she would be free, when she would flow uninterruptedly into the embrace of the sea. And now here she was, midway on her journey, already having forgotten her true destination. Like Sahiban, she was whimsical. Sahiban who, as soon as she sat on the blue horse of her beloved, Mirza, on their way to be one, forgot all about her destination and began reminiscing about a past that was slowly moving away. Her reminiscences, her reluctance to shed her former identity, got Mirza killed and Sahiban martyred. She too is a lover from Punjab but how different her love is from mine.

Just as Mirza had to pay for her lack of devotion, the people of Jhang had to suffer for the Chenab's capriciousness. Like a wildfire, she spread from one village to another, sowing seeds of destruction wherever she passed. Intoxicated in her new-found love, her touch became the touch of death, the death of the former self.

Finally, reaching her destination, finally reaching Jhang, she prostrated outside its tall towers, its tall buildings and its tall mound. She pleaded and begged for just one sight of her

Heer, for whom she had broken her journey, for whom she had delayed her union. Like an invading force of Afghans marching into Punjab, she had progressed uninterrupted, until she had reached Jhang, the crown jewel of all cities, glorious as Lahore was once. If only someone had stopped the Afghans the way Jhang halted her journey, the way Jhang humbled her. She had come not as a conqueror but as a beggar, she said. 'All I want is just one glimpse, one touch, of the most beautiful baby that has been born in the house of Chuchak, on this fortunate night. A baby that is destined to be the most beautiful girl in the world,' she pleaded.

My father, the most kind-hearted man, sire to the most beautiful girl in the world, could not ignore her wishes. Chenab was a guest now, and a guest of the Sials is never turned away. Appearances have to be kept up. He took Chenab's hand in his own, placed a little flood water in the palm of his hand and poured it over my forehead, as if this was not the water of the Chenab but of the Ganga or the Abe Zamzam.

She caressed my face and ran her fingers through my hair. She was assured that the rumours were true. That I was indeed the most beautiful girl ever to be born in Punjab. For if there is a river that knows beauty, then it is indeed the Chenab. She was a witness to the love story of Sohni and Mahiwal as they met every evening on her banks. She had held a drowning Sohni in her hands, sung her lullabies and put her to sleep as she became one with the divine. She had seen Mirza and Sahiban as children, falling more in love with each other every day as their childhood transitioned into the splendour of youth. If there was a river that knew love, then that was the Chenab.

On that fateful night, as she held my face in her hands, she saw before her eyes the unfolding of my complete life. She had already become a participant in the love story of Punjab. She changed her direction permanently that day so that she could see for herself this immortal love legend that was to unfold on her banks. It wasn't an easy transition, for the river had to change its course; it had to make a bend. While it earlier flowed like an arrow on its path, it now flowed like a bow, with a curve, as the river flowed close to Jhang. It was as if the city was pulling the river towards it and she was finding it hard to resist its charm. This was a secret she had whispered in my ear the night she had come as a guest to my home. Through that arch, she had promised to look after me; she had promised to be a witness, a participant. Chenab sat eyeing Jhang, as if it were a black cobra, guarding an ancient Persian treasure, an incarnation of Gugga Pir.

Flowers bloomed on the land that had been blessed by the daughter of the Himalayas as she receded to continue towards her beloved. All these flowers faced Jhang, for they too wanted to see the most beautiful thing there was to see. These flowers did not have to wait for spring to come. They smiled, sang and danced in the breeze and celebrated *basant* the day I stepped on the ground. The trees turned greener and their shadows became darker. Migratory birds lost all sense of season, pattern and direction on seeing me. For them, I became the spring they had been searching for when they fled from the brutal winter in Siberia and Alaska.

The fish in the river hopped around me when I descended into the water. Seeing my love for the river, my father, may God grant him all my lives, built me a special boat, a boat with a beautiful couch on it, a boat as splendid as the boat of Prophet Khizr. I would spend my mornings bathing in my guardian river and my afternoons floating on it, lying on the couch in this beautiful boat, with my friends around me. Luddan, the boatman, to whom my father had entrusted this boat, was permitted to use it to make a living. He was allowed to take passengers to and fro for a little sum, but warned to always protect the sanctity of my couch.

Assured by my laughter, the sun rose from the east. Throughout the day, it travelled through the sky to catch a glimpse of me from different angles. The moon existed to guard me. All night long, it kept the world illuminated, on the lookout for anything or anyone who could threaten me.

I had spent many nights with the moon in its loneliness. I had lent it my ear to hear its tale of woe. Sometimes when it had cried to its heart's content, it stared back at me with enquiring eyes, urging me to share with its lonely heart some stories of my misery. I had nothing to share, nothing to cry about. What pain did I have in the house of my father, where I lived the life of a princess? His only daughter, I am his pride. As the head of his tribe, the chief of Jhang, he could punish people, banish entire tribes, without batting an eyelid, but he would weep a sea if a thorn even pricked my feet.

When with the moon, I did not have the heart to tell it that I had no complaints in the house of Chuchak. I could never summon up the courage to tell it that I did not need any protection. As the daughter of the chief, I was always accompanied by a lot of friends. It had mistaken my soft-heartedness for a weakness. I let it live with that illusion.

I did not tell the moon the tales of my fierce character, of my bravery. I had waged wars and led armies in the qissa penned by Damodar. That battle is not part of this qissa so I will not delve into it any further. I had fought to protect the character of Luddan whom you were just introduced to in the previous section. I will only say that it is not I who needed protection.

While I don't fight armies in this qissa being penned by our Waris, I still retain my valour. I am a symbol of beauty and pride, but don't forget that I am also a metaphor for rebellion, for action and agency. Our Ranjha might be the symbol of the divine, but what will happen to the divine if there is no devotee? Would the divine be able to retain its divinity, if that divinity is not recognized, not worshipped? The divine is an object of worship and without being worshipped, it is nothing but an object. It is through the finite nature of the devotee that the infinity of the divine is recognized.

The devotee is not a helpless, passive partner in this relationship, but rather the agent, the shaper of events, who makes this relationship progress. Have you forgotten how Hiranyakashipu, a humble devotee, became so powerful, as powerful as the divine, through the power of his devotion? Do you not recognise the spiritual prowess achieved by Baba Fareed Shakarganj after his lifetime of devotion?

A true devotee is a powerful devotee. A true devotee is the shaper of destinies. A true devotee is divine.

Don't be mistaken. This is not the story of *Heer–Ranjha* but rather the story of Heer—Waris's Heer, from Waris to Heer. You might be tempted to see the parallels between Ranjha and our poet, our creator, our Waris, but it is really I who truly represent him. It is in my voice that the devotees speak—from Shah Hussain to Bulleh Shah, and now Waris. Sometimes I take the form of Radha, sometimes that of a nameless housewife, but it is always I, at the centre of it all, who become the symbol of a Sufi, a devotee, while Ranjha becomes the symbol of the divine. I make possible the union between the devotee and the divine, the disintegration of the male in my female body. For neither is there a distinction between a devotee and the divine, nor is there any distinction between the male and the female.

I am Waris and Waris is Heer.

Have I convinced you enough of my proud, arrogant youth? Do you understand now the nature of Heer's personality before she encountered the divine, before she met her Ranjha? This is a Heer aware of the majesty of her beauty, a Heer who derives her power from her father, the chief of the Sials. This is a Heer who is pampered and protected but also a Heer who is unafraid of a fight. This is a Heer who knows that she deserves everything, and that the world exists to serve her.

News spreads fast in this world. I hear a mendicant lies on that sacred space. Wearing tattered clothes, he dares put his feet where Heer puts her face. How else is Heer supposed to react but by picking up a stick to beat the intruder who has dared pollute her couch on Luddan's boat? How is this intrusion different from a Shudra entering the temple, a menstruating woman entering the sanctum of a Sufi shrine, a Syed being taught by a kanjri?

Is this not the biggest threat to dharma? What else was preached to Arjun by Krishna when he expressed his reluctance to wage a war against his cousins and uncle? Why else did Ram invade Lanka, if not to protect this dharma? Would a true believer ever allow the worship of al-Lat, al-Uzza and Manat in the true house of God? Can lowly peasants, Jatts, ever take the place of the mighty Mughals? Then how dare this fakir, this dervish, forget his status, and invade my space?

Beating him with a stick, I will bruise his body in the same manner as he has defiled my peace. Poor Luddan, too, whom I have rescued in a previous incarnation, will have to suffer, for how dare he, being the guardian of my boat, allow this atrocity to occur. In this endeavour, I will be accompanied by my friends, my army of Amazons, my valiant soldiers, who have stood by me in every stage of my life and promise to do so till the very end. I don't necessarily need them to fight my battle or my war. For when it comes to valour, do you seriously think this fakir or the poor Luddan really stand a chance?

We reached the bank of the river, the edge of that curve where the Chenab promised to bend. There was a strange silence in the air, an awkward moment, like a drought before a flood. The chirping of the birds had died down, the sun quickly looked away. The entire world braced itself for this battle; the entire world waited for this takedown. Without a care, the mendicant slept on my couch. It looked like he had been born on it, so comfortable did he appear. Little did he know that it would now host his dead body, in the final moments of his life. In my swift vengeance, he would die without a scream.

Like Indra with his thunderbolt, I lifted the stick, high above, almost touching the heavens. I brought it sharply down, just as the unconscious mendicant moved. I saw his face and dropped the stick. I was smitten, struck to the ground. I was like Moses on Mount Sinai, when he caught a glimpse of the divine. I opened my mouth to find an excuse, but words evaded me. For what words do you recite to the being who is the creator of all languages? I felt life slipping out of me. My soul had abandoned me, or was it my body that was failing me? I shivered with cold. I sweated as if I was in the middle of a desert. I felt oxygen escape my lungs. I felt life flowing through my being. I felt heavy, incapable of moving. I felt light, as if I were flying.

And then he got up from the couch and put his hands around me. I died in that moment, became a martyr. I was truly born in that moment. I had met my divine, I had met my Ranjha. Like Mansur al-Hajjaj, I had discovered the Absolute Truth; like Radha, I had found my Krishna. I am no longer Heer. I am no longer the daughter of Chuchak. This boat and this couch don't belong to me. These aren't my friends; this isn't my home. I am no longer Heer, but Ranjha. I am now just a body and Ranjha is my soul. In that divine encounter, I lost all my possessions. It is the death of a former self and the birth of the whole. I am Bulleh Shah dancing in the streets of Kasur. I sit by his feet, my Ranjha's, and take them in my hands. I massage them gently and with my tunic, I wipe the sweat from his brow.

'All that is mine is now yours. We sit here under the watchful sky, in the temple of the divine. I take you as my husband. We are married now, for the rites and the rituals of the world are meaningless. You now take me as your wife,' I said.

'I was married to you the moment I cast my eyes upon you,' Ranjha replied. 'Our union was fated. Our love is centuries old. But you have to promise me that you will not betray me as women do.' Even after all our previous incarnations together, my Ranjha still doubted me. 'I have seen much pain and agony in my life. I have been cast out of my home, with envy sown in the hearts of my brothers, through the mischief of the daughters of Eve. Will you, like Zulaikha, like Luna, have me thrown into prison, as was the destiny of Yousuf and Puran Bhagat? Will you, like Sahiban, hide my bow and arrows, as she did, so that her brothers could easily kill Mirza?'

'My fidelity to you will be an example. Our love story is destined to be legendary. I know of the pains and travesties you have experienced because of the cunning ways of your sisters-in-law but don't cast all women in the same mould. How else can I assure you of my loyalty when I have already given you everything I own? Come with me now, take my hand. Let me take you to my father's house. There you can take care of our buffaloes. We will pretend to the world that you are our servant but in reality, it will be I who will be serving you. Every morning, you can take our herd, that my father has reserved for me, to the jungles. There you can drink the milk of our finest buffaloes. Every day, I will meet you there, where we, away from the prying eyes of the world, will be together. I will feed you *churi*, that symbol of love, with my own hands and we will spend the rest of our lives in marital bliss.'

Darkness surrounded him. There was a certain comfort in its smoothness. It was here that he usually met his mother, a figure in white clothes and an indiscernible face. Now sometimes, in that same space, he also met his father. Together they sat on a dark bench, hand in hand, talking about things he could never remember. Waris enjoyed being in this darkness. He wanted to be here more than anywhere else.

He felt a pinch on his waist. It was Aftab sitting behind him, his teeth and the whiteness of his eyes gleaming in the darkness. Waris held his partially grown beard in his hand. 'Do you want your uncircumcised penis up your ass?' he asked, angrily. Aftab was taken aback by this sudden reaction. Waris never reacted this way. He was always patient, soft-spoken and agreeable to be around.

Umer, the third student in the room, sitting next to Waris, chuckled, trying to make sure that their teacher, Maulvi Ghulam Murtaza, had not heard, but he had. 'Are you at it again, boys? When will your obsession with penises, vaginas and asses end?' He spoke impassively, preoccupied with his thoughts. 'There are other concerns as well in this life, other unaddressed philosophical enquiries that need to be discerned.' Waris laughed along with the rest of the students, more to hide his awkwardness. He was upset not only for being pulled out of the comfort of the darkness, but also for losing his temper.

The students were used to hearing their teacher talk in this manner. He would often curse them when irritated. Having failed to understand a particular theological or metaphysical explanation, he would slap them hard on the back of their heads, calling them donkey's balls or camel's cunt, among other things. With his growing age, the beating was getting less severe but the curses more inventive. The students dared not laugh when he was in that mood.

The most innovative expletives were often reserved for Umer, a scion of one of the ruling Pathan families of Kasur, who also happened to be one of the patrons of this madrasah, Jamia Kot Androon, the most prominent religious and educational institution in the heart of the city. Umer's family controlled vast agricultural fields, collected revenue from trade and all other economic activities in the city, which had increased in the aftermath of regular attacks on Lahore, while his cousins and other family members held important administrative jobs. Higher education at the madrasah was a formality for him. He could not stop thinking about the day when, sitting on a white horse, he would inspect his lands, collect taxes and throw lavish parties at his home. To these parties, he would invite the leading poets, musicians and dancers of Punjab. He would shower them with silver and gold coins and would be remembered as the greatest patron of the arts in Kasur. Later in the night, having gulped down the sweetest wine, he would lie with the most beautiful women. When Umer was in this frame of mind, Waris and Aftab would fantasize along with him. Umer could hardly stop talking when he was with them, but would become embarrassingly quiet during a lesson.

Aftab, on the other hand, could not stop talking during a lecture. He would make comments, ask questions, make comparisons. He had a religious dedication towards his studies and was a favourite of all the teachers, particularly Maulvi sahib, as the students referred to Maulvi Ghulam Murtaza. His real name was Kanhaiya Kumar and he belonged to a minor trading family from Firozpur. From an early age, he had shown an intellectual promise that his siblings did not, so his family had allowed him to pursue higher education and find some sort of employment with the Mughal court. When he was leaving for Kasur, someone had suggested the name Aftab to him to increase his chances of employment.

Waris, the third member of this cohort, enjoyed listening more than talking, whether he was in their company or in a lecture. The three of them could not be separated. They ate, drank, slept and studied together. They adored each other's company and, more than that, they cherished the privilege of being taught by Maulvi sahib.

Maulvi Ghulam Murtaza had been the head of this institution for over three decades now. Under him, it had grown tremendously, with hundreds of students coming to study here from as far away as Agra. Further away from Kasur, the popularity of the madrasah was linked to its connection with Bulleh Shah. His poetry and songs were being sung in Delhi. They resonated on the banks of the Indus. They had become part of the city of Multan, the city of Prahlad Bhagat, Shah Shams Sabzwari and Bahauddin Zakariya. He was the poet of the eighteenth century, a celebrity even before there were any.

As a young man, when Bulleh Shah was a student at the madrasah, Maulvi sahib had been much more involved, teaching classes to all levels of students. He had a bottomless well of energy then. He would wake up well before fajr and teach till *maghrib*, leading all the prayers in the middle, after which he would consult with the other teachers of the madrasah, discuss different students, their individualized needs and other administrative issues.

Sometimes he had to go to the havelis of the leading families
of the city to personally appeal for more funds for the madrasah.
A highly learned man, he was one of the most respected
individuals of Kasur and no one could refuse him. In fact, when
Bulleh Shah had initially got into trouble with the political and
religious elite, he had interceded with the Pathan rulers that
restraint be shown to his student, while he convinced Bulleh
Shah to migrate to Lahore and continue his studies with Shah
Inayat Qadri. He had the unique ability of producing subverts,
even as he dined with the hegemons.

Older now, Maulvi sahib mostly looked after the
administrative and financial needs of the madrasah. Time that he
earlier spent teaching, he would now spend re-reading the texts
that he had read as a young man. He wanted to discover new
and newer esoteric secrets that these books contained. Inspired
by Ibn-Arabi, the thirteenth-century Arab scholar whose books
he particularly enjoyed, Maulvi sahib was of the opinion that
each text contained several secrets and mysteries, and each time
a text was read, a new truth emerged.

From one moment to another, nothing remained the same.
Life was like a flowing river that was constantly changing. It was
created, destroyed and created again, each time with the divine
breath, the source of all existence. Everything in this world
was this divine breath. It emerged from divinity and contained
divinity. Everything changed between two moments even
though it looked the same. When an individual approached a text
he had already read, it was the beginning of a new relationship,
an unveiling of a previously veiled secret.

The Quran, of course, being the most important book, he
would read over and over again. But he would also read other
texts—the Upanishads, the Gita, the Granth Sahib, love legends
and works of Greek philosophy. Life was a journey, a journey

that took us closer to our destination, perfection and divinity, and it was the duty of an individual to pursue that perfection. Only one man had achieved that perfection and that was the Prophet of Islam but there were others who, either through spirituality or philosophy, had got close.

One such individual, according to Maulvi sahib, was Socrates who, using philosophy, had got close to the same truth that Mansur al-Hajjaj and other mystics had reached through spirituality. Often in the morning after his fajr prayers, following which he read the Quran for an hour, he would revisit some of Socrates's dialogues. His favourite was *Apology*, Socrates's conversation with his accusers in Athens, who had charged him with corrupting the youth. Tears would begin flowing from the maulvi's eyes each time he read those powerful words. For over three decades, Maulvi sahib had walked the fine line between imparting an honest education to his students and keeping the political and religious elite of the city satisfied. How would he respond if he was ever called to defend himself in front of the city? Would he be able to articulate as clearly as Socrates? Would any student of his, like Plato did for Socrates, capture his words, his arguments, in his writings and make him immortal?

It was perhaps his love for teaching or his quest to find that perfect student, ignited by a reading of *Apology* that morning, which had inspired Maulvi sahib to take a class with his seniormost students. He had sent a message to them to meet him in his room, an hour before the *zuhr* prayers, when the sun was at its zenith. Waris, Aftab and Umer knew that this was going to be a special class. Maulvi sahib had always taught them in the open courtyard where all the classes happened. His room was reserved for his private use, office by day and lodging at night, and hardly anyone was invited into it.

Maulvi sahib's writing table was placed in the centre of the room, an unfolded paper laid on it, weights holding it steady. His wooden pen, cut at the nib to beautify the writing, was resting in an ink pot on top of the table. Several scrolls and texts were scattered on the floor around it. His sleeping mat had been folded and was standing in the corner of the room, while a few of his clothes were hanging on a nail next to it. It was a small space, flooded by the sunlight that came through an open window looking out towards the courtyard and the open door in the same direction.

'Sit down, wherever you can find some space,' he told them. 'Waris, shut the door and window completely.'

'Do you want me to light the lamp?' Aftab offered.

'No. I want this room to be engulfed in complete darkness. I want your eyes to see nothing but its depth.'

Maulvi sahib had never taught them in this manner. His classes were usually lectures, explanations of texts and ruminations on ideas. It was mostly he who spoke while his students soaked it all in. Sometimes towards the end, he would allow a question or two, but it was never a conversation. For the first time, in the twilight of this career, he was trying something new. In all his readings of the Socratic dialogues, he had always been concentrating on their philosophical essence. Today, however, while re-reading *Apology*, he began thinking about the Socratic manner of teaching. He wondered if that style from Athens could work in Kasur. He wondered if instead of imparting knowledge to students, he could glean it out of them. He wondered if through this teaching method, he could prove, like Socrates had in his time, that knowledge was within us; that all of us, irrespective of our stations in life and our subsequent education, were born with knowledge. If all of us were born with knowledge, as the philosophers had argued, then it would also prove what the Sufis had argued—that we all contained within ourselves divine radiance. For what else is divine radiance, if not knowledge?

'Divinity lies within you,
If only you realize,' in the words of Bhagat Kabir.

With the room completely engulfed in darkness, the darkness eventually getting a hold over the students and their teacher, he asked them to imagine. 'Imagine,' he repeated. It was as if Maulvi sahib was speaking an alien language. For students who had spent days memorizing the verses of the Quran, philosophical arguments and their counterarguments, the term 'imagine' seemed to have no meaning. It was like a blind man being asked to see or an unlettered man being asked to read.

'Imagine that this room is the entire world and that nothing exists outside it. Imagine that the only people you have ever known in this world are those who are now the occupants of this room. Imagine that the only things you have ever seen in this world are those that lie in this room. Imagine that this darkness that you see is the only light you have ever known, the only truth that is true. Can you imagine such a world?'

In a strange way, Waris felt that this imaginary truth was truer than the truth.

'The thought of only knowing this reality all your life might make you sad,' continued Maulvi sahib. 'That's because you might find it hard to forget a reality that you know outside this room. You might find it hard to forget the green of the leaves, the blue of the skies, the smell of the rain or the touch of water. But what if you had never known these sensations? Would it still feel like a loss? What if you had found a way to be happy and content in this room, as humans do, when they have no alternative? I don't want you to imagine this as a forlorn existence but rather imagine being satisfied. Imagine loving this alternative reality. Imagine the beauty of this existence.'

'Recall what Ibn-Arabi said—that there are three worlds. The world of the senses—the material world, the world that you occupy. Right now, this dark room and everything in it is the material world. Then there is the spiritual world, the metaphysical world, the world of the heavens. Can you remember how that world is referred to by Socrates?' asked Maulvi sahib and then, without waiting for the answer, blurted, 'World of Forms. He believes that that is the true world, the unchanging world, while the material world is constantly changing and because it is changing, it is unreliable.'

'Maya,' offered Aftab.

Smiling, Maulvi sahib said, 'Yes, indeed, maya, an illusion, as Vedanta philosophy would say. The question then arises as to how do you move from the material world, the world of illusion, maya, to the world of metaphysics, the world of ultimate truth, the world of the divine, the world of Forms or the all-pervasive reality of Brahman, if you may allow me to say so, dear Aftab.'

Aftab, wide-eyed, the skin of his face tingling with anticipation, his heart pounding faster, nodded enthusiastically.

'Al-Arabi says we can bridge these two worlds through the imagination,' Maulvi sahib almost whispered the last word. He allowed his silence to linger on for a little while longer. He knew that he had the fullest attention of his students. He felt as if the three of them were young mares and he held their reins in his hands. He experienced a lightness in his aged body, something he had last experienced in his youth. He felt as if the entire weight of his body had shifted to his chest, settling in his lungs. He felt as if he was carrying a big secret, the mysteries of the universe. He wanted to guard it, hold on to it for just a little while longer.

Floating on the lightness of his weight, he tiptoed around the room, his books and scrolls, and the students, and opened the door and the window without giving the students any kind of warning. 'Follow me,' he said, as he exited the room.

Assaulted by the sudden exposure to the sun, the students were still squinting and covering their eyes with their hands, when Maulvi sahib held Umer's hand and forcefully pulled it off his eyes. 'Look at the sun. Don't shy away from it.' Umer tried, but couldn't. He squeezed his eyes tightly and looked away. 'What is happening to all of you? Have you all turned blind?' he asked.

'Yes,' shouted Umer.

'Of course, you will go blind. Because you did not prepare your eyes to receive the light of the sun. Your mind was accustomed to the truth of that darkness and suddenly it has to conceive of a new reality, a reality which your mind did not know existed. This new truth is too strong for your mind to handle. Some it drives mad. This is what a divine encounter feels like. This is what Moses experienced on Mount Sinai, what our Prophet experienced in the Cave of Hira. It can blind you, take over your existence if you are not prepared for it, if there is no one to usher you into that experience. And how do you prepare yourself so that you can eventually experience and survive a divine encounter?'

'You search for a master, a guru, who can take you across this treacherous river,' said Aftab.

'Yes, of course. You need a master. That is the message of all the saints and philosophers, from Socrates to Baba Fareed, from Guru Nanak to Shah Hussain. Okay, now instead of the sun, I want you to look at the tree,' he said, pointing to the banyan tree in the centre of the courtyard. It was here that the three of them often had lunch in the afternoon and took a brief nap. In the evening, just before the maghrib prayers, all the students of the madrasah sat around it, while one of the students volunteered to tell a story. Sometimes these were stories from *Shahnama*, the Persian epic that contained several legends. Of all the stories that Waris had heard from *Shahnama*, he enjoyed the tale of Rustam and Sohrab the most, the tragic story of father and son. On other occasions someone would recite a story from the Mahabharata and they all listened with interest.

Standing alone under the scorching sun, all three of them found it much easier to look at the tree. 'Now I want you to look around. Look at the rooms around the courtyard. Look at the minaret of the mosque. Look at the ground and the trail of ants that you see on it. Look there, far away in the courtyard, that thirsty bird with its parched throat, searching for water to drink. Can you see all of this, without going blind?'

They all nodded.

'Why do you think you are able to see all of these things? What makes them visible?' Maulvi sahib asked.

'The sun,' Aftab spoke again.

'Perfect. It is through the sun that this reality is made manifest to us. It is because of the benevolence of the divine that we are able to comprehend the world around us. It is because of divine reality that we are able to see, think, imagine and discern. Everything around us, in the material as well as the spiritual world, reflects in its radiance, in its glory. Beauty exists in this world, because God is beautiful and allows His beauty to be reflected onto an object which we then perceive to be beautiful. If beauty did not exist as an essence of God, as one of his divine traits, then there would be no beauty in this world. The ninety-nine names of God are these various essences, these perfect forms, that reflect on this world, in various objects and individuals which we then perceive. The world becomes incomprehensible without divine radiance. Knowledge is divine radiance.'

For a moment, Waris felt as if he were back in Jandiala, in the company of his father. He heard his voice in the voice of his teacher. He saw his face in Maulvi sahib's face. He tried putting away the thought, for he feared that if the image of his father stayed in his thoughts any longer, he might break down.

'Now, one last thing,' he continued. 'The life that you see around the courtyard. The ants, the birds, the tree, we know are alive and breathing. They are representatives of life itself. What if there was no sun? Would the tree be able to survive? Would these birds still be alive?' Maulvi sahib was looking towards Aftab, knowing quite well that it was he who would end up answering on everyone's behalf.

'Absolutely not,' said Aftab. 'Their life emanates from the sun. They exist because the sun exists. The sun allows them to participate in its existence. All the creatures of this world, those who are sentient and those that are not, carry within themselves a part of that sun, a part of that radiance. This is what was stated by the learned scholar, Adi Shankara. This is what is at the essence of the Rig Veda and the Upanishads. This is the concept of Brahman, the divine existence, the only unitary existence, out of which all existence emanates and which it is a part of. Everything that exists in this world, us humans, animals and plants, are part of Brahman. They are a part of that ultimate reality.'

'Excellent,' said Maulvi sahib. 'You are absolutely correct. Not just the Vedanta or the Upanishadic philosophy but this remains the central feature of the philosophical ideas of Socrates, as well as the Arab scholar Ibn-Arabi. These are all different paths, different ways. Vedanta, Upanishads, Islam, philosophy, mysticism, to get to the same destination. All is One and One is all. There is nothing but God.'

'But I thought that Hindus worshipped several gods, several idols. Isn't that what separates Islam from the pantheism of Hindus? Our belief in one true God and theirs in multiple false deities,' asked Umer, sounding convinced by his own statement.

'We do have multiple gods and deities but the belief is that they are all different manifestations of one divine existence, Brahman. Did you know that Al-Beruni, the first Arab scholar to ever study our religion, came to the conclusion that Hindus believe in one God? He called us people of the Book, like Christians and Jews. You should try visiting the library more often,' said Aftab, with a certain pride. Umer listened quietly.

'Our entire world and all its experiences are like the darkness of that room. Truth, reality, as we perceive it, is that dark room. However, when we access divine reality, we realise how little we know about true reality, the true world. Now that you have accessed this truth, now that you have learned that there is a world beyond the world of that darkness, would you go back to that room, to that same darkness and forget about this world, its trees, this courtyard and the sun, to spend the rest of your life in that darkness again, content as you were before you had this encounter with the sun, the divine?' Maulvi Ghulam Murtaza was enchanted by his own charisma and almost singing the words.

'Not at all,' replied Umer.

'So, in other words, you have been transformed. One is never the same after a divine encounter. It is the death of the former self and the birth of a new, enlightened self. If there is no transformation, then it is not a divine encounter, for how can you be touched by the divine presence and still be the same?'

'Now you can truly imagine the life of a Sufi, a philosopher, a Qalandar or a Bhagat, who has experienced divine reality, who has drunk from the fountains of the eternal truth. Once these people discover divine truth, the trappings of the material world lose their significance for them. Once that divine reality has been unveiled to them, the fickleness of the material world manifests itself. They lose all interest in it and refuse to engage with it. Others, people around them, those who are still stuck in that dark room, look at these people and think they have lost connection with reality, that they are madmen, but it is in fact these people stuck in the darkness of that room who are actually deluding themselves by believing in a reality which is not real at all.'

Waris's mind conjured up an image of Bulleh Shah dancing on the streets of Kasur. He recalled his initial embarrassment on his behalf. He understood now that Bulleh Shah was ecstatic in his exposure to a divine reality, under the radiance of this metaphorical sun, while Waris was still living in that dark room, content in his ignorance. He began feeling the rhythm of the dhamaal in his feet. He could feel the swirling of his head. For a brief moment, when he understood what his teacher was trying to teach him, Waris too participated in that ecstatic divine existence.

'Well, if such prominent scholars, philosophers have proved that we are all part of that divine existence, then why do people still take offence at Bulleh Shah's poetry? Why do people accuse him of being a kafir or blasphemer, when all he is saying is that there is no distinction between a devotee and the divine? Why was Mansur al-Hajjaj killed for his statement "I am the Absolute Truth?" How is that any different from what is said by Adi Shankara, Socrates or Ibn-Arabi?' asked Waris.

'Waris, my son, I love your passion for poetry. Here I am talking about philosophical concepts and how beautifully you have brought in the poetry of my favourite student, Bulleh Shah, and the spiritual master al-Hajjaj. It is a special gift you have.

This ability to see philosophy in literature, to understand the depth of mysticism in poetry. I can teach you philosophies but I can never teach you that skill. You have raised an important point. Even though the poets and the philosophers were saying the same thing, the poets experienced a backlash unlike the philosophers, well, except for Socrates.'

Maulvi sahib continued, 'The problem is not what you say but rather how you say it. Despite all their efforts, the language of a philosopher remains elusive. They make important and critical points but only those who have mastered their language understand. On the other hand, a poet takes an elusive concept and presents it in a language that everyone can understand. Everybody in Punjab understands what Heer is and what Ranjha is. Everything that I have just explained to you can be summed in this one line, "Call me Ranjha, as I am no longer Heer." The same could be said about legends and stories. They all have a message, a higher philosophical point they are trying to make. What do you think Damodar was trying to do when he wrote *Heer–Ranjha*? Was he just trying to tell us about a love story or was he trying to make a certain philosophical or even political point?'

'It is in this intermarriage between philosophy and politics that your answer lies. All philosophers have certain political opinions that are expressed in their philosophies. Plato wanted rule of the philosophers. Ibn-Arabi also wanted something similar. However, they don't draw the ire of the rulers because their language remains mysterious, erudite, for even the most learned ones. But when al-Hajjaj, Shah Hussain or Bulleh Shah express these philosophical and political ideas in their simple language, the ramifications are very different. Don't make the mistake of thinking that al-Hajjaj was killed for his religious views. He was martyred because his was a political movement, a challenge from the downtrodden to the ruling class. No one cares about Bulleh Shah's religious views. It is his message of equality, his rejection of all hierarchies, of this distinction between a Syed and an Arain, master and servant, between the rulers and the ruled, that threatens them.'

Nothing comes from nothing. Neither Valmiki's Ramayana nor Jayadeva's *Gita Govinda*. Neither Shah Hussain's *kafi* or Damodar's qissa. Like living beings, like humans, these legends, these stories have a soul that resides in heaven, in that world of limbo, called *barzakh*, where all unborn souls live, before they are blown into the womb of the mother. From that heavenly existence, these legends and their characters are conjured into this world. They are therefore both immortal and mortal, similar to how the divine being is both veiled and unveiled.

These legends, these characters, as an immortal entity, are universal symbols. In their heavenly existence, they are archetypes, the qissa of *Heer–Ranjha*, the most perfect love legend, Ranjha, the perfect lover, and Heer, the perfect devotee, but in their earthly existence, when they are summoned by a particular author or a poet, of a particular time period, they cease to be archetypes and become representatives of a particular context.

Just as these legends and their characters, as archetypes, have an existence prior to their worldly life, they continue to have an existence even after their bodily death. They are born over and over again, reincarnated as they are in multiple lives and multiple characters. There is a connection between one incarnation and another. Sometimes this incarnation from one life to another is explained through karma. Sometimes this cycle of life, birth, death and birth again, *samsara*, is explained as the root of misery, from which emancipation, *moksha*, needs to be achieved.

As a universal symbol, an archetype, I too have a pre-existence, somewhere in that world of barzakh. Now if I was a philosopher or a jogi, I would have spent my entire life contemplating my pre-existence, about my life in that heaven. That would have been my purpose, my mission, my dharma. But I am not a philosopher or a jogi, even though I am someone who can quote these mysteries. Perhaps you can think of me as Umer, from the previous section, well versed in all this literature, aware of the complex debates that have been raging across generations, but uninterested in answering them. I am a man of this world, tied to its social, political and economic relations. I have too much at stake, too much to lose if I am ever, God forbid, consumed by that divine ecstasy. As a man of this world, I am aware of these philosophers, these mystics and their musings, for they are also a part of this world even if they vehemently reject it.

I am the leader of the Sials. I am the chief of Jhang. I am Chuchak.

If we were interacting through a different medium, let's say, if you had come to Jhang as my guest, then I would never have given you my introduction in my own words. My servants would have looked after you, prepared your bath, and presented you with new clothes. They would have fed you. Then in the evening, you would have been told about me, about my greatness, about my wealth, the multiple villages that are under my command, the hundreds of buffaloes that I own. My scribe or my family Mirasi, the keeper of our tradition, would have sung to you the songs of my bravery and that of my ancestors. He would have told you the ancient history of the Sial tribe, how we have been rulers of Punjab for centuries, how we were Rajput Hindus, prior to our conversion en masse at the hands of Baba Fareed Shakarganj of Pakpattan, and how we were bestowed economic and political privileges by the greatest Mughal emperor, Akbar the Great.

The nature of our relationship, however, does not permit such formalities. We share an intimate bond, a deep connection which perhaps can be explained through that example which drove Shah Hussain, that young poet from Lahore, insane. As a scholar of the Quran, one day when he came across this divine truth that God is closer to us than our jugular vein, he truly understood the nature of the relationship between the devotee and the divine. He understood that God knew his intentions, even before he knew of them, and if that is the nature of their relationship, if that is the extent of their intimacy, then what need does he have for appeasing God through these outwardly rituals. God knows what is in his heart and that he worships Him with each and every breath. Our relationship is somewhat similar. As a two-dimensional character on these pages, being read by a creature, an entity, far more complex than I, how can I possibly elude you?

As you probably know, my first worldly incarnation was bestowed on me by Damodar Das. Oh, that was a tricky time for Punjab, similar to what the situation is today in many ways. Punjab was experiencing a cataclysmic change. The young Mughal emperor, Akbar, was expanding his kingdom in all directions and many areas that enjoyed autonomy were losing their independence. A new administrative structure was implemented, and new tax regimes were introduced. The Mughal state was centralizing control and many zamindars and *jagirdars* didn't like it one bit.

Those familiar with Punjab would have heard the tales of Dulla Bhatti, the valiant zamindar from Pindi Bhattian who

fought against the mighty Mughal emperor. In his bid to
retain his freedom, he continued a battle that had previously
been fought by his father and grandfather. Even today on the
occasion of every Lohri, when winter begins loosening its grip
over our plains, people sing songs about his bravery and the
humiliation experienced by Akbar. Of course, I don't allow any
such profanities in Jhang or any of my villages. For I understand
much better than the regular, uncouth resident of Punjab the
benefits that came with the Mughals. I recall well the tales of my
ancestors, of how wilderness, insecurity and mayhem had Punjab
in its grip before Akbar extended his majestic gaze upon us.
From darkness, Punjab was ushered into brightness. Prosperity
reigned where once there was chaos. The Mughal ruler had
appointed several representatives all over the province to ensure
that it was protected. My family and I are some of those proud
guardians who were given this glorious task.

If you ask me, rebels like Dulla Bhatti were nothing but
self-interested landowners who wanted to protect their own
economic and political interests. What need is there to celebrate
a man like him, a common criminal? He deserved his fate, a
public execution in Lahore with his body displayed publicly.
It would be a warning to those who were attempting to keep
Punjab in darkness.

What do you think my archetype is in this old tale told
by Damodar? Do I represent the status quo? The political and
economic elite, challenged by ridiculous rebels like Dulla Bhatti
and others? What is the connection between my previous
incarnation and the current one? Are my lives connected by some
sort of karmic divinity or is my soul, my character, searching
for moksha? As in Damodar's time, the Punjab of Waris too is
experiencing unprecedented change. The old structures raised
by the mighty Mughal emperors are in a state of collapse. A new

political force is emerging, a force of the downtrodden, a force of the oppressed, the followers of Guru Gobind Singh. Much has changed between these two Punjabs. Much more remains the same. Is my universal symbol, my archetype, still of the status quo, the political elite in the time of political unrest? Who do you think represents the rebel?

It is a strange thing talking about oneself. It is like flowing with the current of a river. It requires no effort. It takes a life of its own after a little while, and no matter how uncomfortable one is in engaging in this arrogant activity, it is easy to lose oneself in this river of self-love. For that I seek your forgiveness, as I am not an arrogant man and contrary to what you might think, I abhor talking about myself. So let us turn to the topic that I want to discuss.

My Heer, my daughter. A tide of emotions overtakes me, every time I think of her. My body begins to melt, my heart sinks into my stomach, my eyes begin to glitter, and a smile spreads across my face. I am overwhelmed, impatient and satisfied, restless because every particle in my body yearns to be with her. Like a fish out of water, or a soul separated from the body, I become desperate, eager to be with her, in her presence. The rhythm in my heart yearns to hear the beat of her running feet on the ground. The seedlings of spring ache to hear her laughter so that these flowers in my heart can finally sprout, and cocoons can turn into beautiful butterflies. The desert of my existence becomes the lush green fields of Punjab, when Heer, like the Chenab, flows through it.

I am serene when she is in my thoughts, for she is in my presence every time I think about her. The rivers stop flowing, the birds stop chirping, the humdrum of civilization dies down, the sun and the moon halt in their tracks and the earth stops rotating. Time ceases to matter. There is no more regret for what has been and no breathless anticipation of what is in store. All that there is, is just that moment, where only I exist, and in the I of my existence is Heer. Only she exists.

She is our firstborn, born after years and eras of desperation. We prayed at every temple, walked barefoot to every shrine, fed all the Brahmins and distributed langar to every fakir. I consumed all the plants and other remedies, while Maliki, my wife, recited every verse given by the hakim. We tried every medicinal science, Unani, Ayurveda and even the magic spells of jogis. Just when we had begun to think that this season of drought would never end, that God Almighty had destined us to be like trees that bear no fruit, a miracle happened. Maliki got pregnant.

Wrapped in a light blue cloth, she was brought out and put into my arms. I didn't know how to hold her or how to respond. She was smaller and lighter than I had imagined, the tiny features of her face, her fingers, her curled foot, all spoke a language I could not understand. I knew that I had become a father, but I still did not understand what it meant to be one. I felt the trembling in my knees, the bending of my back. My shoulders that were once broad and proud, for the first time, began to slouch. This was not what I had imagined it would feel like. She was light as a feather, but I couldn't bear to carry her weight. I wanted to put her away, and run away, run away to a life which did not exist any more.

Now that we are being honest, allow me to share with you a truth I wish I had long forgotten. In those early months, I could not bring myself to be alone with our infant daughter. I had held her the day she was born, and not again, for several months. I would rush away from home, as soon as I woke up, only to return late in the night. I could not bring myself to confront her, for through that confrontation, I was being made to confront myself. She was a constant reminder that I was responsible for a body totally dependent on me. A brave, grown man, I was accustomed to lead, to be in control, I hated this new feeling of vulnerability.

If it was up to me, the rest of my days would have been spent in this denial, but my beautiful Heer had other plans. It was one of those chilly mornings, when the winter is not completely free. I had woken up early, earlier than usual, disturbed all night by the thought of a land dispute among my tribe that I had to address in the morning. For an unusual reason, for it was not something I had ever done before, I looked into her crib. Unaware of my anxieties, she was wide awake; her eyes, detecting mine, found a sparkle. Her face brightened up, a wide smile spread on her lips. She became restless, playful, fighting with her arms and knees. I picked her up and kissed her on the forehead. In that moment, I experienced true love. I can try to explain to you what that feeling was for, if anything, our Waris knows how to write about love, but in this case, even he, the master poet, would fail. It is an emotion that can never be expressed, only felt. She had me in her spell. There is magic in her being. No one is like her, nothing.

From that day onwards, I became her little toy. My shoulders were her first ride, my lap her perennial bed. It was my finger she clasped when she discovered her feet. She was always in search of me when I was not at home and would greet me with exuberance when I returned. From that time till the time she slept, it was just the two of us; nobody else mattered. Maliki and I soon had another child, a boy this time, whom we named Sultan, king of the world. He would be my successor, the inheritor of my wealth. One day he would sit on the seat of the chief of the Sial clan. I loved him as well, perhaps as much as Heer, but found it hard to express it to him, with the kind of ease that Heer drew out of me. In his mother, in Maliki, he found the support that Heer found in me. To an undiscerning observer, it seemed like we had our favourites, an impression we had no intention of challenging.

Of late, however, Maliki has been raising a concern. She tells me that I have to rein in Heer, that I have given her too much freedom and that she has forgotten the true role of women in our society. Heer, she says, is no longer a child. Gone are her carefree days, when she could roam around the streets of Jhang with her friends, run into the jungle and bathe in the waters of the Chenab. She tells me that both her body and her thoughts need to be regulated. She needs to learn how to be docile, submissive to the will of her future husband. She needs to learn household chores, instead of engaging in verbal duels. She tells me that it is my love which has emboldened her and that it is now my responsibility to train her.

My ears hear her concerns but my heart refuses to listen. I see a little girl running towards me with her open arms, when she talks about the growing body of my child. She tells me that I should confine her movement to within this house, while I wonder how to open up the joys of paradise for her, for no doubt while Jhang is heaven, I know that greater worlds abound. She tells me that Heer does as she pleases. I wonder how else are princesses, who are destined to be queens, supposed to act. The norm becomes what the queen desires as all other rules disintegrate. She tells me that Heer needs to learn to be submissive so that one day she can cater to the whims of her husband, and I wonder does divine will ever submit?

O Waris, if only Maliki understood the magnificence of Heer.

She entered the courtyard, thundering with her determined feet. Our household came to life once again as the world began dancing to the tinkle of her anklets. Her face lit up when she saw me, the same way it had on that fateful morning when she first charmed me. There was an unknown man in tattered clothes walking behind her. His gangly limbs hung by his side and his sunburned skin told its own tale. The entire household, Maliki, Sultan and all our servants were thinking about him, sharing secret looks, while I was only looking at Heer. Ignoring the questioning looks of everyone around her, she walked straight to me. She introduced me to Dhido Ranjha and told me that he would be our new buffalo herder. She had already made the decision. She only needed my formal approval.

For the first time, I looked at the boy and registered his condition. He looked like someone from a respectable family despite his appearance, for one can never hide one's paternity, even if one tries. Can a crow ever pass off for a swan, a Shudra as a Brahmin, a Musali as a Syed, or the peasant warlords as mighty Mughal emperors?

'He can run as fast as a cheetah and swim the deepest seas. He has the eye of an eagle and the heart of a saint,' said Heer. 'None of our animals would ever be lost again for we are truly blessed to have found someone like Ranjha to be our buffalo herder.'

'My daughter, where have you found this man? He has a certain radiance about him, a touch of divinity. But how am I to trust a person who has abandoned his own home? You tell me he was dealt a poor hand. That luck has conspired with his brothers to deprive him of his ancestral heritage. The Ranjhas are a respectable lot, even though they are nowhere near our stature, but how can I trust a man who has no other man to vouch for him, so far away from his home. He might have told you all these tales about himself, which you now believe to be true, but my dear daughter, you are still a child, blessed with all of life's fortunes. You are unaware of its brutalities; such has been the reach of my protection. He could have duped you with his words. How can I trust a man not even trusted by his own brothers?' I said to her.

'If you believe in the divinity of the divine, the Oneness of its existence, if you believe in the finality of our Prophet, in the truth of his message, then you should also believe in me. I vouch for him as the saints vouched for the divine. I know that he tells the truth for his word itself is a measure of veracity. He has come from far away, hearing about the generosity of the Sials. We, who once welcomed the Chenab to our threshold, how can we now send away a man in need? What will be said about us, how will the world remember us? We who have earned this pride over generations will lose all our honour in this one swift action. Think very carefully, my dear father, for in this moment lies the future destiny of our progeny. How would we ever be able to wipe out this stain? Even the pure waters of the Ganga will not be able to wash away our sins,' said Heer.

With the passion of the newly converted, my daughter fought her case. I eventually conceded to her demand and hired the young boy as our family servant. He was now to look after our herd and Heer was to look after him. I had made that decision and reverted to my known life, assured that I had salvaged the honour of the Sials.

4

The Season of Love

There was a pattern to its insanity. In the dead of night, it would roam the winding streets of Kasur, howling and cursing, banging loudly on the wooden windows and doors, its sound resonating in the empty lanes. No one would respond to its cries. Shivering under thick blankets, they would pray for the demon to disappear. But it never did. It would get even bolder in the summers, roving across the city, through its labyrinth passages in broad daylight, when the sun was at its peak. It would sing songs of seduction. In a state of mania, it would be at its charismatic best. For the unacquainted, there was a lure in these songs. Sometimes they would step out through the door or peep from a window searching for something that was never there. The majority, however, were aware of these seasonal patterns. They shut themselves up in their homes, waiting for the madness to pass, so that they could step out after that.

It was only in the season of love that it was truly accepted. It would run through the streets, racing with the children who were chasing one another. All the doors and windows would then be opened and it would be allowed to enter and stay for as long as it liked, sometimes even through the night. Passing through the street corners, where the men usually gathered through the day, it would be smiled at, embraced and welcomed. In the courtyards, where women got together for spinning, it would sit along with them, sharing with them stories from the street.

In the open ground, known as *khula maidan*, in the heart of the city, it would dance like a dervish. Partaking of that special drink of the jogis and *malang*, bhang, it would whirl uncontrollably, inebriated, marching from one corner to another. It would carry in its hands colours, the brightest in the world, and blow them onto every passer-by. For these couple of weeks, it was forgiven all trespasses; it was forgiven all sins.

It was the season of *bahar*, the season of basant. It was the season of intoxication, majestic spring. The thick blankets everyone had worn through the dry killer winter were now shunned, revealing the dyed, colourful clothes. There were smiles on everyone's faces, seduction in everyone's eyes. It was the season of lovers, of blooming hearts and secret rendezvous. It was the shortest season in the year. Flowers grew in the most unexpected of places, in between the cobblestones on the paved streets, sprouting from walls and even from the corners of the drain. It was a season when everything was in moderation, the cold, the heat, the length of the day and the depth of the night, everything except people's behaviour. Even those who never consumed it had some bhang, while others enjoyed wine. There was an unlimited supply of fruits and food, for a never-ending appetite.

It was the first and the only time Waris tried bhang. It had taken some convincing on the part of Umer and Aftab. It was after all the festival of Holi, the celebration of spring. It was the only time in the year when the forbidden was permissible, they argued. 'And this is not an intoxicant, Waris,' said Aftab. 'This is the bestower of joy; it is what binds the heart. This is the leaf of insight or, should I say, the liberator.'

They had been given two weeks off from their studies. Kasur, ever since it had become aligned with the Mughals, had formally begun celebrating Holi, merging it with the festival of Navroz. The entire city participated in the celebrations, as all other activities came to a halt. In recent years, even though the city only maintained a nominal relationship with the court in Delhi, the tradition survived. All across the city, everyone, men and women alike, consumed bhang. It was the season when everything was sacred; nothing was profane.

Waris understood well the significance of bhang in the ascetic tradition. He knew that it was important to consume it sometimes to access a higher truth, a higher realm of reality. He had seen many a dervish and Sufi engage in its consumption several times, but he found it hard to convince himself to do it. He still struggled with the legality of it. He knew that there were several scholars who disapproved of such intoxicants, who argued that just like wine or alcohol, hashish, bhang and other intoxicants were not permissible in Islam.

Perhaps, if the question only came down to its legality, Waris wouldn't have felt much inhibition in trying it. He was never one to obsess about rituals or the permissibility of things even though he followed all of them; he did it because he didn't know it was possible not to do so. This is how he had grown up. This is what he had seen his father do. Now that he was an adult, the practices that had been rooted within him had grown into a self-sustaining tree.

Particularly after the death of his father, these religious rituals and rules had acquired a greater significance for him. They allowed him to connect with Gulsher Shah, to imagine him and converse with him, not with words but through thoughts. He was happy and satisfied when he was offering his namaz. He didn't know what would become of him if he abandoned it, or the other religious rituals, for that matter. It wasn't Waris who was rejecting bhang but the voice of this father that now dwelt within him.

However, while Gusher Shah's voice resided within him, there was another voice in him that was beginning to assert itself, the voice of youth, excitement, possibilities, rebellion and self-belief. This emerging voice overpowered Waris so much that he could no longer hear the voice of his father. It helped that this voice found a certain resonance with the external world.

Like the rest of the city, he too was seduced by the gentle breeze. As if overcome by lust, after being united with one's lover after a season of separation, he was losing control. His inhibitions were melting away and his defenses were being defeated. His words continued paying lip service to his values, but his heart was already convinced. Umer and Aftab, who had by now spent several seasons with their friend, knew about this losing battle that Waris was constantly engaged in. Just a little push and Waris would be off the precipice. He wouldn't fall but fly, wouldn't crash but soar. Crushing the hemp leaves into a paste, they mixed it into almond milk and gulped it down. Once the fortress of inhibition had been breached, there was no moderation.

Waris saw the motion of the arm. He noticed the hand, clenched into a fist, the red dust falling out of it, thrown rapidly towards him. It happened in a flash, or so it seemed. Waris didn't have the time to look away, or shut his eyes. The red dust however had other plans. It had realized Waris's vulnerabilities, his helplessness. It slowed down as soon as it left the hand, hanging languidly in front of his face, staring back as intently at Waris as he saw it. Waris smiled at the dust. He could see a relaxation of its muscles. Its eyebrows arched intently, as a smile spread on its lips. He extended his hand, wanting to touch this beautiful red face, but it dismantled. Waris felt a rush of blood to his head; a lethargy seeped into his body. He felt his hand hanging in the air, realizing that he was trying to hold the spring breeze, draped in a red cloak. He felt a sense of embarrassment and looked around to see if anyone had noticed his strange behaviour.

He was standing in a corner of the khula maidan. The three of them had come here after drinking some bhang. While walking towards the ground, Waris was constantly trying to observe his own behaviour to see if the hemp was taking effect. He did not feel anything at all and wasn't sure if he was relieved or disappointed. Umer and Aftab too seemed like themselves, just a little happier than usual, but that could very well be due to the weather or the excitement of the festivities. It was at that moment that Waris, realizing that he had been seeing a smiling face in the red dust, understood the potency of the bhang. A smile spread across his eyes and lips, as he felt a jolt of happiness run through his body.

All across the ground, he saw the spring breeze swaying the colourful clothes that it wore and took off, one after the other. These clouds of colours all had unique shapes, fascinating figures. They took on various incarnations, lived various lives in a short span of time, from rats to full-grown human beings. He saw horned demons become angels with wings, peasants on bullock carts transform into soldiers on chariots on the battleground of Kurukshetra. There were all kinds of scenes, as if the river of time had ceased to flow and everything that had ever happened on earth was now laid out on the ground. This was a strange place, an alternative reality, where the creatures of heaven and hell mingled with the animals and humans from this world.

In this chaos, Waris caught her eyes. They were questioning him with reserved anticipation. They were brave, resisting the expectations of decorum and staring straight at him. For a moment, Waris almost looked away, afraid that he might infringe upon her modesty, but he sensed a defiance, a jettisoning of societal inhibitions. Summoning up all his strength, he looked back at them. He felt his weight drop and an excitement rush upwards from his knees. His heart fluttered, something it had never done before, as if in that moment, a beautiful butterfly was discovering its wings in his chest. It seemed as if, at any time, this butterfly would tear through his body and fly into the sky. He wanted to say something. Her eyes wouldn't let him, though.

He saw the sudden movement of the arm as yet again, another cloud of red dust was thrown at him. This time, he closed his eyes. The red dust fell all over his face. It caressed his skin, planted gentle kisses and held his face in its hands. Waris opened his eyes to see her eyes still looking at him, this time laughing loudly. They urged him to follow her, almost challenged him. She turned around and ran away, stopping at a little distance to see if he was up to the duel.

Waris followed her, his hand closed in a fist as if he was carrying colour in them. She skirted around the edge of the ground and stopped in front of a stall where coloured powder had been placed for anyone to pick up. She continued running in front of him, while Waris ran after her, without any idea of what he would do when he finally caught up. As he neared her, she slowed down, turned around and threw another cloud of colour at him. His face was now covered with yellow kisses. For the first time, Waris noticed her face, as round as her eyes, her thick hair tied in a braid, jumping against her back, like the waves of an ocean crashing against a cliff. His heart followed the poetry of her oscillating braid. Her face was covered with multiple colours, with a predominant shade of purple. He couldn't tell if he had seen her before or if she even belonged to Kasur. Perhaps she was a goddess, a devi, an apsara or a houri that had descended from the heavens, in this mixing of the worlds.

Having been defeated twice by her, Waris was now finally ready to engage. He filled both his fists with green and red powder and chased after her. Her pace increased and so did his, as they ran from one part of the maidan to the other, their young legs riding upon the gentle spring breeze. She slowed down a little, allowing him to catch up. He discarded all his armoury upon her, the red and green settling on her purple face, transforming it into silver and brown. Their eyes met once again, as the lips remained silent, more comfortable and familiar in each other's embrace. On this crowded ground, where the entire city had gathered, they only saw each other, played Holi with no one else. They remained engaged in this battle for what felt like an eternity at that moment. He didn't ask her name or anything else and neither did she; the longevity of their love story was confined to this occasion, to this battle which had completely subsumed them.

The story ended as abruptly as it had begun. It was Waris's turn to chase her, to respond to her affront. With only her braid in sight, he ran through the crowd, eager to catch up with her, to unleash upon her the colour of love. He banged forcefully into a body, as the colour that he held in his hand fell to the ground. For the first time in a while, he took his eyes off her and saw who he had run into. It was Aftab, who had been searching for Waris from the moment they had come to the ground. They were worried about their friend. He had got separated from them in the rush of the crowd, and they were concerned he might begin to panic, as those who have had hemp sometimes do. Aftab's eyes lit up, when he realized he had found his friend. He held Waris with both his hands and gave him a tight hug.

Waris's heart, still beating to the rhythm of the braid, looked over Aftab's shoulder to search for it, but it was gone. Her brown, silver and purple face was lost in the crowd.

'Have you been alright? Where have you been?' Aftab asked Waris, but Waris was in no position to respond. He could only nod and say, 'Hmm,' his eyes still scanning the crowd, looking for those colours and the braid.

'Come with me. The best part of Holi is about to begin,' said Aftab, as he held Waris's arm and dragged him along. Waris allowed himself to be led, convinced that he would see her face again. How could he not? They had been brought together by fate, by divine will. He was still looking around trying to locate her as they moved to the middle of the ground, where a huge crowd of mostly young men had gathered. Hanging atop the ground by a thin wire that ran across two buildings was a *matka*, an earthen pot. Aftab put one of his arms around Waris's shoulder and the other around that of Umer. 'Hold on tight,' he warned Waris. Waris felt another arm come around his shoulders, while a set of hands held his back tightly from behind. He wanted to turn around to see who it was, imagining her standing behind him, but Aftab instructed him to look straight ahead and lower his head.

It felt as if an army of bodies had mounted his back and shoulders. There was no end to it as the human pyramid above him began to grow. He cemented his feet on the ground and tightened his arms. He was wondering how many layers had formed above him, but there was no way of knowing. He thought about the height of the and figured it would probably take about four or five tiers of people to get to the top. For a little while, his mind focused on the matka-breaking game.

After two unsuccessful attempts, the matka was finally broken on the third attempt and Waris, along with the rest of the crowd, let out a loud cheer. The boy who had achieved the feat at the top was the youngest of the lot, no more than twelve. A group of boys carried him on their shoulders and began yelling, 'Here is our Krishna, here is our Krishna,' as he sat proudly on their shoulders.

That night, Waris tossed and turned. The window in the room was open and the gentle breeze blew silently in, taking Waris in its embrace. He thought repeatedly about the day's encounter and felt the sensation of the coloured dust on his face and remembered the mischief in her eyes. He wondered where she was right now and if she too was thinking about him, if she too was confessing to the breeze her love for him.

I was there even before time, as an idea, existed. Before the first cities, Harappa, Mohenjo-daro and Mehrgarh. I was there before there were humans, before they colonized the world with their ideas. They found a beginning where there was none, and proposed an impending end. They created time, in their own image, manufactured an illusion of control, imposing finite limitations on a phenomenon that flowed infinitely. I was there before the misconceptions of linearity, chronology and history took root. Before there was mythology. I was a witness to the birth of civilization, the rise of distinction between what was wild and what was cultured. I saw the gradual dissemination of norms and values, the first set of rules and other impositions. I saw the violence of their stifling grip over people's imaginations and the wrath of the guardians of these holy laws and sacred traditions.

They came running to me, the first set of rebels, from Siddharth, Mahavira, Gorakhnath, to Fareed, Nanak and Waris.

I offered them respite and removed the blinkers of preconceived notions from their eyes. I am reminder of a time before time, of a world before it was conceived. I am pure existence, untainted, unrestrained. I have no past; I have no end. I am what life was intended to look like before it was tamed. Couched within self-created constraints, the mortal finds comfort. My boundless vitality frightens them, it takes away all semblance of control. It is to shed away this pretence, to relinquish this control that the jogi, the dervish, the Sufi, turn towards me. In my peripheral existence, on the margins of society, the Sufis find their goal. I represent chaos, ferocity to the ordinary members of society, but to an ascetic, I symbolize a break from all traditions, all conventions. Here, in the forest, amidst the unorchestrated growth of the trees, in the company of wildings, all religious laws, conventions, familial bonds cease to exist. I represent a life oppressively free, a life full of possibilities, a life full of threats.

It is I, the forest, that is the site of our next scene, the rendezvous between Heer and Ranjha. Here, in the forest, Heer is not the daughter of Chuchak. She is no one's sister or honour, and Dhido Ranjha is just Dhido, a blank slate, an empty sheet of paper, on which he would write his own story, his own tale, unfettered by the baggage of his past, or the burden of expectations. In the forest, where the rules of the world disintegrate, it doesn't matter that these two lovers are not married. I, the forest, bear witness to their union, without demanding any societal sanctions. To me, every union is pure, every act of love legitimate. In my world, the lovers set their own limitations; they decide their own rules.

The same morning descends upon Jhang and me, but it represents two different things. While the morning is a reminder to the city of its responsibilities and compulsions, to the forest, it is the beginning of a celebration. Young leaves wake up from slumber and search for the rays of the sun, as if it was the love of a mother that poor Waris never experienced. The birds dance in the air, feeding off the spring breeze as if it was their breakfast. Carrying the message of morning, the butterflies travel from one flower to the next, scattering colours on their way. A congregation of animals gathers by the river, as if it were arriving for the fajr prayers. The sound of the river echoes throughout the forest, like melodies from the flute of Krishna, and all the creatures on its banks, his gopis, arrive to quench their thirst.

Sitting under a banyan tree, next to the river, our Ranjha plays the flute. Lying on his lap, with her dishevelled hair scattered around her face is Heer. With her eyes closed, she is lost in meditation, reciting the name of the divine, reciting the name of her Ram. Next to them is the empty utensil that Heer had brought from her home, containing churi made of ghee, gourd, butter and milk. She had made it herself, one of those rare moments when she had sat by the hearth cooking. Her unusual behaviour had not gone unnoticed. Maliki, her mother, and the house servants, while busy with their own chores, had noticed. She used to visit me earlier as well, with her friends, when she would swing upon my branches, and run around my trunks. She would chase the deer and rabbits and dive into the river. But this was a different Heer. Her eyes were fixed upon her Ranjha, her focus pinned on his comfort.

She had fed him with one hand, while fanning him with the other. She gave him two bites and then took one herself, upon his insistence. The forest that had once captured her imagination did not interest her any more. Nor did her friends who, like an army without a general, scattered around the forest without purpose. Some swam in the river among the fish, chasing the brightest of them, eager to feel their smooth skin on their palms.

Some sat by the riverbank, caressing the swans, eyeing Heer and her Ranjha resentfully. Some hid behind the trunk of the tree, where the lovers sat, and put their hands around Ranjha's eyes, asking him flirtatiously if he remembered their names. Some ruffled the hair on his head and challenged him to chase them, while some placed a gentle kiss on his cheeks, expecting Ranjha to do the same. Our Krishna was surrounded by beautiful maidens. They vied for his attention; they overwhelmed him with their pleas. Krishna, however, was not interested. His love was reserved only for his Heer.

Our Radha, our Heer, would have had a cause for concern if he had reciprocated. Like Radha, she would have complained to her Krishna, if Ranjha, this deity of love, had held their waists, caressed their breasts or planted gentle kisses on their necks. If that had been the case, then this poor Waris, like Jayadeva as Radha's advocate, would have penned Heer's pleas, as Radha's were recorded in *Gita Govinda*. Waris would have expressed her lamentations and would have made Ranjha realize, like Krishna was made to before him. But that was not to be. Our Ranjha had learned from Krishna's mistakes. His gaze was fixed upon Heer, as if he was Arjuna, the marksman, eyeing the bullseye. Can Arjuna ever miss his aim? Can Radha be forgotten by Krishna? Can Ranjha's love ever be for someone else but Heer?

With these two lovers lost in each other, I took it upon myself to look after the buffaloes. It was the most beautiful herd in the entire city of Jhang, composed of the best breeds of Punjab. There were buffaloes of all varieties. They offered the sweetest, densest milk and produced the gentlest of offspring. They too had fallen in love with our Ranjha. In the morning, when he set off from the city, they formed a straight line behind him, not even one straying away. They had experienced several buffalo herders before him, but never one as kind as Ranjha.

They swayed their heads to the music of his flute, chewed their fodder to the rhythm of his raga. They spread all over the forest, as if sentries on patrol. They knew that while the world thought it was Ranjha who was looking out for them, it was in fact they who had to protect his secret.

It was a secret that the entire forest conspired to preserve. The predators, who would have keenly feasted on their meat, deliberately kept away. The river, which had earlier accepted the sacrifice of so many beasts, slowed down as it passed through this part of the forest, careful not to consume anyone. Our Ranjha, who had never worked a day in his life, who had been mocked by his brothers and his sisters-in-law, was turning out to be a splendid buffalo herder. The herd thrived under him. Their milk became sweeter, their attitude even more passive. The entire forest and the city were enamoured with his charm, while he was in love with Heer.

In the night, when the sun receded and darkness wrapped its chaddar across the sky, and a veil of ignorance was wrapped around the eyes of Chuchak and Maliki, Heer would sneak out of her home, out of the chokehold of the city's rules and regulations, and meet Ranjha in the hut of Mithi, located next to the river, in the embrace of the forest. Mithi was the family servant, a loyal attendant of her mother, but her commitment had been shattered; her fealty had been bought. Five gold coins had been dangled in front of her eyes, more than a year's wages, and so Mithi had offered her hut to the lovers.

Every evening, she would prepare their bedding, sprinkle it with rose petals, as if Heer was her daughter and Ranjha her son-in-law. She was there to answer all questions, to explain all the intricacies of love. Before Heer's arrival, she sat Ranjha down and told him about women, about their fidelity and ferocity, about their generosity and animosity. She explained to him about love, about its gentleness and its wrath. She described for him the sweet taste of its nectar. She warned him about its poisonous nature. She told him about the strength of the bond and its weakness.

With his arm under her head, their bodies clung to each other, they lay on the bed of roses. 'I have been searching for you all my life,' said Heer to Ranjha. 'Without you, I was a soul without a body, a boat without a boatman, a cart without a bull, a devotee without the divine. I am yours, forever, in this life and that which is reserved in heaven, in all my other incarnations, those that I have already lived and those that I am yet to experience.'

'It is in your search that I have roamed as a mendicant from one stop to another. Like a stray dog, I have been shooed away; in your love, I have shed my pride, my prestige and relinquished all pleasures. I was once Dhido Ranjha, the scion of Mauja Chaudary. Look at me now. I am your family servant. But I fear sometimes. Sometimes I doubt your loyalty. It is not you who is to be blamed, but rather your womanly nature. For you are made of a disloyal gene. No man can ever trust a woman completely, even when she is a part of his being.'

'O Ranjha, you are the wisest of them all, but sometimes you talk like a fool. Were not both Adam and Eve created from the same mould? Were not all the saints and gurus borne by women? Did not Zulaikha renounce her kingdom for Yousuf, or Sohni drown herself for Mahiwal? Did not Sassi become a martyr for Punnu, or Shirin sacrifice herself for Farhad? I am your slave for now, and forever. Sell me to a brothel, or carve me into tiny pieces with a knife, and dispose of me in a body of water. Your name would still resonate from the depths of the river; Chenab will provide you with testimony to my commitment.'

They renewed their vows to each other, before the break of dawn, before the light could carry the secret of their union to the rest of the town. Heer would leave shortly, to return once again later in the day. Secretly they met in the forest, as I took an oath to keep them shielded, promised to keep at bay the norms and values of society. Their love prospered in the forest, a love rendered impure outside my sanctuary. For now, all was well in this universe, for their secret was secure in my bosom.

5

A Storm Brewing

Her eyes transformed into fish and leaped out of the manuscript. Waris shut the book in frustration. For months now, he had turned to Jayadeva's *Gita Govinda* during his free time in search of the girl he had had a brief encounter with during the Holi celebrations. He hadn't needed the inspiration in the beginning. Her face would appear in front of him, at the first memory of the sensation he had experienced on that beautiful afternoon. Gradually, however, the face, covered in colour, became harder to recall. The eyes lingered on for a little while longer before they too disappeared. In his desperation to keep alive the physical memory (he had no difficulty remembering what that experience felt like) he turned towards the greatest love story there ever was.

Since the past couple of weeks, the students had had much more free time on their hands. Maulvi sahib had been engaged with another student—Bulleh Shah. For some time after his return to Kasur, the Pathan families of the city had tolerated his idiosyncrasies. As long as his taunts were riddled in poetry, he was allowed to be. But for the past month or so, Bulleh Shah had become more direct. The frequency of the dhamaal had decreased and that of his sermons had increased. He spoke against the ever increasing taxes and the violence committed on the bodies of peasants. He had begun speaking in favour of the Sikh guerilla groups, and against the brutalities committed by Zakariya Khan in the name of the Mughal empire. He lambasted the silence of the religious leaders, the mullahs and the priests, dependent on the generosity of the ruling families. He criticized their obsession with religious rituals, and the unjust political system that prevailed owing to such patronage.

However, more than the behaviour of Bulleh Shah, it was the political situation in Punjab that had changed. Various Sikh groups now controlled vast tracts of land including several villages and towns all over Punjab. The city had become an island surrounded by areas under the sway of various Sikh rulers. With an extension of the Sikh stronghold also came control over the trading routes which had brought Kasur its economic prosperity. Fear now resided within the ruling elite families of the city, fear about an imminent storm; fear of losing their independence.

If this was not enough, there was also a fear of the Marathas. The Marathas, the strongest political and military force in Hindustan, were now heading north-westwards, towards Punjab, Kasur and Lahore. It was only a matter of time before this invasion. Even if the Pathan ruler somehow found a way to halt the progress of the Sikh groups, there was no way they would have been able to hold their position against the mighty Marathas. Only a divine miracle could save them.

Finding themselves stuck in the middle of two powerful forces, the Pathan rulers began doing what all autocrats do in a similar situation—crack down on any local dissent. Perhaps at a different time, Bulleh Shah would have been allowed to be. His words would not have threatened the existence of this political system, but this was unlike any other time. This was a time of fear. The religious establishment responded to Bulleh Shah's attack by resorting to its previous tactic of calling him a kafir. The political establishment began spreading rumours that he was a Sikh agent. He was a spy, they said, who had been planted here by the Sikh leadership to disclose Kasur's secrets to them so that they could capture the city.

Once again, it was Maulvi Ghulam Murtaza who came to his student's rescue. He asked the ruling elite for some time to intercede with Bulleh Shah on their behalf. Bulleh Shah, being Bulleh Shah, would have listened to no one else. For days on end, the teacher was in the company of his student, engaging with him, trying to make him realize the severity of the situation.

With Maulvi sahib away from the madrasah, the regular structure and discipline that he had ensured at the institution, mostly by his presence, began to disintegrate. It was the seniormost students, Waris, Aftab and Umer, who experienced the greatest rupture in their routine, for it was they who were taught most frequently by him.

While Umer began spending most of his newly discovered free time in the city, Waris and Aftab were often found in the library. With *Gita Govinda* in his hand, Waris would find a quiet corner and read this iconic love legend of Radha and Krishna. Reading Jayadeva's description of Radha's face and her body, over and over again, Waris, without realizing it, had supplemented the image of the girl in his mind with the image of Radha as described by Jayadeva. It was now in Radha's image that he began imagining his beloved. It was Radha's fish-shaped eyes that he would see, instead of her rounder ones. It was Radha's full breasts he would imagine, instead of her partially formed ones. And then, slowly, his mind stopped playing along.

No matter how many times he read the description of Radha's physicality, he could not conjure up an image in his mind. He had finally accepted that, no matter how hard he tried, he could not remember her physical features.

Annoyed with himself, he shut the book and looked up. Aftab was still sitting in his corner, his head buried in a manuscript. Waris could see slanted sunrays cut through the open window, as they fell and dispersed on the floor. Through their angle, he knew it was late afternoon. He continued staring at those rays, as tiny particles performed dhamaal in the spotlight. He was lost in his thoughts, when Umer entered the room and sat next to him.

'I have some bad news,' said Umer, panting. Hearing his voice, Aftab lifted his head up. 'Maulvi sahib will be returning to the madrasah tonight. It's back to our routine once again.'

'Has Bulleh Shah agreed to tone down his rhetoric?' asked Waris.

'No,' Umer said, angrily. 'If only. That imbecile is stubborn as a donkey. You won't believe what he has done now. I have just heard from my uncle. It's not public knowledge. He has run off and found refuge in Daftu.'

Umer's uncle was head of the *hifazati majlis,* for the city. Umer sometimes shadowed him when he had the time, riding along with him, as he inspected the troops, sitting next to him when he received intelligence reports. Through his family, he had inherited the fear that had spread within the ruling elite. He had inherited their revulsion for Bulleh Shah. When he opined on Bulleh Shah, the words were his, but the opinions were those of his uncles, his father and other relatives.

'Did you hear me? Daftu! Of all the places, he had to choose Daftu,' continued Umer, convinced that by repeating the name of the village, he would be able to persuade his listeners of Bulleh Shah's crime.

'You know why he choose Daftu, right?' he asked, unsure if his words were having the desired impact. 'He is a kafir at heart. Why else would he run off to Daftu, and why would those Sikh infidels of Daftu, its so-called chiefs, take him in? He left like a coward, under cover of darkness. Our soldiers chased him when they discovered his escape, but abandoned the hunt when he entered the vicinity of Daftu. That would have started a battle between the two neighbouring towns. And for what? One irrelevant mendicant? Let him go to hell,' he said, feigning indifference.

Waris was crestfallen to hear the news of Bulleh Shah's exile. He had found comfort in the fact that Bulleh Shah was in the same city as he was. He had felt a sense of security and now it was gone. He wondered what role Maulvi sahib had played in Bulleh Shah's escape. He wanted to ask Umer but did not want to cast any suspicions on their teacher.

Aftab and Waris were surprised by their friend's passionate outburst. Umer never had strong opinions about anything. They didn't know how to respond. Busy with their reading, they had been unaware of the conversations that had been taking place outside the library, beyond the walls of the madrasah. Both of them remained quiet as Umer spoke. It was Aftab's silence, rather than that of Waris, that was stark. He was hardly one to shy away from a discussion. Here was a perfect opportunity but he remained quiet. There was something in Umer's tone that deterred him. Waris noticed this silence but couldn't understand the reason behind it.

'You know, this Diwali, perhaps we can celebrate the exodus of evil and tyranny from Kasur,' said Waris, trying to diffuse the tension. Aftab laughed awkwardly.

'You know, this is the problem with us Muslims. This is the reason Allah is punishing us by taking power away from us, and giving it to these uncouth Jatts—the Sikhs—and the infidel Marathas. They control vast tracts of lands now, entire villages, towns, cities, places that were once ruled by the Muslims. We have lost everything and there is so much more we'll lose if Kasur is lost.'

Umer became quiet, staring intently at the floor, and then continued after a little while, 'Oh, they'll try. For sure, they will try. How long before they enter our city, challenge our sovereignty? How long before they make us their slaves, bar us from practising our religion, taunt us for worshipping the true God? They will defile our women with their impure bodies, play Holi with our blood. They will bar the sound of the azaan from all mosques and cut off the head of anyone seen offering namaz. We'll be left with no other option but to pretend to be Sikhs or Hindus. We have to stop them now. It has to begin by strengthening ourselves from within, by rooting out all traitors that are part of our society and purifying it.'

Aftab felt as if his entire weight had decided to move to his stomach and then rush towards his head, blurring his vision. He felt a light-headedness as drops of sweat appeared all over his body. He could feel the rate of his breathing increase, his heart pumping faster, but he didn't want to show his emotions, didn't want to remind his friend that he was indeed a Hindu who had taken on this name to blend easily into this society. He noticed how Umer looked at him, trying to look for signs, for any allusions that Umer was making.

Of course, Umer knew Aftab's real name was Kanhaiya Kumar and that he was a Hindu, but it hadn't ever mattered. To Umer, it still didn't matter. Aftab was a part of his definition of us, so comfortable was he with his presence, but Aftab had no way of knowing that. He found signs in Umer's tone, words and body language, where there were none.

'What are you talking about, Umer? What has got into you?' asked Waris, a little annoyed, but also afraid. 'I know the Sikhs now control large parts of Punjab. They control my village. They are the reason I am here, removed from the land that contains the graves of my ancestors but how can you blame these political changes on the religiosity of Muslims? That is a ridiculous idea. What impurity? What traitors are you talking about?'

'Waris, open your eyes and see what is happening around you,' Umer said, patronizingly. 'The world is changing. God has abandoned us. He has left Punjab and settled in the west. For five hundred years, kings from Delhi ruled over the barbaric Afghans, and now Delhi lies in ruins, and Afghani cities flourish. God is with them because they are true to him. They are true Muslims. They follow a pure Islam, untainted by corrupt pagan practices. Look at us here. We consume bhang and break matkas on Holi as if it is an Islamic ritual. We celebrate the works of pagan scholars and poets, and fool ourselves into believing that we are expanding our intellect. Our ways have become corrupt. There is now no difference between us, Hindus and the Sikhs. We revere the same saints, go to the same shrines, celebrate the same festivals. It is disgusting. We have lost our religion and adopted paganism. Can we continue calling ourselves Muslim? Can we continue calling this Islam? The sun now rises in the west and it is towards the west that we need to turn. Our king is now Ahmad Shah Abdali, the true Muslim King, like Mahmud Ghaznavi before him. He is our only hope. Only he can save us from ourselves and the infidels amidst us. Only he can restore our lost glory.'

'You know, Aftab, you always used to make fun of me that I didn't spend enough time in the library,' continued Umer. 'That is true. But that doesn't mean I haven't been reading. I was at my uncle's home last week when he handed me a bunch of books by Shah Waliullah Dehlawi. Oh, what an experience it has been. I read several of his writings this entire week. I feel like a new person. He has opened my eyes to the truth that I was blinded to. I am full of regret that I have spent all my life without discovering his wisdom. It feels like a life wasted. I would highly recommend that you read his work too. You need to.'

At the mention of Shah Waliullah, Waris and Aftab exchanged a brief glance that Umer didn't notice, a glance that expressed surprise but was also a validation of a prediction that had been made earlier.

A few months ago, Aftab had discovered one of Shah Waliullah's books in the library and, upon reading it, had shared it with Waris. Shah Waliullah was an Islamic scholar who believed that the purity of the religion had been compromised in Hindustan, as it had mingled with the pagan religions, and it was this purity that needed to be recovered for a true Islam to emerge. That one book had led to a further exploration of his literature, following which Aftab and Waris had had a passionate discussion about his ideas, sitting right here in the library.

It was late afternoon, similar to the one right now, and both of them were alone in the library as was usually the case. 'So how would Shah Waliullah respond to Baba Fareed Shakarganj, for example?' Aftab had asked Waris that day. 'Coming from the Chishtiya silsila, you know that Baba Fareed celebrated *qawwali* and dhamaal. Where do you think these traditions are coming from? Do you not see the connection between the qawwali and the bhajan, or between the dhamaal and Shiva's tandava? Are the Chishtis then corrupting religion by incorporating pagan practices, by expressing these practices in the language of a new religion? Would Shah Waliullah dare say that Baba Fareed was not a true Muslim or not following a pure Islam?'

'I don't think so,' Waris had responded. 'I think he would instead argue that Baba Fareed or other Sufi saints borrowed from pagan traditions because they had to. Because Islam was still new to the subcontinent at that point and these Sufi saints had to use local pagan symbols to make the new religion comprehensible to the local populace. He would argue that now because Islam is firmly established in the region, there is no need to use these tactics. So, to conclude my point, Shah Waliullah, in response to your question, would say that Baba Fareed had to do what he had to, to popularize the new religion.'

'Sure. But as my counterpoint, wouldn't you agree that it is impossible to search for the original religion that he wants to rediscover? Isn't his perception of that original message tainted by his personal experiences of eighteenth-century Delhi? You know you just mentioned that Baba Fareed had to preach a new religion to the people of his time, so he had to speak in their spiritual language. This spiritual language borrowed from pagan religions. So basically, the religion that developed in the twelfth and thirteenth centuries reflected the context of that time, the mythologies, religiosity and expectations of the spirituality of that time. Why would the eighteenth century be any different? We are now living in a particular era, a different context. So, our understanding of religion today will be a product of our context today.

'The same logic applies to Shah Waliullah,' Aftab continued. 'He is a product of this context—this political context, a time of social upheaval and uncertainty, when it seems as if Muslim rule in India is being weakened by the Sikhs and the Marathas. What does he do to respond to this political uncertainty, to explain the loss of political power? He blames their religiosity. Were the Mughal Kings better Muslims than many around us? Was Alauddin Khilji the perfect Muslim? Of course not. The rise of Muslim power in Hindustan, and what you are seeing right now, cannot be so easily explained away by the religiosity of the protagonists.

'And if I may,' continued Aftab, 'haven't there always been disagreements about what true religion is, right from the beginning? I mean, the Kharijites accused Hazrat Ali, the Caliph, of straying away from pure religion. Can you believe it? Hazrat Ali?' he said, with emphasis. Despite being Hindus, Aftab's family had a particular association with Hazrat Ali and his sons, Hassan and Hussain. Every year on Muharram, they only wore black, cooked the simplest of meals, and did not partake in any celebration. 'The divide between Shia and Sunni has only increased following the Karbala. Both believe they follow the true religion. Then there are all of these philosophical differences. How do we know which one is correct and which one is wrong?'

'Well, Shah Waliullah would argue that we should go back to the fundamentals—the Quran and the Hadith—to decipher the original religion,' said Waris. 'You know, personally, I find no merit in his arguments as you very well know but I feel there is a need to engage with these concepts. It is powerful because of its simplicity. I don't appreciate it at all for I know that simple explanations for complex things are gimmicks. But it will resonate with people. I have seen with my own eyes how the people of Punjab are suffering. I am sure you are aware of that as well. His ideas will provide them a reassurance—that they can reclaim what is lost if they become better Muslims.'

'Good point, Waris. Now to come back to your argument about fundamentals, doesn't everyone think they are following the fundamentals of religion? All these schools of thought have found justifications for themselves, based on these fundamentals. I mean, those who believe in monism, the Ibn-Arabi school of thought, have used the Quran to justify this belief, and those who oppose them—those who believe in monotheism, also use the Quran to counter these claims. All these scholars bring in their own interpretations to the Holy Book.'

'Well said, my friend,' said Waris. 'You know, your argument about monism and monotheism got me thinking. We know that early Arab scholars were influenced by Greek philosophy. There is a direct connection between Plato's theory of form and the Islamic philosophy. Similarly, Aristotle had a huge impact on medicinal science. Many hakims still master Unani (Greek) medicine, which has its roots in Aristotle. I don't know if I ever told you, but my father was a hakim and he taught me the basic principles of Unani medicine. Anyway, the point that I want to make is this: weren't these Greek philosophers pagan? Should we then get rid of the entirety of Islamic philosophy because we don't want it corrupted by pagan philosophy? Why then is this argument being made in the context of the subcontinent by the likes of Shah Waliullah? The Islamic culture in Hindustan benefited immensely from the pagan philosophy here—the Upanishads, the Gita, the Vedas, the philosophies of the yogis, Shiva's ascetics. Are we to abandon these centuries of the intermingling of the cultures? How do we even begin this disentangling? Is that even possible? Would there be anything left if we removed all these influences?

'You know, I have been reading Jayadeva's *Gita Govinda* these past few days, and I cannot help but see parallels between his poetry and Punjabi Sufi poetry. Would you still have the poetry of Baba Fareed without Jayadeva? Would you still have Shah Hussain's Ranjha, without Krishna?' asked Waris.

Unaware of this comprehensive discussion about Shah Waliullah that had taken place between Aftab and Waris a few months ago, Umer continued expressing his admiration for the scholar. Aftab wanted Waris to engage. He wanted Waris to disrupt this narrative but, to his disappointment, Waris didn't say anything. Aftab wanted to remind him that if he could, he would have responded to Umer but his passion frightened him. It reminded him of his non-Muslimness and the precarious position he would be in if he invoked Umer's or his family's wrath. He wanted Waris to come to his rescue, to challenge his notion of impurity, but Waris disappointed him.

'I have been told by my uncle that Shah Waliullah has written a letter to Ahmad Shah Abdali, asking him to invade Hindustan, asking him to salvage the fate of the Muslim community in this country,' said Umer. 'I think we need that. We need that powerful force to restore order, to show all these groups that are now daring to raise their heads their true position.' Umer finished speaking and looked towards Aftab.

Here, hold my hand. Tell me, what are you thinking? Who do you think of when you say you are thinking about nothing? Who resides in your thoughts like a guilty memory? What is his name? How did you two meet? Who else knows your secret? Where do you meet him? How often do you meet? What does he say to you? How does he express his fidelity towards you? And what do you say? Where does he kiss you? Does he touch you there? Is he gentle? How does his breath smell? Does his moustache tingle your neck? Does he bite you softly on your nipples? Does he swirl his tongue around them? Don't you cover your face with your hands now. Don't you dare feign shame. You weren't embarrassed when he rode you like a bull? Why are you trying to pretend now? Oh please, don't stop, tell me everything. I won't tell a soul. Your secrets are safe with me.

Here, here, have you heard? The daughter of the chief meets the family servant in the jungle. She takes him food, churi, that she makes with her own hands. She feeds him and he bites her fingers. In the thick foliage, their bodies mingle. The entire universe knows of their union; it conspires with the lovers to keep it hidden. I am telling you this in confidence. Now don't you go about blabbing to the world. Swear upon my life and that of your beloved that you will not talk about this with anyone, anyone!

You did not hear it from me, but my source is true. The buffalo herder and Heer are secret lovers. He is not what he says he is and she keeps the cover. Together they have cast a spell over the entire city. They lie together in sin, in bright daylight and in the shadow of the night. Oh, I feel bad for her poor father, a man of such pride. How would he bear this stigma? I feel his plight.

I am not one to be swayed by town gossip or a trivial scandal. I am a man of religion. I spend my day lost in contemplation. I am free from the trappings of society. I have no wife, no children. Rumours of this storm brewing enter my hut. I would have paid no attention had I not heard the name of my niece. Aloof I may be, but I am still a Sial. My honour is bound to my tribe, my loyalty to my cousin paramount. But more than that, if what I hear is true, then this is also a religious sin, the gravest of crimes. Without the bond of marriage, a formal sanctification, their relationship is illegitimate. Caught in their bodily lust, they forget the laws of God. How can I allow this sin to occur on my watch? What face would I show to my brother and his wife, if I, despite knowing of this transgression, did not do anything to stop it? How would I present myself in the court of Heaven?

Dressed as a mendicant, with beads around my neck, I grabbed my walking stick, and limped my way to the forest.

I saw Ranjha sitting alone, next to the river, eating the churi that my niece, it seemed, had prepared. She was nowhere to be seen. I saw my opportunity. I rushed over to him, as quickly as I could, and presented my woes of hunger to him. Despite his infringement, he is a kind soul. He gave me his bowl of churi. With evidence in my hand, I was off to Jhang. For if these two are not lovers, then why does she bring him churi every day? Is this a meal that is prepared for the family servants by the daughter of the chief? In the aroma of the butter and the sugar, I could sniff their secret. How would the council of the Sials refute my testimony?

I was still halfway from Jhang when Heer pounced on me. I was a hapless prey to her ferocity. Ranjha had told her the story of the mendicant and she had realized that it was none other than her uncle, Kaido. She took the bowl of evidence from my hand and threw it on the ground. She pulled my necklace of beads and scattered them all around. She pulled my hair, slapped my face and tore my clothes. She showed no respect for my age or my status. Neither did she pay any heed to my sacred stature. As she let go of my feeble body, I ran for it. She continued calling me obscenities as I moved away from her.

Without even allowing myself to catch a breath, I presented myself to the council of Jhang. Sitting amidst the other elders as their chief was Chuchak. Look how proudly he sat, with his broad shoulders held back, his oiled moustache turned upwards. His turban was freshly starched and stood tall. Here he broke bread with his friends without any knowledge at all. Let's see how long his broad shoulders, his arched back can carry the weight of Heer's youth. Let's see how long he can sit here arrogantly among his peers, while his daughter besmirches his reputation. She has cut off his feet and Chuchak still feels he stands tall. His laughter, as he spoke to his friends, pierced my ears and added salt to all the wounds his daughter had inflicted upon me.

'O, you leader of the Sials, our pride and honour, the protector of our lands and our buffaloes, look at what your daughter has done to me,' I said to him. 'This is my punishment for telling the truth. This is my award for ensuring God's law.'

Chuchak turned away from his friends and looked me up and down distractedly, the residue of the hearty laughter still hanging on his lips as a tilted smile. 'Look at you, Kaido. What happened? Did you find yourself chasing sheep in your slumber again, or did you cross paths with some other intoxicated jogis? You should have at least washed your face before coming to us. Why don't you go home, change your clothes and come back to recall for us what travesty has fallen upon you this time? I assure you, we will avenge this crime. I promise you, we will salvage your honour.' The rest of the council laughed and Chuchak looked satisfied.

'It is not my honour that needs to be protected, but yours, my brother. While you sit here carefree, your daughter roams the jungle with that buffalo herder you've employed. She brings him churi every day. The tide of youth flows through their veins. Theirs is not a harmless relationship. If you don't intervene right now, I can't say what travesty would fall upon you, upon us, upon this town.'

'Shut your filthy mouth, you rumour-monger,' he said, his face turning red. 'How dare you talk about my Heer in this manner? Have you no shame? Do you have no one else to talk about? Is your appetite for gossip not satisfied that you talk about our daughters, our honour, in this manner? Do we not already tolerate you enough?'

'My sire, my friend, my brother, my heart bleeds as I utter these words.' I maintained my composure. 'I would rather have seen my tongue fall off before having to talk about Heer, our daughter, in this manner. For is she not my daughter? Is she not my honour?'

I felt my voice cracking and wondered if Chuchak noticed it.

'I have been hearing about these rumours for a long time but I wanted to be sure. So, I went to the jungle to see for myself and lo and behold there was Heer feeding that buffalo herder churi with her own hands. She attacked me like a wounded beast when she saw that I had witnessed her secret, her crime.'

Tears were now welling up in my eyes.

'I would have got you more evidence, my brother. I would have even brought you some of that churi but my old bones could not withstand the blows of your ferocious daughter. Consider my bruised face, my torn clothes as evidence of her trespass.'

'I don't believe a single word that comes out of your filthy mouth,' roared Chuchak. 'My Heer is my pride. She can never betray my trust. But I will still call her here so that she can respond to these allegations you make. But mind you, Kaido,' he continued, 'if what you say is a lie, I will bury you alive with my own bare hands.'

Chuchak whispered something to a servant standing nearby. He bowed his head and left immediately. I stood there, all eyes on me. A slight fear entered my heart. Had I been too hasty in coming to Chuchak? Should I have waited to collect more evidence? Beads of sweat appeared on my forehead that I knew Chuchak noticed.

Heer arrived shortly after, not alone but with the daughters of Iblis, like the members of Satan's *baraat*, like the army of Nadir Shah entering Delhi. I knew right then that she had brought these fake witnesses so she could craft a web of elaborate lies.

'Don't believe a word spoken by this wily creature,' said her friends, pointing towards me, staring at me in disgust, even before a question could be posed. Heer, it seemed, knew that she would be called here shortly and she was prepared. Her friends interceded on her behalf. 'We see how he looks at us with his lustful eyes. He stares at our chests and pinches our backs when he finds us alone. Calling us daughters and wearing that religious garb, he passes his hands over our bodies. He makes lecherous comments and describes his secret fantasies. He picks up his dhoti and bares his penis, asking us to vitalize his lost virility.'

Of course, they were lying. I swear to God they were lying. I swear on the dead graves of my parents they were lying. My body was shaking as I heard these baseless accusations being thrown at me and the lies being told to protect the honour of their friend. I tried to intervene. I called them liars, for that is what they truly were, but Chuchak gestured at me to stop. They are lying. Liars. Fabricating tales about me in front of the council, in front of all Jhang and I couldn't respond because the chief was partial towards his daughter. I felt as if my body was about to give up, my feet unable to withstand my weight. This was too much for me to handle. Too many lies. I kept on shaking as they kept on lying. Of course, they were lying. Believe me they were lying.

'This is not a man you should trust; his entire existence is that of treachery,' they continued. 'Like a stray dog, he roams through the streets of Jhang, listening at closed doors for any gossip, any news that he can trumpet through our community. He is evil personified, the ultimate symbol of perfidy.'

My evidence was judged as inconclusive and I was reprimanded for what I had done to the girls. Liars. Crafting tales to save their friend. I will show them. This has got out of hand. I will show them. Don't be misled by my disabled leg that forces me to limp. I will show them. I can still protect my honour. The honour of the Sials. The honour of divine laws. I will show them. This will not go unanswered. Their accusations will be responded to. I will show them.

I will never forget this, Heer. Never. You will see. You will have to pay. I will show you.

I rushed to my sister, Maliki, and told her all that I had seen and the lies that were told to save Heer and defame me. In the privacy of her home, she confronted Heer. She told her that a matter that should never be discussed is now being discussed in every nook and corner of the city.

'You are a sinner, a shame for our family,' she remarked.

Her words sounded like an accusation, but she spoke as if she was asking her a question. As if, through her accusation, she wanted to check if the rumours were true.

'You spend your days in the arms of that buffalo herder. You present yourself to him as if he is your husband and you are his lawful wife. Do you have no sense of propriety? Or honour?'

'Heer is Ranjha, and Ranjha is Heer,' was Heer's unabashed reply. 'We are married to each other and have been since the day of his arrival. With Allah as our witness, we have accepted each other as husband and wife. Don't mention to me the trivialities of these worldly rituals, these rules and regulations. Our love is pure, our union legal.' What she couldn't say out in the open, in front of the council, in front of her father, she had no shame saying in the privacy of her home, in front of her mother. She trusted her mother with this confession, trusted her with her truth.

'Listen to her talk like a whore from Kasur,' said Maliki, in a state of disbelief. 'You should bless your stars that it is I who am being exposed to this blasphemy, not your brother or father. Do you wish to be sacrificed, do you wish to die, like thousands have before you?' She sounded genuinely concerned for the fate of her daughter. 'Your brother will kill you with his bare hands;

your father will drown you in the Chenab. We will tell the world we had no daughter. There never was a Heer.'

'Don't frighten me with this talk of death. I died the day I merged with Ranjha. You can get rid of my body, burn it at the stake.' Heer felt emboldened since her secret was out. 'I will never stop speaking the truth. I will never lie. What is the status of the body, without the sanctification of the soul? My soul resides with Ranjha. I can never die.'

Later that night, Maliki whispered Heer's words into her father's ears. She censored a few of her blasphemous comments and kept back some details of that interaction for she was afraid, afraid of what might happen, afraid of how Chuchak might respond. She couldn't imagine. Didn't want to imagine. She spoke in hints, in allusions, to raise enough suspicion, to raise enough doubts. Chuchak, whose mind had already been perturbed by the public discussion of his daughter's relationship with the buffalo herder, was more responsive this time. Even if all of this was a lie, a rumour had been born, a rumour that now engulfed them, that had spread all over Jhang and beyond, a rumour that needed to be dealt with.

Together they devised a plan. Next morning, Ranjha was called and relieved of his services. 'I hired you to take care of our buffaloes, but you became a bull among my herd. Your presence raises voices; people have come to us with concerns. I am the chief of the Sials; my honour is impeccable. You are a blot on my reputation. I can no longer tolerate this scandal.'

Casting away the woollen shawl from his shoulder and putting away the staff in his hand, Ranjha spoke with indignation. 'I have served you with utmost loyalty. I have been your most faithful servant. Is this how the honourable Sials treat orphans, those who have already been rejected? I will never show my face in this town again; I will never see Heer again. I consider a morsel or even a drop of water from your courtyard haram. I will leave immediately. To hell with you and your buffaloes! If I could cast magic spells, I would recite those charms. May this town never prosper; may its honour never be redeemed.'

Out in the wilderness, sat a forlorn Ranjha. Sitting on a rock next to the river, he played the instrument of the devil; he played the flute. Through his flute, he told stories about what had happened to him, about his departure from the Sial household. These stories became rumours. Rumours that ran through the streets of Jhang. They sang songs at women's spinning parties. They sat under the shade of the banyan tree in the presence of the elders. They smoked hashish in the company of the ascetics. They danced at religious fairs. They performed dhamaal to the singing of the qawwals. In these stories, Ranjha somehow managed to salvage his pride. He became the victim and the Sials the offenders. 'Have you heard how the Sials treated their family servant? Have you heard how he was turned away without his pay?'

It was not because of the effect of these rumours that Chuchak called Ranjha back. He had to send for him when his herd of buffaloes too expressed their lament at Ranjha's departure. A herd that had prospered under Ranjha began to thin out. Some were lost to the river and others to hungry predators. The delicate balance that had been maintained was now lost. Rumours our Chuchak could handle, but what would happen to him without his buffaloes? What would his position be in society? What would the Sials be? Would they still be respected and loved all over Punjab? Something had to be done before this loss became unmanageable. A message from Chuchak was sent to Ranjha with perfidious apologies and a plea to return. He was asked to take care of the buffaloes again, to revive the wealth of the Sials that was slowly slipping away from them. However, with this message left another messenger in the direction of Ranganpur, to the village of the Kheras.

The council of the Sials had accepted their proposal. Heer would marry Saida, the son of the chief of the Kheras.

6

The Resistance

The sun refused to rise. Its head was enveloped by a brown chaddar of dust. From the rooftops of the tall buildings of Lahore, it looked as if the horizon was on fire. Brown smoke slowly climbed the walls of the sky. All the residents of the city of Lahore gathered to see the spectacle, thousands of them on rooftops, including the governor, Mir Mannu. No one spoke, not even the children. There was absolute silence. The loud prayers that had resonated for several days prior to this impending attack had become quieter and quieter with each subsequent moment till they completely vanished.

From across the river, beyond the veil of the horizon, came the muted sound of drumbeats, panting and puffing as they rose to prominence. It was the sound of multiple hands, numerous fingers casting their magic on one giant drum skin. As the beat became louder, it broke down into multiple sounds, all playing the same tune, but at a different pace. The cloud of dust began to swirl as the earth began to dance. The thick ramparts protecting the city began to shake as the floors of the rooftops reverberated. From behind the obscurity of the horizon and the dust, the army finally manifested itself. Hundreds of horses and thousands of hooves tapping on the ground, creating a rhythmic ecstasy akin to the dhamaal of a Sufi, the tandava of Shiva. Leading all the horses was a white horse, its long white mane flowing behind it, ridden by the leader of this army, the Afghan king, Ahmad Shah Abdali.

The sheath of the sword rubs against the trunk of my body. It's an ornate design, red in colour, with gold markings on it. The sheath is fit to host the swords of kings or generals. This rider riding me is none of these. He is the one and only son of the Kheras and goes by the name of Saida. If I were to talk about him objectively, he is not really as despicable a character as I would make him out to be. I mean he is from a respectable family, doesn't have many vices, or any more than men of his status usually do. He is not evil like Heer's uncle, Kaido. In fact, you might even say he is misunderstood, a victim of the Heer and Ranjha-centric focus of this narration. Perhaps in a spin-off story, he might come across as the tragic protagonist. But that would be a different qissa, which we will not discuss here. So, for now, let us return to the archetype of this character, as he was intended by Waris.

Sitting atop my beautiful, graceful body, this idiot thinks he is a soldier. Look how stiffly he sits, holding the handle of the blunt sword in his hand, as his mother, sister and aunts shower coins over him. A trail of beggars follows this splendid baraat to gather these coins.

I have known Saida since he was a child. We almost grew up together. I am the foal of his father's favourite horse. I was Saida's first ride. I remember how he wet my back the first time he sat on me. I am of the purest Arabic breed. I can run faster than the wind, outpace any animal and run for miles and miles without a break. And here I am, decked like a bride—with a red cloth draped all over me and my face covered with a strange red mask. All for what? Saida? So that he can fulfil his desire to feel like a soldier on this important day of his life. This man, who has never even hunted a squirrel, thinks he can conquer the heart of Heer. I have heard stories about her, including the love legend with the buffalo herder, and so have the other Kheras. But here they are, presenting their son to Jhang, lured by the wealth the Sials will give them in return.

You know, long ago, in a time lost to antiquity, a wedding ceremony was a war. In that ancient age, husbands-to-be were expected to come on a horse and capture their bride-to-be by force. If they were successful in getting away with it, the couple were married. This is how my ancestors got intertwined in this ridiculous human ceremony. Here we are, on the outskirts of Jhang, re-enacting symbolically that ancient custom.

With his hands on his waist, the Afghan king, standing over six feet tall, his turban rising almost a foot above that, stared intently at the rampart around the Lahore Fort and the walled city, as if he intended to crush it by the sheer force of his glare. For weeks now, the Afghan army had been trying to infiltrate the city. His soldiers had arranged for tall ladders to climb the wall, but boiling oil was poured on them before they could reach the top. None of the cannons in the Afghan artillery had been effective.

In frustration, Abdali had come up with the futile plan of capturing *goh*, giant monitor lizards, from the wilderness around the city. A thick robe had been tied to the body of the lizard, while the other end of the robe was held by individual soldiers.

In the darkness of the night, these lizards were made to clamber up the walls of the fort, attempting to pull the soldiers along as they climbed. But even before the soldiers were off the ground came burning oil from the ramparts.

All day, bands of soldiers walked around the circumference of the wall, searching for any unattended or weaker sections. There were none. The governor of Lahore, Mir Mannu, had witnessed the fate of Delhi at the hands of Abdali in one of his previous raids. He had also heard stories from refugees ejected from the villages, towns and unprotected cities that were on the important route connecting Afghanistan with Lahore and Delhi. Mir Mannu was well aware that no mercy would be shown to his city, its property, its ruling class, its wealth and its people. He stood against the Afghans on behalf of the Mughal empire, but he was essentially fighting to save his own life.

The Durrani army, under the capable leadership of Abdali, had the reputation of being ferocious fighters. Mir Mannu knew that this was a battle-hardened army which had an edge over his forces. So instead of trying his luck on the battlefield, Mir Mannu decided to strengthen his defences. Weeks prior to the attack, he stood next to the workers as they renovated the weaker sections of the ramparts. Hundreds of new soldiers were recruited to patrol these sections of the wall. Mir Mannu understood that even if these soldiers were not as trained as the Afghan army, given their vantage position, they would be able to withstand the attack. His strategy seemed to work.

Abdali's face showed no sign of emotion as he looked at the impenetrable wall in front of him. It was this lack of expression in his eyes, on his face, that intimidated his subordinates and enemies alike. But despite his composure, the fear of defeat played havoc with his mind. What would it do to his reputation, his legacy? He was no longer obsessing about strategies to penetrate

Lahore, but thinking about ways to replenish his diminishing food supplies. Abdali had always preferred speed and swiftness as a military strategy, which is why his army travelled light. In order to obtain food supplies for his soldiers, they raided towns and villages.

But more than the diminishing food supplies, it was the idleness of his soldiers that scared him. The fate of his former king, Nadir Shah, and how he was assassinated by his own guards, haunted him. A soldier himself, he understood the need of his soldiers for battle and knew well enough that if an external source for this need was not found, then it often turned inwards. Abdali had ambitious dreams, of a splendid Afghan empire, independent of the Persians and the Mughals that had been their fate for centuries. No, he would not allow these dreams to die on the walls of Lahore. Something had to be done.

Think of every possible meal you can imagine—pulao, roasted lamb, dal, chicken, gobi, kaddu, baingan, bhindi. An array of sweets—laddu, barfi, halwa, jalebi. Drinks unlimited—lassi, milk, rose water, sharbat. Imagine their aroma travelling through the streets of Jhang. Think of an endless line of chefs standing over cauldrons cooking these delicious recipes. The fire under these cauldrons has been burning continuously for weeks, feeding the thousands of guests who have come to attend the greatest wedding Punjab has ever seen.

Think of every possible colour. Imagine these colours laid out in front of you in the form of clothes in separate baskets, a basket for every member of the baraat. These things don't just spring up overnight. They need years of careful planning and strategizing. I began thinking about Heer's wedding the day she was born. I began collecting these clothes and storing them away for this auspicious day that has been blessed by all the brahmins of Jhang and Ranganpur.

I know you've already heard from her father. You already know that he dotes over his daughter while I am connected to my son. He is a man, the wise Chuchak, leader of the Sial clan, but how can he ever understand the thread that joins together my daughter and me? I love her more than love itself but how can I truly love her? How can I ever allow myself to express, or even acknowledge this love? This is a strange bond that connects us. A bond that makes us transparent to each other. Naked in our mutual gaze. We know each other more than we are comfortable acknowledging. We understand each other better than we understand ourselves. The thought pricks at my conscience. Guilt overwhelms me.

I look at these clothes displayed in front of me, some of which came with my baraat when I entered the house of the Sials as a bride. Memories of that day come rushing back to me as I prepare to welcome the baraat of my daughter. Memories of my mother warning me to always think of my in-laws before anyone else. Memories of my father, my dear father, putting his hand on my head, his expressions holding back the flood of emotions he was hiding, his lips saying nothing. How happy they would have been today to see their granddaughter, their Heer, become a bride! Allah took them away too soon. Mysterious are his ways.

Upon my arrival in the Sial household, I had been presented numerous jewellery sets, weighing more than I did. As the sets were being presented to me, my mother-in-law, may Allah grant her the highest place in Jannah, told me to keep them safe for my daughter. And here they are, these sets, next to the hundreds of baskets of clothes that we will send back with Heer to her marital home, her *sasural*. Today our daughter, the life of our home, will cease to be our daughter and become the pride of the Kheras. I hope the Kheras look after her as we have. I hope her mother-in-law loves her as I have; that Saida brings her everything she deserves, for she deserves the world.

Please forgive me if I shed a few tears, for these are tears of joy, tears that are a gift of motherhood.

I was still sitting in the courtyard, supervising the preparations for the baraat, when our family servant, Mithi, who is like a mother to Heer, whispered in my ear that Heer was refusing to wear the wedding dress. I snapped out of my fantasy world and jolted back to reality. I could hear the baraat entering the city, the loud drumbeats, the high-pitched wail of the shehnai, and the singing of the Mirasis. I needed to be out there, leading all the Sial women in welcoming the baraat, a grand welcome for a grand baraat. What would the Khera women think if the bride's mother did not step out to meet them? Wouldn't that add fuel to the scandal that already surrounds this wedding and refuses to die down? It seems as if all of Punjab has heard about Heer and that wretched buffalo herder. Has she not brought enough shame to us that she is creating yet another scene?

I entered the room where Heer was sitting alone, still in her nightclothes, her hair dishevelled, her kajal melting on to her cheeks. 'Why mother, why?' she yelled upon seeing me. 'What ancient grudge do you hold against me? What kind of strange tradition is this that ties all women together? Why have you become my oppressor today? Why are you bent on ensuring that I have no choice, a choice that was also once taken away from you? Why do you want to ensure that a custom which once took away your freedom now takes away mine? Is this why mothers have daughters so that they can pass on this legacy upon them as dowry?' Her voice cracked as she finished the sentence. She buried her face in her lap and began to cry.

My heart melted as I heard her words. How helpless I felt, my knees buckling under the pressure! I held onto the edge of the bed to steady myself. I wanted to walk up to her, take her in my arms and wipe away her tears, tears that my mother never wiped away from my face, that were also left on my mother's face by her mother. Could I, all by myself, end this cycle once and for all? What if I took a stand, what if I supported my daughter? The thought sent a shudder down my spine, as beads of sweat appeared on my forehead. No, I had to be strong. I could not succumb. I had to do this for her, for her future, her survival, her own good. And that of the clan! Yes, I had to do the right thing. I could not be weak.

'How long is this ghost of that buffalo herder going to dominate your existence? You will be wedded to Saida in a few minutes. You will be leaving for Ranganpur with the Kheras today. Give up this futile resistance and become the bride that you are supposed to be.'

'I will not go with the Kheras. I cannot go with the Kheras. Please don't send me with the Kheras. What kind of mother sends Sita to Lanka herself? That Ravana doesn't deserve me. My heart is only with my Ram, my Krishna, my Ranjha.'

'Shut up, you harlot, I should have buried you with my own hands the day you were born. I understand today why the birth of a daughter is deemed a curse and that of a son a boon. I wish you were never born; I wish God had spared me this day. Be assured that one of the two will leave this house today, either your baraat or your *janazah*.' Saying this, I stormed out of the room. Standing outside the door, I took a couple of minutes to compose myself. I pasted a smile on my face as I exited the house to welcome the baraat.

A grand welcome, for a grand baraat!

Yousuf Khan took a deep breath and almost immediately began coughing. The smell of burning bricks, wood, utensils and human carcasses still hung in the air. He looked around to see if his coughing had awoken anyone. All the soldiers around him were sleeping peacefully. He cast a glance at the royal tent; its light was finally out. The king had been up for much of the night. He whistled to the left and then to the right to check with the other sentries. The Afghan army had camped on a vacant ground, next to the river. Facing them were the remains of what had once been the village of Maraka, a Sikh-dominated village about thirty kilometres south of the city of Lahore.

Leaving a well-equipped contingent in Lahore, Abdali had decided to travel south along the river to replenish his food stocks. Frustrated at the siege taking longer than planned, the soldiers were given free rein to vent and gather whatever they could from the many villages that lay along the way. Most of these villages had already been abandoned, fearing an attack by the Afghans. Some people had found refuge in Lahore, some had travelled to Kasur, while others had found temporary abode in other fortified towns.

The Durrani army did not engage with the fortified towns. Abdali understood that his soldiers could not bear the stress of another siege. So, he deliberately picked softer targets, small villages, towns, unprotected by soldiers or ramparts. Some of these villages were Muslim-dominated, and others Sikh- or Hindu-dominated. The Abdali army did not discriminate. Since it was the harvest season, the army had gathered more than enough food after only a couple of raids, but they continued moving south nonetheless, burning villages down after having extracted everything worthwhile.

Arriving at the village of Maraka, Abdali sent his soldiers into the village while he camped outside, with the orders that all the villagers be gathered in front of him. With hundreds of people standing in front of him, guarded by a handful of soldiers bearing swords, a group of soldiers were sent back to search the houses for valuables. A few more soldiers were asked to bring in the bright golden, freshly cut wheat, stored in the communal granary of the village.

The villagers watched helplessly as their precious belongings, clothes, jewellery, that they had cherished for decades, were brought out and placed in front of the king. The king always had the first choice. After choosing a few select pieces, it was the turn of his generals, and then his soldiers, all following the proper hierarchy. In one fell swoop, the villagers of Maraka had been reduced to poverty.

'Finish the job,' said Abdali to his soldiers as he turned back and returned to his tent. His soldiers, swords in their hands, descended upon the unarmed villagers, transforming breathing, living bodies into piles of limbs and a mass of blood in a matter of minutes. The remains were then set on fire as was the village.

Yousuf could still see embers from the fire where the village had once stood. He looked at the human carcasses to see if the vultures that had been feasting on them had scattered. It was too dark to make out.

He heard a whistle back from the left but none from the right. He looked deep in the darkness for any signs of his fellow sentry. There were none. He blew another whistle but there was still no response. He held his sword, checked his breastplate and headed right. He heard some movement as he got closer to where he remembered the sentry being stationed. He grabbed his sword firmly and began breathing heavily, straining to capture any signs of intruders when he felt a sharp prick on his back and a strong grip over his mouth. He could smell wet mud on the hand that was covering his face. The prick of the sword on his back got sharper. And then he noticed in front of him, emerging from the darkness, about twenty Sikh soldiers, with their long beards, thick turbans and ferocious eyes.

'Tell us where you've stored the wheat,' whispered the man holding his hand over Yousuf's mouth. He had now moved the sword to his neck. Yousuf could feel his breath on his face. He pointed towards a tent in the middle of the courtyard, surrounded by hundreds of sleeping soldiers around it.

The Sikh soldiers looked at each other and began walking towards the tent, skilfully negotiating the sleeping bodies. They entered the tent, got as much of the wheat as the few soldiers could carry, looked around to ensure that the soldiers were still sleeping and walked back carefully. Once the Sikh soldiers got back to where Yousuf had been held, they disappeared into the darkness once again. Yousuf could feel a trickle of piss in his pants. He shut his eyes, reciting the first *kalma* in his mind. He heard his captor shout, 'Waheguru ji da Khalsa, Waheguru ji di fateh'.

Perhaps when this drama is resolved, I should spend a week reciting holy verses on the banks of the Chenab to get rid of this problem once and for all. I would need powerful verses to counter this spell. God knows which *tantrik* has cast his magic spell upon this river. From every generation, it seeks a human sacrifice, the blood of a young maiden. Before Heer, there was

Sahiban, and before her, there was Sohni. If I were a pagan, I would have suggested that these three sisters are but one, a reincarnation of one soul in multiple bodies but thank God, I don't believe in such blasphemies. May Allah always protect me from these impieties!

I was sitting in a room with Heer, her father, brother and mother alongside her, while outside the door, everyone awaited the splendid baraat from Ranganpur. For now, it seemed they were unaware of Heer's recalcitrance. In this room, where silence lurked in corners as it does after the death of a beloved, I could hear the sounds of laughter and celebration outside. The sound of the fireworks punctuated the stillness of this room. I could imagine the different patterns in the sky—stars, rain, peacocks, elephants, coloured circles and many more. Further down the street, out in the open space where the baraat waited for the bride, was Saida, sitting on the stage, surrounded by young girls, flirting with him, asking him absurd questions, finding reasons to hold his hands or touch his face. Even from this distance, I could hear the seduction in their giggles.

If I were outside, I would have brought to an immediate end these unlawful practices, traditions that have taken us away from the purity of our religion. I would have put all these girls, showing their bodies in their newly stitched clothes stuck tightly to them, in purdah and ensured that there was no intermingling between the genders. I would have reminded the Sials that it is these immoral practices that have resulted in this situation today, that has brought ignominy to the threshold of their home.

'Heer, my child, my daughter, why are you being stubborn? Why are you rejecting this blessing that stands outside your door? God has destined for all of us to find partners and live in marital bliss. It is the tradition of our Prophet. It has been instructed in the Quran. Refusing to marry is a rejection of this command. It is a violation of the highest code, a grave crime,' I said to her, convinced that she would respond to my words of reason.

'When have I rejected marriage? How have I threatened this institution? I believe in its sanctity, and it is for this reason that I refuse to accept Saida,' she replied, with conviction. 'Ranjha is my husband and I his bride. The Quran says that each creature is created in pairs. These pairs were created when Brahma split himself into two. Without one, the other would cease to exist. How then can you expect me to forget my Ranjha and tie a knot with a stranger? Wouldn't that challenge God's divinity? For is it not God who brought us together?'

'I see how you have lost all shame.' I could feel my ears warming. 'It is the height of immorality to talk in this manner in front of one's father and brother but to bring in God to justify your lust for your lover? If I didn't know better, I would have taken you for Satan's daughter! What marriage do you talk about when there was no maulvi to sanctify the union, no *walima* to announce the contract? Who were your witnesses? Who recited the holy verses? How can you claim to be married without seeking the permission of your father?'

'God was our witness, and it is God who sanctified our marriage. We were wed in the forest and as his wedding presents, Ranjha brought the bounties of the Chenab. The deer, the cranes, the parrots and others were part of the congregation and it is they who recited words of devotion for God to bless this wedding. Who are you then to question the legality of this marriage, the will of God?'

'I am the upholder of God's law. I am the judge who ensures that all the rites and the rituals are followed. From what I hear, your marriage with Ranjha is invalid. None of the criteria of marriage were followed, so I declare it null and void.'

'Have some humility, old man; don't parade your wishes as commandments of God. Many have come before you, from the Pharaoh to Hiranyakashipu, who made a similar mistake. History is rife with examples of men who thought they were speaking on behalf of God, but committed the biggest crimes in the name of ensuring divine justice. Be assured that when Angel Israfil blows his trumpet, when the Earth will be rent asunder, when the mountains will fly like discarded wool, when the snake and the bull that have held the world since time immemorial will be filled with fear, and when Kalki will appear, riding a white horse to bring an end to the Kali Yuga, then you will have to pay for your crimes. You will have to pay for your sins. Rest assured, God has prepared a special place in hell for souls like yours.'

'You would have lost your tongue a long time ago if you were my daughter. With my own hands, I would have wrung your neck till the last gasp of breath was forced out of your throat. Then I would have cut your body into several pieces and fed them to the crows. It is to prevent a fate like yours that infant girls are buried alive or drowned in milk. You should consider yourself lucky that your father entertains a tolerance that I do not possess.' I stopped talking. Words failed me.

I turned towards Maliki and said, 'My sister, bring me a glass of water before I lose my control.'

I took small sips from the tumbler, using this break to compose my thoughts. I hate being angry, hate it with a vengeance. I could still hear the sounds of festivities outside the door. How unaware were the guests and poor Saida about the scene unfolding here! Cursed was the day when the Kheras decided to have their nose rubbed on the ground by sending the *rishta* of their beloved son for this daughter of Iblis.

'Maulvi sahib,' whispered Maliki in my ear, while I was still drinking. 'We need to do something quickly. I have been getting frequent messages from outside. The guests are getting impatient. There are rumours about Heer's resistance to this marriage. There are voices that it is because of that ill-fated buffalo herder, may God destroy his future. If this marriage is not solemnized soon, we will not be able to put an end to this scandal and, God forbid, the baraat might return without Heer. Imagine the hell that would befall us, the Sials and Jhang, if that happens. Who would ever want to marry our daughters? We would forever be remembered as the city of this hapless girl.'

Realizing that there was no point in rationalizing with Heer or instilling in her the fear of God, for her heart had been shut to the true light of religion, morality and divinity, I tried another strategy. I took Maliki, Chuchak and Heer's brother, Sultan, to one corner and told them about my plan.

A piece of cloth was brought and handed over to Maliki. Sultan held Heer's hands while Chuchak stood behind her, holding her head. Maliki tied the cloth around her mouth so that no more blasphemous comments could escape those doomed lips. We covered her head with a dupatta and called for two witnesses from the community who were already aware of the situation. After reciting the required verses, I asked Heer if this marriage to Saida was acceptable to her. Her head, which was being held by her father, nodded. I interpreted that as her acceptance. I asked her this question twice again and she acceded.

I exited the room and declared to the congregation that Heer was now legally wedded to Saida. The baraat rejoiced, as if they had conquered the fort of Lahore. They distributed sweetmeats among themselves while both sides presented me copious gifts. However, instead of staying at the festivities, I returned home immediately and the two witnesses who were present in the room also disappeared. I had performed my duty; now it was up to the Kheras. May God bless this marriage.

Waris felt the grip of a hand around his wrist. It pulled him down. More than anything else, it was the suddenness of it that caught him by surprise, and he felt a sharp pain in his shoulder. He felt anger wash over him and glared at the person responsible for the action, now sitting on the ground in front of him. It was a man, probably in his early thirties, his eyes drooping, with red burn marks on his face. He had a long face and a sharp nose, with only a few grey hairs in his beard and head. He held his face with dignity but his eyes, red with exhaustion, with thick dark circles under them, told a different story. The words that came out of his mouth caught up with the plea evident in his eyes.

'Please, give me one extra roti today. My body cannot survive on just one. This is my only meal of the day,' he pleaded.

'Two? You must be out of your mind,' said Waris. 'I could take this back from you and give it to someone else who would appreciate it more than you.'

Waris was still finishing his sentence when he felt a slight nudge behind him. It was Umer, carrying a bucket full of water. Aftab was behind both of them, pouring dal on the roti that Waris was handing out. Umer silently nodded to Waris, signalling that he should move on.

Every evening after maghrib, Waris, Umer and Aftab would feed the refugees who would gather outside the madrasah. They had begun doing this with the arrival of the first set of refugees a few months ago. Coming from neighbouring towns and villages, these refugees brought with them tales of the Durrani army, the siege of Lahore and the plunder of Punjab. They came only with the clothes on their backs and a handful of precious items, leaving behind their harvest and other possessions. They were the lucky ones, still alive to tell their stories. The tales that they told merged with tales of previous experiences of being displaced from their homes during Abdali's previous raids, and those of Nadir Shah before him. Among the refugees were many who were accustomed to losing it all and starting from scratch, over and over again.

A few of the refugees, with extended family in the city, found a place to live, but for the vast majority of them, the bare streets of the city, under the open sky, served as their abode. They were seen in every street, every corner, in every vacant ground and outside every mosque, temple and *mazaar*. They lived in groups, in clusters of families, replicating their household structures in their new situation.

In the beginning, their physical condition wasn't as bad, as traces of their past prosperity lingered on for a few days. Their clothes were not as tattered, their bones not as protruding, their eyes not as hollow. They looked not very different from the people of Kasur. In those initial days, the citizens of the city had enthusiastically supported them. All households prepared extra food which was distributed to the refugees. Any extra clothing or bedding was handed over. The richer citizens began commissioning daily food for the refugees, as the city of Kasur exhibited its glorious self.

But soon, reality returned, as the philanthropic spirit of the early days began receding. The richer households were the first ones to pull back. With hundreds of refugees pouring into the city every day, the looming threat of an imminent Abdali attack, at least in the imagination, increased. It played havoc with the minds of the people, as they began hoarding their possessions. It was around this time that the physical condition of the refugees began changing. Soon they transformed into an army of beggars, roaming from one part of the city to another in search of sustenance—an army that was increasing exponentially all the time.

Maulvi Ghulam Murtaza's madrasah, along with several other religious institutions around the city, mosques, temples and Sufi shrines, continued providing daily meals to the refugees. However, without the support of the citizens and due to the ever increasing number, they were now finding it hard to fulfil the demand. Every day, Waris, Umer and Aftab distributed food to hundreds of people who gathered outside the madrasah and had to turn away hundreds of others who could not be supported. Some refugees began queuing up early in the morning to get one roti and some dal for dinner after maghrib. Sometimes fights broke out in queues, demanding the intervention of Waris and others. Usually, the threat of no more food worked.

In these past couple of months, as Waris devoted himself fully to serving the refugees, his friends began noticing certain changes in his behaviour. He no longer engaged in intellectual discussions with Aftab or even with Maulvi sahib. He would toss and turn on his bed all night, gently massaging his exhausted arms and legs, finding it impossible to sleep. He had also become increasingly short-tempered, often yelling at refugees to behave themselves if they broke the queue. Once, he pushed a man who wanted food out of turn.

Aftab, noticing the altered behaviour of his friend, tried having a conversation with him several times. He tried talking to him about political developments, about the future of Punjab, the future of the Mughal empire and the Sikh militia, but Waris would never engage. He would often notice how Waris's legs and hands began shaking during any such discussions.

'The dal is getting more and more watery every day,' said Aftab to Waris, as they returned to the madrasah after running out of supplies to feed everyone yet again.

'I'll talk to Maulvi sahib,' said Waris. 'We need to do something about the situation. These people have no one, no home. They are like orphans. They need our protection. They were once respectful citizens, zamindars. Look at them now.' Aftab noticed that Waris trembled as he spoke. Then without waiting for Aftab to respond, he headed straight to Maulvi sahib's room. Maulvi sahib was sitting on his low table, writing in the light of the lantern. 'Ah, Waris,' he said, smiling, as he put down his pen and asked him to enter. Waris wanted to smile back but found it physically impossible to do so. 'Waris, do you know what I am writing? I am translating Saadi's *Gulstan* into Punjabi. Can you believe it has never been translated into our language? Imagine it being read to hundreds of people around Punjab, in a language that they can understand, that they can relate to.'

Waris sat next to Maulvi sahib. Maulvi Ghulam Murtaza turned towards him and spoke enthusiastically, 'You know, I often wonder. What good is all our knowledge if it is not shared, shared with everyone out there? We keep it locked up in madrasahs like these, happy in our island, exchanging ideas among ourselves, without really spreading these ideas as they should be.' In his excitement, Maulvi sahib had failed to notice Waris's sombre expression.

'Maulvi sahib, I have come here to discuss an urgent matter with you,' said Waris, not responding to Maulvi sahib's enthusiasm. 'You need to talk to the ruling families. They need to do something about this crisis. Hundreds will starve to death on the streets of Kasur if they don't respond. Please ask them for just a little more money. That's all. We will do the rest. Where will these refugees go?' Waris's voice quivered as he spoke.

'Waris, what do I tell you?' Maulvi sahib replied, as he placed one of his hands on Waris's shoulder. Waris instinctively began massaging it. 'The ruling families don't like me or support me the way they once did. This whole Bulleh Shah fiasco has really brought a lot of focus on me and many uncomfortable questions are being asked of my loyalty, my patriotism, my religiosity.' Maulvi sahib said the last word mockingly, laughing sarcastically. 'You are talking about increasing our funding and here I am struggling to even maintain what we have. I think the time is nigh when I will be no longer welcome in Kasur. Perhaps then I will return to your home, to your Jandiala with you. Will you take me in?' said Maulvi sahib, still in good humour.

Waris could not muster a reply. His face reddened and he averted his eyes. His teacher noticed how Waris increased the pressure of his massage. 'Waris, is everything alright? Have you heard any news from Jandiala? Is your family safe?' Waris shook his head, still finding it hard to speak. 'Waris puttar, I think you should leave Kasur.' Waris looked up, his eyes swollen, filled with tears, staring back at his teacher.

'Why, Maulvi sahib? Why are you turning me away from your abode, from my home?' His voice, that he was struggling to maintain, had finally cracked.

'Because this home is slipping away from us. Our house is on fire. We just cannot see it. The entire city is afraid of Durrani. But I am not afraid of him. I know he won't attack Kasur. It's not Durrani I am talking about. It's these monsters who rule us. They will use Durrani as an excuse, similar to how they used the Sikh militia before him. They will come down hard on all they perceive as their enemy. Unfortunately, at this point, I might be one of them. But they won't end with me. They will go after my students. They will go after you, to make sure that no other

Bulleh Shah emerges from this madrasah. Kasur is no longer safe. You have to leave. I will tell Aftab to do the same.'

'But, Maulvi sahib, where will I go? I can't go to Jandiala. I can't go westwards in these circumstances. Do you want me to become a refugee again?'

'Puttar, you are not a refugee. You are an explorer, a wanderer, a dervish. The entire world is your playground. The entire world is your home. Your roots are scattered everywhere. You are tied to no ground. I think it's best if you head south, towards Pakpattan, at this point. It is far away from this political circus. There you'll be able to live peacefully and find some comfort. There you can spread some of this wisdom you have acquired here. Apply this knowledge to some practical use. It'll do you good to get out of this ivory tower we have around us. Baba Fareed Shakarganj will look after you.'

In the act of breaking, I am able to unite the lovers once before they are to be separated again. I come to life in my death. It would have been a passive existence otherwise, the life of a lifeless object, the bangle on the wrist, or the anklet around the leg. Together with these ornaments, I would have been stored away, in the secret chambers of the inner recesses of the house, where not even light falls. Perhaps Heer would have taken me out and worn me around her neck, like her mother had done before her, if Heer had ever decided to embrace her new role. That would have been my role for the rest of my inanimate existence. Maybe she would have passed me on to her daughter as her wedding gift as I was passed over to Maliki by her mother. I had become the property of the Sials through that interaction and now I was on my way to becoming a Khera. Along with the other jewellery and other hidden treasures, I, a pearl necklace, would have been a symbol of their wealth, their prosperity, their power. I use the word symbol deliberately, to identify that there is nothing inherent in my value, my worth that represents wealth, but what humans associate with me. They connect their aspirations with me, aspirations that are linked to wealth, wealth that becomes a symbol of prosperity and power, one symbol giving birth to an endless chain of symbols, with a lifeless object at the centre of it all.

There I was on that fateful afternoon, in the middle of the two lovers, as they embraced each other, inside Heer's bridal palanquin, on its way to the abode of the Kheras. Ranjha touched me as his hand moved from her neck to her breast. Their passion told a story of a long separation, of many nights spent in isolation, even though that wasn't the case.

Only a day before, Heer had met Ranjha in the forest, exhorting him, pleading with him to run away with her, to cut off all societal ties and live as ecstatic dervishes who had found their divine.

'What do you have to lose, my lover?' Heer had asked. 'You have already abandoned your family. It is my name, my honour and my family that people will mock. I am ready to face it all. I have relinquished all these ties.' But Ranjha was reluctant.

'I am not a thief. We have committed no crime.' He spoke stubbornly. 'I have already lost one home and lived the life of a wanderer. I cannot become an itinerant once again. Wedded we already are, in a pure, true union, but I will marry you once again with all the proper rituals, bringing a baraat that the world will remember.'

'Oh, you callous of heart, why don't you understand?' Heer implored him. 'The opportunity is now, for tomorrow I'll be wed to Saida. You will be forgiven yet again, while the world will blame me for having led you on and abandoned you for the Kheras' wealth, as they accuse Sahiban of betraying Mirza.'

But Ranjha was not to be swayed.

The next day, Heer's wedding procession set out. Throughout the procession, Ranjha walked right at the end, carrying on the top of his head, in a wooden basket, gifts that her parents had sent for Heer's new home. Like a loyal family servant, he was performing his last role. Heer was crying silently in her palanquin, and at the end of the baraat, Ranjha too shed a few tears. As the procession stopped for a break and the men guarding the bride closed their eyes temporarily, Heer signalled for Ranjha to enter the palanquin.

'You have already forgotten me. You have chosen the Kheras over me,' said Ranjha as he entered the palanquin.

'If you were so eager to wed, if you were so eager to become Saida's bride, then why did you cast your spell over me?' complained Ranjha, as lovers usually do. 'Countless days and countless nights I have spent as your family servant and how easy it was for you to forget me. Are women only created to tempt the fate of men?'

'We should have eloped when we had the opportunity. What use is this pointless remonstrance now?' Heer sounded annoyed. 'Listen to me carefully, for we only have a few precious moments,' she whispered. 'I will wait for you at the Kheras', I will never be his bride. My body, my soul, my wealth belong to you and only you are my shepherd. Go to Tilla Jogian, that ancient mound where jogis congregate. Shed off these worldly clothes, and shave off that beautiful hair of yours.' She ran her hand through his head one last time. 'Cut a deep hole in your ear lobe and wear that stone ring in it, the embellishment of jog. Carrying a begging bowl and a staff in your hand, come to Ranganpur and meet me there. Your bride, your Heer, will spend every waking hour staring at the door for you. There we will be reunited once again.'

Only a day separated these two meetings, but it was as if an entire eternity had passed.

In that embrace of lovers, when the world became oblivious to them, the world caught up. The Kheras and their bearers became aware of the sounds of a man coming from the palanquin of their prized possession. They gathered around it and asked who it was. It was then that Heer held me in her hand and pulled me from her neck.

My precious pearls scattered on the ground as the string that held me together broke forever. 'I had broken my necklace and had asked my family servant to help me collect the pieces,' responded Heer, slightly panicked. The Kheras were no fools, for they had heard stories of the family servant. They wondered if this family servant was Ranjha.

'Should we kill him and get rid of his body in the jungle right here?' they whispered to each other menacingly, but Heer heard them.

'I will kill myself on the spot if a soul touches this man,' she roared. 'He is our loyal servant, the most loyal we have ever had. He carries within him the soul of Jhang and I am connected with him with an invisible thread. Let him go in peace and I will go with you to Ranganpur and be the bride that you need me to be.'

The Kheras were not convinced but they did not want to take the risk. They allowed Ranjha to linger at the end of the baraat till they reached home. There he was rid of his baskets and warned to never show his face there again.

7

Renunciation

On the flat plains of Punjab, the mound looked like a mole on spotless skin. It was a lone structure like the solitary hump of a desert camel. It rose gradually, evenly, from all sides as if it had been crafted by the hands of a potter. The city of Ajodhan was spread around its base, in concentric circles, looking upwards towards the mound, towards the shrine at the top, for sustenance, like a brood of birds calling for its mother's attention.

Waris found the sight comforting, familiar, as if he had been here before. He had only visited Pakpattan in his head, through the stories that were told to him by his father and later by Maulvi sahib. Stories about Baba Fareed Shakarganj and how he made sugar appear miraculously under his prayer mat, stories about his *chilla*, his meditation, his years of hanging upside down inside wells and from trees. Stories that Baba Fareed told about himself, through his poetry, about his devotion, his religiosity, his philosophy, like a humble dervish waiting to be united with the divine.

These stories were scattered in the alleys and streets of Ajodhan, which later came to be known as Pakpattan because of its association with Baba Fareed, the pure. It made Waris nostalgic. It reminded him of home, not Jandiala or Kasur, but home, a warm sensation in which he was whole, complete. It reminded him of his loss. He wished he could share this moment with his father, wished that he could share the joy of seeing this mound, this shrine, with him.

The city was only a few hundred yards away from the top of the mound. On quieter afternoons, the wind brought with it cries of the hawkers from the city. Every day, hundreds of pilgrims ascended the mound, bringing with them offerings— pots of water, food and other gifts.

The shrine was a different world. Time stood still here— days merged into months, months that became years. All day long the qawwals sang the verses of Baba Fareed, songs that sometimes continued late into the night, nights that transformed into mornings and then afternoons. There was always a group of qawwals waiting to take over after the previous group had tired, groups that had travelled from different parts of Punjab and beyond for the opportunity to seek the saint's blessings. At the shrine, no other world existed.

Waris would watch these qawwali performances. He would shut his eyes and listen to the verses being sung in a loop by the qawwal, over and over again, for hours, days, eternity. These verses would reverberate throughout his body, overwhelm him, take over his existence, until there was nothing on his mind, his lips but these verses. Waris became the verses.

There was always a group of devotees around him. Their heads, like Waris's, responded to the rhythm of the music. Every day, devotees would lose themselves to this rhythm— the rhythm travelling from their heads to their bodies, until the body was completely in its thrall. The body would then react in all sorts of ways. It would exist only in its physicality. It would run around the courtyard, or jump at the same spot, as if the floor was on fire. It would wriggle on the ground, shaking, exhibiting the unique sight of divine ecstasy. The body, in those moments, did not belong to the devotee but to the divine, a conduit through which the divine engaged with the world. Back in their bodies, the traumatized devotees were consoled by other devotees around them.

Later in the night, lying on the ground, in a corner that he had made his own at the shrine, Waris would repeat the verses in his head. He would play around with them. Change their order, replace words. He would borrow a line from Shah Hussain, take another from Bulleh Shah and merge it with the verses of Fareed. He would create new verses in the process, verses that were an amalgamation of these three poets and more. Some of these verses he would forget in the morning; others he would remember, reciting them in his mind as he served langar to the pilgrims at the shrine.

Waris couldn't say with certainty how long he had been at the shrine. It could have been a month or more. In the mornings, he would busy himself at the langar hall. All day long, he would walk up and down the many aisles, serving food to devotees. Here in the midst of activity, his mind was far away from the intellectual discussions of the madrasah. What was the difference between monism and monotheism? Were saints born with inherent divinity or was it a boon bestowed on them? Could divinity be accessed rationally? Waris had spent days and nights arguing over these differences with Aftab. Now these varying points of view that had resulted in major schisms seemed irrelevant, a fool's errand almost. Waris wanted to reach out to his friend, tell him how pointless some of their discussions had been, but of course that wasn't possible.

The more he missed his friends, the harder he worked, trying hard to keep the feelings from overwhelming him.

He discovered joy in service, a kind of joy that he had once experienced at the madrasah when Maulvi sahib, through his lectures, had opened up a new world to him. This joy that he felt brought back even more memories of Kasur and Jandiala and of his childhood, but Waris found an effective way of distracting himself through work. With a smile on his face, he would distribute plates, serve food, and later wash the used plates. Through this work, he discovered a strange sense of fulfilment, one that all the intellectual discussions had not given him. The realization that he could be happy without delving into deep philosophical debates surprised him.

He philosophized, reflecting on why that had been the case, for philosophizing was second nature to him, something he did instinctively, after years of training. For several days, he found no answer until one day he noticed a large family sitting together at the langar, enjoying one another's company. Their smiles increased as Waris put food on their plates. There was his answer. It had always been in front of him. It had been there all along in the poetry of Fareed, Nanak, Bulleh Shah, Shah Hussain, Kabir and many other poets, verses that Waris knew by heart, verses that he now interacted with every night through the performances of the qawwal, in a closeness he had never had before.

He realized that one may be able to access a version of divinity rationally, which he had been doing all these years at the madrasah, but this knowledge would mean nothing if one lacks an intimate relationship with the divine, a bond of love that can only be truly experienced by loving another human being wholeheartedly, by discovering the scattered traces of divinity in them, by bringing happiness to them, by being of service to them. Waris, in that moment, felt as if he had truly experienced divinity. Perhaps this is why Maulvi sahib had told him to go to Pakpattan. It seemed that by sending him away, he was imparting his last lesson.

Once he began reflecting on the experiential nature of divinity, a lot of other questions emerged, questions about rituals and their significance. What was the purpose of religious rituals? Didn't these rituals create fear, instead of love, of the divine, scarring an individual with their threats of the fires of hell, or bribing one with the rewards of heaven? Didn't they defeat the purpose of worship, he wondered, which is to love the divine, unconditionally. For the first time, Waris understood the meaning of an old story he had heard from his father about Rabia Barsi, a female Sufi mystic from Iraq who wanted a cup of water to quench the thirst of hell, and fire to burn heaven, so that she could truly pray to God, for the love of God itself, and nothing else. He understood the criticism of religious rituals that ran through the poetry of Guru Nanak, Shah Hussain and, of course, Bulleh Shah.

There was something about the atmosphere of the shrine that fostered these thoughts—the lax rules, the disintegration of society's values in its vicinity, bhang being consumed everywhere, unmarried men and women sitting together with no scruples, men dressed as women, and women dressed as men. Often, the time of prayer went unnoticed. There was no jamaat. Here there was no defined way of being, as if the rules of society, of convention, did not matter in this space.

Why did all these poets move away from an emphasis on heaven and hell and focus on the materiality of this physical world? Why was there so much importance given to the here and now, and the self, as opposed to what was out there, beyond this world? What if there was no heaven or hell? What if all that is is this world? What if heaven and hell are nothing but symbolic representations of our experiences here? What if angels and demons lived among us? For wasn't Ahmad Shah Abdali the devil himself? Wasn't Zakariya Khan, on whose orders Bhai Mani Singh was executed, an execution that Waris witnessed in Lahore, a demon? Could hell be any worse than the situation in Punjab? Waris's mind spun under the weight of these thoughts. He began questioning everything, everything he held sacred.

Often, Waris found himself thinking about Shah Waliullah, the scholar from Delhi, who had invited Ahmad Shah Abdali to invade Hindustan to restore Islam in the subcontinent (as if Abdali needed an invitation). What was the pure religion that he wanted to extract from impure influences, the corruption of rituals, as he defined it? Waris saw every day hundreds of Hindus and Sikhs expressing their religiosity, their love for this Muslim Sufi saint, sitting together without distinction at the langar hall for food, responding similarly to the music of the qawwal, treating the grave in a similar manner irrespective of their religion. The more he observed the intermeshing of traditions in the courtyard of a Sufi shrine, the more the ridiculousness of Shah Waliullah's arguments angered him. In his thoughts, he would argue with him and come up with replies to his counterarguments.

Sometimes he would think about writing something in response to Shah Waliullah, to present his point of view, highlighting the beauty and divinity in this intermingling of traditions, which gave birth to new traditions. He wanted to show how, what we saw as religion today, was a product of hundreds of years of this intermingling, of Yousuf interacting with Krishna, of Musa overlapping with Prahalad Bhagat, of Isa being imagined as Buddha. One would cease to exist without the other, as night without day, as black without white. Nothing would survive if these threads were disentangled, he wanted to write. None of the purity would be retained. But the thought of writing frightened him. Where should he begin? What language should he write in? Was there even a point to writing? Would anyone read his work? Who would take him seriously, in front of the renowned scholar Shah Waliullah?

Sitting among the pilgrims, Waris would sometimes overhear how the Sikh militia attacked the Abdali army as it was on its way back with all the bounty it had looted. Despite his anger towards these groups, given his personal experiences with them while he was in Jandiala, and the information he would get about them in Kasur, about what they were doing in different parts of Punjab, almost always through Umer, the news cheered him, made him feel a tinge of pride. He was glad that there was someone in Punjab who could in some way inflict pain upon the Abdali army, be a symbol of resistance.

While engaged in *sewa*, Waris would observe the images and sights around the langar hall—the clothes of the people, their demeanour, their behaviour. He would imagine stories about these pilgrims, live their lives vicariously—discover his father in a stranger, imagine his friends in groups of young men. He would imagine himself taking the role of a groom who had come there with his bride. What would it be like to be married, he wondered. Increasingly this thought found space in his mind. He wanted to get married, he decided, but didn't know how it would happen. How would he ever find a suitable bride, so far away from home, without the support of his family? The thought reminded him of his loss, his loneliness, his orphaned state. He considered returning to Jandiala sometimes, but couldn't act on it, afraid of what he might discover there, afraid that his brothers and their families might not be alive.

At the shrine, Waris was a silent observer, happy to recede into his reclusive self. He was a regular sight. When not helping the devotees, he could be seen scribbling on a piece of paper in his corner. No one made an effort to get to know him. Nor did

Waris attempt to make any connections. There were a few like
him, permanent members of the shrine, all reclusive, all carrying
tales no one wanted to share.

Waris would observe from a distance the daily arrival of the
diwan, the caretaker of the shrine, as all the devotees and pilgrims
gathered around him. He was a young man, perhaps even a few
years younger than Waris. He always wore white, with a long
cloak that dragged on the floor behind him, purifying it with its
sacredness. The cloak would occasionally be held by the long
line of devotees walking after him, who kissed it and touched
it to their eyes and forehead. He would enter the shrine just
before maghrib and then stay there until late at night listening to
the qawwal. Devotees would place a few coins in front of him
when they placed coins in front of the qawwals, coins that his
entourage would swiftly remove. The diwan usually had dinner
at the langar but Waris never found an opportunity to serve
him, beaten always by those more eager than him.

Even though Waris kept his distance, the diwan noticed
him. Perhaps it was the dignified way in which Waris held
himself. One day in the langar hall, while Waris was serving
other devotees, the diwan sent for him. Waris put away the
bucket he was carrying and walked towards him. He sat in front
of him, his legs folded under him and his eyes on the ground.

'Where are you from?' asked the diwan, in an authoritative
voice.

'I am originally from Jandiala. But I was a student of Maulvi
Ghulam Murtaza in Kasur. I was living there at his madrasah
before I moved to Pakpattan.'

'Who are you?' the diwan asked, a little surprised by
the response.

'I am Waris, a Syed, a descendant of Muhammad al-Makki,
who traces his lineage back to Imam Ali al-Hadi, who was a

descendant of Imam Hussain, the grandson of the Prophet. Peace be upon him!'

Upon hearing Waris's response, the diwan straightened his back, while his disciples gasped with surprise. 'You are a Syed Badshah?' he asked, sounding slightly doubtful. 'Why are you living like a beggar here? You should have come to me earlier, told me about yourself. I would have taken you to my haveli. I would have treated you as my guest. It would be my greatest privilege to serve you.'

Waris pressed his palms together in front of him and looked straight at the diwan. 'Maharaj, I am your guest at the shrine as well. All I need is a quiet corner and a spare change of clothes, both of which I already have. Your langar provides me with more than I can eat. Here I can perform sewa. Please allow me to remain here. Baba Fareed himself is looking after me.'

The diwan held Waris's hands and then put his hand on Waris's head. 'As you wish, my son. Please don't hesitate to let me know if you ever need anything.'

Waris bowed his head lower. 'Saeen, I cannot thank you enough for all you have already done for a poor soul like me. What more would I need? I would however like to formally enter the fold of the Chishtiya Sufi Silsila. Please do me that honour and I would be grateful to you for the rest of my life.'

Waris wasn't sure why he had asked to be formally included into the Chishtiya Silsila. The thought had just entered his mind. It wouldn't have changed anything but now that he had expressed the desire, he wanted it; he wanted to be a part of the Chishtiya Silsila, be a part of the six-hundred-year-long tradition. He wanted to be a part of this community that had followers all over Punjab and Hindustan. He wanted to belong with them, now that he belonged nowhere. He would be at home wherever there were Chishtis. He would no longer be an orphan, no longer an exile or a refugee.

'Of course, that would be my privilege.' The diwan extended his hand to one side and a disciple placed a red thread in it. The diwan gripped it, shut his eyes and began reciting something under his breath, his lips moving silently, sometimes allowing an incomprehensible sound to escape. He then blew on the thread and gestured to Waris. Waris extended his arm in the direction of the diwan who tied the thread around his wrist.

'You are now one of us. Part of the rich tradition that connects back to Nizamuddin Auliya, Baba Fareed and Moinuddin Chishti. Their shadow will always be over you, will always protect you, but you too have to defend their legacy, their honour, through your actions, your thoughts and intentions. You have to carry yourself as a true Muslim, following in the footsteps of these saints, for it is not you the world will see but a member of the Chishti Silsila. They will judge us through you. You are responsible for all of us and all of us are responsible for you. This thread is your bond with us. From today onwards, your hands have been tied such that they cannot cause anyone harm. Do you promise to live by this code, dear Waris?'

'I do.'

What is a thought disentangled from distractions? A thought that is pure. A thought that does not hook onto other thoughts, other reference points. A thought that exists on its own. It will be hard for you mortals to conceptualize this thought, to imagine this solitary existence where the body, the mind and the soul converge, where the world around you disintegrates and so do all your physical needs, leaving behind the trueness of that one thought.

You might ask me if, by thought, I mean the divine. I will answer that question with some more questions. What is the divine? What does the divine look like? Where does the divine reside? What are the characteristics of the divine? Many thinkers have defined the divine through human traits, as a jealous, angry, merciful, kind being. I disagree with them all, for these are human attributes and concepts imposed upon a being that exists outside these limitations. I am not even sure if we can use the word exist because even that is a human concept.

I define the divine as a thought, an unrestrained, unbound thought. The thought has no boundaries, no end, no beginning. It can take any form, create anything from nothing. The word 'divine' is corrupted, imbued with layers of meanings, placed one atop another over centuries. The word carries baggage that is impossible to shun. It conjures up images that don't do justice to it. I have therefore disassociated with the word and use thought—*dhi, buddhi*.

Don't fret too much if this is too complicated for you. Sometimes it takes years, and sometimes lifetimes, to comprehend the basics of this thought. And sometimes even all that time is not enough.

It requires years and years of training, of preparation, of negation of the self, to become one with that thought. Siddharth lost his kingdom, his family and even his name in his search for that thought. Mahavira spent years in meditation, until birds formed nests in his hair and plants grew around him. Baba Fareed hung inside a dark well for twelve years with nothing but his thoughts, following which he hung on a tree for another twelve. Some spend days buried within graves while others find it scattered in the ashes at cremation grounds.

It is the hardest of journeys but don't worry, you've found the best among teachers. I could teach you a few breathing exercises, certain bodily postures to help you align with that thought. For this is not just a thought that resides purely in the mind. It cannot be accessed just through the brain. That would be a foolish thought. It requires the participation of the entire body. It begins from our breathing and then circulates through our blood. It animates our limbs and then finally it enters the brain. It requires a harmony of soul, body and mind. It requires physical exertion, controlling one's impulses and regulating one's mind. It requires yog and through that, one acquires the status of jog.

I could teach you everything but before I take you on as a student, you'll have to pass certain tests. You'll have to convince me of your commitment. For this is not a journey for the faint-hearted, or for those who lack perseverance. Many have jumped into this river without adequate preparation. Many have tried climbing this mountain only to fail. Like Sohni, you will drown in the Chenab if you are not careful.

For those unacquainted, this journey might seem easy. Many a youth, exhausted by the toils of their daily chores, run to me, to become jogis. What lures them is the charm, the itinerant lifestyle, no family compulsions to hold them down. They see their elders bow at our feet and seek our blessings. They see the magic in our spells, the power of our charms and they are drawn to us. They see how we can control the patterns of the seasons, the will of animals and the hearts of humans. They hear our enigmatic words and they see our bowls filled with food as we move from one house to another in the midst of civilization. But what they don't see is our starving bodies, our protruding bones when we are meditating in the wilderness. It is not jog that draws them to us but an abhorrence of their sedentary lifestyle. They think they want us but what they really want is an escape from their self-imposed prisons. Caught in an illusion, maya, the two might seem the same but they are not.

I have spent my entire life in this jog, sitting on top of this mound of jogis, Tilla Jogian. I am part of this mound; I reside in each and every corner of this place. In some parts of the world, in certain social circles, this mound is known as the mound of Balnath. I accept this honour with joined palms and utter humility, for I am not worthy of this honour. I have spent my entire life in self-effacement. I would rather refer to this mound as the mound of Gorakhnath, our spiritual guru, the Maha Yogi, who, learning from Lord Shiva, himself taught us the basic percepts of yog and jog.

While his existence has escaped the confinement of his physical body, he does, in his multiple forms and incarnations, visit me. Sometimes he speaks through me and I, Balnath, become Gorakhnath. Some of my disciples call me the next Maha Yogi, but I ignore all these claims. Completely. For they are meant to flatter so that I bestow on them the power of jog that they have been in search of for the better part of their lives. Some of these disciples came to me as children and now they are standing on the threshold of the last phase of their life still waiting. If only it was that easy.

But enough of this conversation. I had no intention of going off on these tangents. This is what happens when one tries to concentrate and connect with that thought. Even a trained jogi like me sometimes gets distracted. I am sitting under an ancient acacia tree on the top of this mound, my eyes closed. All around me are my disciples, sitting in a similar posture. I don't remember how long I have been in this pose. Time is of no significance to us jogis. My stomach has now been disciplined so that it no longer growls with hunger. My disciples' bodies, however, are not as trained and I can occasionally hear the pleas of starvation. We will boil a few leaves and drink that water when our bodies are about to give up. I can feel vultures circling the sky above

us, mistaking us for carcasses. The sun is glaring at us from its
highest point.

Silence wraps itself around us, not an absolute silence but
the kind of silence that amplifies sounds. A silence that has a
rhythm, a silence that is harmonious, a silence that carries the
sound of the crawl of an insect and the rustle of leaves. This
silence is intruded upon by the sound of shuffling feet. Perhaps
it is one of my disciples who has lost concentration. For the
first time in I don't know how many days, I open my eyes, the
bright rays of the sun blinding me. I shut them again and open
them after a few seconds.

What is that I see? Is that the head of a young man emerging
from the edge of the mound? I can see his curly hair, swaying
in the wind behind him, his dense mustache, its edges turned
upwards as if he is a proud scion of a Jatt. His face radiates
with beauty in a way that everything that the face turns towards
becomes beautiful. The plants around him look greener. The
vultures above our head have disappeared and swans have
appeared out of nowhere.

Who is he and what does he want from me? Is he in search
of jog? What travesty has fallen upon him that he is trying to
forget? He walks towards me.

'Even before you place your head on my feet and ask me
what you've come to ask me, my answer is no,' I tell him. 'You
carry within yourself the baggage of your love for the world. I
can see the weight it exerts on your shoulders. You should have
left it at the base of this mound before you began your ascent.
You are not meant for this rigorous life that you've come to
pursue. Do you even know what it takes? Look around you.'

All my disciples were now looking at us.

'Look at the faces of these disciples who have spent their
entire lives here and still they wait. The jog begins with ripping

out the ego from within and trampling it under one's feet. It requires forgetting about everybody and everything that you've ever loved and cremating that life as if it were dead. What makes you think you are ready for this arduous journey?'

'Maharaj, Mahayogi, Guru Balnath,' said the beautiful man, with his palms pressed together. 'Don't turn me away from your sanctuary,' he begged. 'I am an orphan, a victim of the world's atrocities. I have severed all my ties, I am devoted to you like Sita was to Ram, Radha was to Krishna, and Heer is to Ranjha. I have killed my former self, murdered him with my own bare hands. I am a blank slate, presenting myself to you. Write your lesson of jog on me, accept me in your fold.'

His words fell on me as if they were the songs of Prophet Daud, as if it was the flute of Krishna. I could feel my heart melt. I looked into his eyes and his passion stabbed at me. It sent a jolt through my body and I began to shake. Drops of sweat began dripping down my forehead. The beautiful man took the edge of his shirt and wiped it clean. I felt the freezing breeze of the Himalayas in his touch. In his shadow, I could see the silhouette of Mahadeva, of Bhagwan Shiva.

I held both of his hands in my hands and embraced him. I wanted to fall at his feet and acknowledge him for what he was, but his eyes stopped me. 'How can I stand between you and your jog? It would be our honour to have you in our midst. You are a gift of the gods to us; how can we turn you away? I will make you a jogi right now. I will teach you the secrets of yoga and bestow upon you all my magic skills. You will be able to control the seasons, tame animals and read people's hearts. You will know of their deepest secrets and will be able to find the cures to all their ills. You will become the most powerful jogi in the world.'

My disciples could not understand my behaviour. Of course, they could not see what I could see. In unison, they rose up in fury and cried, 'How dare you decide to bestow the secrets of jog on this man, whom you have just met, while we have sat at your feet for years? You told us we were not prepared and here you think this man is worthy who has just climbed up the mountain? We refuse to be a part of this unfair order; you know no justice. Together we will beat you up and your beloved devotee and seek vengeance for the torture you have inflicted upon us.'

'Be quiet, you imbeciles,' I raged in indignation, blood rushing towards my head. 'You know not what you say. Your behaviour has just demonstrated why I think you are still not prepared. Who you see as an untrained novice, I see as a learned man,' I said, as I held his arm. 'He may not wear the robes of jog yet, but don't be mistaken; he is already one of us. He has been a jogi since time immemorial. While you will always be known by the name of your master, I will be known through him.' I wanted to bend down in front of him, acknowledge him for who he was but didn't, to keep up a pretence of master and devotee. 'He asks me for jog but it is nothing but a ritual. He is already a jogi. This is only a confirmation.

'You dare raise your voice against me? You threaten me with violence?' I continued. 'It seems that you have completely forgotten the powers that reside in me. With one small spell, I can transform you all into toads. For the rest of your lives, all you will do is croak. Without lifting a finger, I will break your hands and legs. I will make a necklace out of your limbs and wear it around my neck. Don't challenge the wrath of a jogi; you idiots should know better than that. You can bring the entire army of Ahmad Shah Abdali in front of me; you know it will not stand a chance.'

My threats achieved their purpose. 'Forgive us, master, we were consumed by our envy. We are blind to that secret world that you have access to. We accept all your wishes, all your commands. If you want to make this man a jogi, we will humbly accept. We will serve him as we serve you, without the slightest quibble. Tell us what to do and it will be done this instant,' they said, in unison.

So, on my orders, Ranjha's clothes were stripped off, as if this was his former body, his former self, that he was abandoning. His beautiful hair and his proud moustache were shaved off, as he had no use for these notions of beauty in his new life. Ash was smeared on his face and his body to purify him with the symbol of death, the only thing that is true of life. His ears were pierced and two stone earrings were placed in them to remind him of his bond with us.

Upon completing these rituals, I summoned all my magical powers and transferred them to him. I saw his eyes light up, his body becoming taut as he experienced this powerful force run through him. He looked at me through his transformed eyes and then saw himself. In that moment, he knew that he had changed. He had become a jogi.

'Now that you have become a jogi, you must remember all your vows. You must never think about establishing a household; never must you marry, or sire children. You should look at all the women in the world as if they are your sisters or mother. You must live a life of purity and help whoever you can,' I told him.

'Old man, what ridiculous lessons are you giving me?' he replied, with contempt. 'I have become a jogi for the love of my Heer and now you are asking me to forget her. Take back this jog for none of this matters, if I am not with her.' He knew well enough that once he had been given this boon, it could not be taken back.

'You preach your message of renunciation. You search for the divine in the wilderness. Clad in your saffron clothes, you roam around the world with a bowl in your hand, feeding off other people's labour. You talk about service but who do you serve except yourself? I don't see an orphanage at your ashram, neither do I see any meal for the starving. You wear this garb of humility, but you don't take off your crown of pride. God has made us so that we participate in the world, to live a married life. Who has given you the authority to challenge this divine right? You cover your eyes with this ash so that you become blind to the beauty of the world. Its glory lies in living. There is beauty in work. There is worship in hard labour. There is joy in spending time with loved ones, in seeing the smile of a child, in the warm embrace of your beloved. No jog can ever compete with that experience.'

'Oh, my dear child, don't you understand,' I replied softly. 'The world is a mere illusion. You have been caught in its trap for so long that you are finding it hard to forgo it. There is no moksha without abandonment; otherwise, you remain trapped. Women were created to lure you to keep you imprisoned in your body. To become one with God, you have to rise above this physicality. This lust is the curse of Satan. It keeps you from the true light.'

'What you are referring to as lust is an eternal bond. What do you know about love when you have remained deprived of its delights?' he said, mockingly. 'Your life is not worth living if you haven't tasted this nectar. I experience divinity in the eyes of my Heer. I belong forever in her arms. For I am her soul and she is my body; separated, we yearn for each other. I came to you to become a jogi so that I can go and get her back. Like Sita, she is stuck in the lair of Ravana. I have to go to Ranganpur to wage this righteous war.'

In the intensity of this young man's arguments, I could see the purity of his love. I realized that this was not an ordinary love, between two mortals, but rather a spiritual union between two sacred souls. Their bond was ethereal. God had destined that they be together and had fated them to become symbols of lovers. They were to become the ultimate example of love, its ideal form, through which all other loves, and all other love stories, were to emerge. Their jog lies in them being together, for what else is jog but true love?

'Forgive me, my son, for I doubted your intentions. I see now that you are incomplete without your Heer. I shall not stand in your way. You have my permission to go to Ranganpur and claim what is rightfully yours. I will personally present myself in God's court and pray for your success.'

The air around him began to thicken, exerting its weight on his shoulders and back. His lungs struggled for air, sucking heavily to pull in traces of oxygen from his surroundings. Beads of perspiration appeared on his forehead. The din around him became incomprehensible. The laughter began to blend with the cries, the humming within the hall mixing with the fading sound of the qawwali coming from outside. Waris was sitting inside the langar hall. He had a piece of roti in his right hand, dal in a plate in front of him, but he could not seem to lift it to his mouth.

All day long, and for several days prior to this one, Waris had been running up and down the langar hall, feeding an army of devotees who arrived without end, as if they were limbs of a rakshasa replacing themselves after being cut. It was the occasion of the annual festival at the shrine, the urs of Baba Fareed, the celebratory day when his soul abandoned his body and became one with the divine. The shrine shone like the sun, radiating in its sacredness, to greet all these visitors. Oil lamps had been placed all over the courtyard, in every available niche, on windowsills, around the lone berry tree that rose next to Baba Fareed's grave. It was under this tree that Baba, more than five hundred years ago, had moved his madrasah, when he became the head of the Chishtiya Silsila, away from the power centre of Delhi. This was the only thing protecting him and his students from the heat and the rain, its fruit their only sustenance. However, power came chasing him. It now resided at his shrine, originated from his grave and those of his descendants, exhibited itself through the splendid structures that had been constructed over these graves and lent authority to the caretaker of the shrine.

It was late in the night. Waris was carrying the heavy bucket of dal in his hand, serving pilgrims, when he felt a sharp pain in his shoulder. He occasionally felt this pain, but it was always manageable. Today, however, it was excruciating. He needed to stop. He put the bucket on the ground and began massaging his shoulder. Daud, one of the hired helps, responsible for cooking the langar, saw Waris and told him to rest. Waris sat in a corner, facing the crowd in front of him, while Daud served him food.

Since the past several days, Waris had completely devoted himself to sewa, leaving him no time to reminisce, reflect or miss his friends, Maulvi sahib, and Kasur. He found it hard to suppress their memories in the beginning, while he was still discovering his place at the shrine. The more he thought about his time in Kasur, the harder it was to cope with all the changes that had been forced upon him continuously since his childhood. He wanted to move on, to fully immerse himself in his new life. Whenever he found himself wandering back to his past, he would engage in intense physical exertion to distract his thoughts. While he found some success in burying his recent memories of Kasur, the memories of Jandiala and his father were harder to avoid. They kept emerging, riding along on the morning breeze, in the sound of the azaan, the echo of the Maulvi's voice in an empty mosque, in the songs of the qawwal. He would shut his eyes and ears to them, try to put them away, work harder, filling the empty moments in his day that threatened him.

But there was a limit to how much he could exert. The exhaustion, it seemed, had finally caught up. Now that he had stopped working, he could no longer avoid these moments. Thoughts, memories now began to surface. They arrived in a surge, deluging his existence. They overpowered him. Thoughts that reminded him of his loss, helplessness, of his insignificance, his lack of control. They formed a whirlpool in his head, mixed with the noise in the hall, and began to swirl, until Waris could no longer feel himself, his hands, his body. Taking short breaths, still struggling to breathe, he dragged his body backwards, towards the wall, and, with his back supported, shut his eyes.

In the darkness that now surrounded him, his mother appeared. It was her usual image, a thin, young woman, in white, with an indiscernible face. Indiscernible not because she was at a distance or had no features, but because it wasn't an image, but a notion.

The image remained with him for some time, calmed him down, held his hand and took his head in its embrace. Slowly the density of the air began to lift itself, his lungs rediscovered breath. The heat radiating from his body was cooled by the breeze coming in through the open windows. The din around him began to fade away as distinct sounds, noises of people talking, laughing, eating, sleeping reappeared.

The rush in the hall had thinned out. Many pilgrims had moved out into the courtyard, while a few remained inside lying on the ground, hoping for a few hours of sleep before the festivities restarted in the morning. There were still a handful of people who were eating and Daud was serving them himself. The rest of the kitchen staff, it seemed, had taken off. Frightened at what he had just experienced, he followed Daud with his eyes, observing his actions, his language, as he moved from one pilgrim to another.

It was in this state that Waris first caught sight of Saraswati. She was sitting with her son in one of the aisles, the only two people in that aisle. Daud had just served them food and moved on but Waris's eyes did not. She was wearing a white sari, no jewellery, no *sindoor*. Waris felt as if he had seen her before. He observed her face. She was dark, with sharp features, distinct, clear, with nothing abstract about it. It was as if the face had been chiselled, a long, sharp nose, a sharp chin and thin, sharp lips. Had he seen her at the shrine earlier? Had he served her food? Waris couldn't be sure. She appeared familiar.

The child next to her was about three. He sat with his elbow resting on his mother's thigh, his hand holding his chin, his eyes looking into oblivion. He had his mother's eyes, Waris thought. 'Here, take one more bite,' she said, love dripping from every word, as she fed his reluctant mouth. 'My good son,' she said, when he took the bite, as if she was the happiest person in the hall. She passed her hand through his hair and kissed him on the head. Her voice appeared comforting. It appeared beautiful. It danced around the room on its tiny feet before collapsing on the ground, transforming into tiny sparks that disappeared after a little while. When the child refused to eat, she cleaned the plate with a few bites.

She found a wall behind her to rest, put the child on her lap and starting rocking her legs slowly. The child slept immediately, as she ran her hands through his hair. She remained in that position for several moments, before she too began to doze off, opening her eyes suddenly after a few minutes, as she caught her neck slipping to the side. She picked up the child, placed him on the floor, her arm under his head, and wrapped her body around him.

Waris got up, went to his corner in the courtyard and picked up his bundle of clothes. He walked back to the langar hall, approaching the sleeping mother and son. Her eyes opened up in fear as his shadow appeared over them. Waris was upset at himself for frightening her. 'Here,' he said politely, the words refusing to leave his throat, reluctantly coming into existence, as he handed her his bundle of clothes. 'Please use this as a pillow.' She didn't say anything, too shocked by the scare she had received. Waris walked away, her eyes following, as he found an empty space in the vast langar hall and lay on the ground, facing the wall, his back towards her. She placed the bundle under her head and went back to sleep.

In the morning, Waris was woken up by her shadow over him. She was returning his bundle. Her child was much happier now, holding his mother's leg and pivoting from one arm to another. 'Thank you,' she said in a shy voice, a voice that carried traces of the love Waris had heard last night. He extended his hands and grabbed the bundle from her, the tips of his fingers catching the tips of hers for a moment. A brief moment in which the day appeared brighter.

Later in the day, Waris saw the mother and the son in the langar hall once again. It was late afternoon and the peak hour for lunch had passed. He walked up to them and put some food in their plate. She looked up at him, her big eyes expanding in recognition. Her upper lip curled slightly in a suppressed smile. Waris noticed that smile, as it found its way onto his lips, blossoming fully like a flower in the spring breeze. The smile on his face surprised him, making use of muscles that hadn't been used in months. It spread uncomfortably on his face, like an insect on his cheeks. He tried getting rid of it but his body would not respond.

'Thank you,' she said, the traces of the smile now gone.

After they had had their lunch, Waris approached them once again and asked, 'Where are you from?' Words struggled against his dry throat as he pushed them out, his breathing stopping in that momentary silence that existed between the exit of the words from his lips, and the wait for a response from hers.

'Malka Hans,' she replied, as she looked at him and looked away.

'Is this the first time you've come to Pakpattan?' Waris felt his parched throat. Perhaps he needed some water.

'No. We come every year.' Waris waited for an elaboration, but nothing came.

'Do you come alone?' he asked, only to regret it immediately.

'I am not alone,' she said confidently. Waris felt a sense of relief. 'Chotu is with me.' There was an excitement in her tone. She patted her son lightly on the back, and laughed gently. 'Where are you from?' she asked, as she finally allowed her eyes to anchor on his face. Waris was glad to hear the question, happy that now this was a two-way conversation, no longer an infringement. Words now came more easily to him, as he answered a question he had answered many times before, and he answered it as if it was rehearsed.

'I am from many places and nowhere at the same time. I was born in Jandiala but I became an orphan at a young age. I lost my home. I found some comfort in Kasur briefly, at the madrasah of Maulvi Ghulam Murtaza but that too was snatched away. I am temporarily from Pakpattan, or this shrine, I should say, but I am not tied to this place.' He didn't know why he had added this line at the end. He had never said that before. Now that it had been said, acknowledged, its reality exerted itself on him. Suddenly he became more aware of his uprootedness, his homelessness. It saddened him, so much so that he wanted to end this conversation and revert to sewa. But he didn't. He continued standing there. The shadow of the statement appeared vaguely on his face. Waris wanted to pull it away before Saraswati saw it. He put his hand in front of Chotu, encouraging him to slap his palm. Chotu responded but Waris moved his hand away right at the end, a smile appearing on his face.

Chotu laughed loudly and said, 'Again.' Saraswati too giggled with the child. Waris and Chotu engaged in this game for some time, Chotu failing each time. Eventually he held Waris's hand with his left hand and then managed to slap it with his right. He raised both of his arms in the air victoriously and began saying, 'I won. I won.' Both Waris and Saraswati laughed along with Chotu.

'Where is his father?' Waris asked casually, as he messed Chotu's hair. Chotu, annoyed at this action, tried to remove his hands from his head but Waris continued bothering him.

'He passed away last year,' she said dryly, with her eyes on her son. The sparkle that was there only a moment ago was now gone.

Waris let go of Chotu's head as Chotu held Waris's hand and tried twisting it. Waris's attention was completely on Saraswati now. 'I am sorry. I should have known. How did he . . .'

'In a battle.'

'Was he a soldier?'

'No. He was a farmer, but then he was ordered to join the army, given a weapon, offered no training and forced to wage war.' She spoke as if the inevitability of his death was a forgone conclusion.

'Who was he fighting for?'

'Our jagirdar. He raised an army to ward off the attacks of the Sikh guerillas threatening his villages.'

They stood in silence for several minutes. Waris unsure about what to say and Saraswati unsure about how much more to share. By now, Chotu had managed to put Waris's hand behind his back. Waris felt a tinge of pain at the usual spot in his right shoulder. 'Hey, you little monster. What are you doing?' said Waris. He picked up Chotu, turned him upside down and put him on his shoulder. 'You are my bag of atta. We will use you to make roti and feed everyone.' Waris began walking towards the kitchen.

'No. Leave me,' cried Chotu. 'Amma, help me.' Real tears formed in his eyes.

'He is only joking, Chotu,' said Saraswati, responding to her son's plea in all seriousness.

Waris put Chotu down, held him by his legs and dangled him in front of him. Chotu's shirt fell on his face, showing his round tummy. 'I am going to eat you,' said Waris, as he put his face on the child's stomach and growled. Chotu's cries of help immediately changed to laughter.

Has any male writer ever been able to write women well? How can you expect poor Waris to be any better? Aren't we all caricatures in the hands of male writers—prideful, arrogant, beguiling, deceitful and conniving?

Alright, perhaps I am being a little harsh on this poet. He does, after all, get a few things right. It's a question worth asking though—how does a man who never got married, who never heard the pleas of his wife, understand the tension between a bride, her *saas* and *nanad*? But then I might be underestimating our Waris. He is someone who has an ear for folk. Our wedding songs are full of these laments.

In any case, my complaint remains. I deserved a much more important role than playing second fiddle to Heer. Maybe, in another life, justice will be done. Perhaps one day, I will be the lead character of my own story, for there is no doubt that I do deserve one.

My apologies, I entangled you in the threads of my thought without a formal introduction. I am Sahiti, Saida's sister. I have been the pride and the life of this house since my birth. My father adores me and my brother would take on the world for me. I am the centre of this household, the most important figure, well . . . until the arrival of Heer!

How should I describe myself? I can call myself beautiful, but I feel the poet has already exhausted his vocabulary of similes in drawing up Heer. Fine, let me resort to the expected clichés, of youth and arrogance. That I am. And I am also resentful and envious of the new bride. The entire village has gathered to see her moon-like face. All the eyes that once searched for me have now lost interest in me. Look at how all these pupils are glued to her.

There she is, sitting in the middle of the courtyard, wearing the bride's red, her hands covered in henna, gold bangles dancing around her wrists. She has her hand in a big bowl, filled with milk, searching for a bracelet. My brother, Saida, is in search of it too. Whoever finds it first will be the dominant one in this relationship. So they say. What is that I notice? Her hand has hardly moved. She sits there, lifelessly, as if without a soul, while Saida is searching for the bangle enthusiastically. The girls around her are asking her to participate, nudging her, but they might as well be talking to a rock. They look towards me, expecting a solution, but I am as surprised as them. Saida manages to find the bangle and yells in excitement, 'I win! I win!' he says, with his hand up. No one but my mother claps for him.

The guests approach the bride, offer her gifts, which she refuses to hold; the gifts fall to the ground. They touch her face to see if she is actually as beautiful as everyone says she is, but she turns her face away, looking annoyed. They try to welcome her, explain to her their relationship with us, but she refuses to listen, looking completely disinterested.

Soon the guests give up and begin to quietly slip away. 'What have the Kheras brought upon themselves?' I hear the whispers. Can you imagine the horror? The shame? Our Khera ears are not made to hear taunts. No one has dared mock us before this. Could it be true? Could the rumours be true? Of course, I have heard them. We all have. Don't ask me that question. It wasn't my decision to make. It was my father and mother who were swayed by this rishta of the Sials. They wanted to bring this Heer to our home (and everything else that came with her).

The drama continues deep into the night. I can hear the sound of falling, screeching and howls of pain from the couple's room, not the kind of sounds one expects to hear on the first night of newly-weds. After a while, the door opens and Saida emerges, bruised and hurt, tears falling down his cheeks. Behind him stands Heer, her hair dishevelled, gold *tikka* out of place, her dupatta lying on the floor. Her teeth are clenched together and there is blood in her eyes. She shuts the door immediately after Saida escapes. Our mother caters to his wounds while I lend him a sympathetic ear. 'She refuses to be my bride. She attacked me viciously when I approached her bed,' he says with a whimper.

'What kind of a man are you?' my mother speaks, mockingly. 'Is this how you were raised? You should take what is rightfully yours.'

I couldn't agree more but our Saida was ineffective. For days, he lumbered around her room not daring to step in. The bride locked herself inside, guarding herself like a wounded lioness. The entire village laughed at us, while Saida became the butt of many jokes. Rumours had started spreading, rumours that had been born in Jhang but had now travelled to Ranganpur, as Heer's *jahaiz*. My brother's head fell in shame, while a fire burned inside my soul.

My blood boiled at the sight of our bride, unaware, unconcerned about the dishonour she was bringing us. She made no effort to share our concerns, to reach out, to extend a hand of friendship to me, or help my mother. All day long, she lay on her bed, as if she was chained to it by Ravana. She refused to wash her face or even change her clothes and turned away all food that was sent her way. 'Have you come here to bring us torture? Do you have no shame? Is this how brides act at their in-laws? Is this how the Sials educate their women?' I say to her one day, as I catch a glimpse of her through her partially opened door.

'Go away from here. Why do you torture a tortured soul?' she replies, reluctantly. 'I have no energy to engage in this conversation with you. I see that you speak out of love for your brother, for you see only his plight. If only you had known what is going on inside me, you wouldn't have been so heartless. You would have sat next to me, crying a thousand tears. Go away from here. Please don't torture me.' She breaks down after speaking, burying her face in her lap.

'Cursed was the day when you were brought into this house,' I reply. 'How happy we all were before your arrival! Where there was once spring now only autumn resides. Dark clouds hover over us at all times. Will we ever see some respite?'

I wish she had responded but she refused to engage, her head still in her lap. 'Have you gone deaf? Are you too almighty to even reply? I understand well enough what games you are trying to play. Don't forget that this is still my house and will remain till the day I die. I swear upon the graves of all my ancestors that I will find a way. One day my brother, the apple of my eye, will make you his bride.' I then walked away, even angrier than I was before the beginning of this conversation.

I went to my mother and devised a scheme. I whispered my plan in her ear, and the same night she called Saida into her room to have this conversation with him. 'Take this stick with you.' The words were uttered by my mother, but the idea was mine. 'Beat her up with it till she is tame.'

'Make sure you don't leave the room until you have consummated your marriage,' I warned him, almost threatening him. I looked him up and down, unsure if my words had their desired effect. Saida was nodding enthusiastically, and there was a determined expression in his eyes. He was eager to go into the room, eager to implement the strategy.

As planned, Saida entered the room with the stick and locked the door. My mother and I stood outside with bated breath, waiting to hear Heer's cries. We heard sounds of thrashing and whipping and high-pitched screams. My mother and I exchanged glances, for we knew that our plan was working. Tonight, our brother would be a bull and Heer his passive wife. We were still flashing silent smiles to each other when the door opened with a bang. It was Saida once again, with bruises all over his face and body, his clothes partially torn. He limped out of the door, holding his swollen knee. As he left the room, Heer threw the broken stick after him.

'What kind of a man are you?' I was the first to scream. Without having mercy on his condition, I began slapping him with both hands. Our mother had to hold me back. 'Can't you control your wife?' I continued as I moved away from him. 'If only . . . if only I was in your place, I would have shown her real might. We should never have got you married. We should have let you chase sheep all your life. You will not be able to control this wild beast.'

'Oh, my poor son, what has that witch done to you?' lamented my mother as she inspected the severity of the wounds. 'Come with me right now, I will tend to your bruises. Come, Sahiti, help your brother; fetch some hot water. I will kill that wench with my own hands, you just wait and see.' Reluctantly, I helped my brother. With one of his arms around my shoulder and the other around that of my mother, he, and we, slowly walked to the other room.

'It's not my fault that I could not overpower her,' Saida finally managed to say, as we were sitting in my mother's room, placing warm rags on his wounds that were now beginning to show. Even as he spoke, he winced in pain.

'She is not alone in there. She is watched over by djinns.' He sounded frightened and shaken up. 'There are devils in the room with her and it is they who beat me up. They took the stick from my hand and unleashed their fury, while Heer stood in the corner, watching the scene unfold. They have threatened that they will do this again if I ever try to enter the room. I have promised them I will never return and Mother, I warn you, neither should you. I will call this my misfortune and accept this as the will of God. Cursed be the day when I decided to marry this woman.'

O Waris, you call us women arrogant and deceitful, but how cleverly you allow a man to defend his ego and retain his pride!

'My in-laws believe I am cursed.' Saraswati sounded amused, as if she was hearing this statement for the first time and was surprised by it. It was late afternoon and they were sitting in the courtyard under the berry tree. The tree cast uneven shadows on their clothes. Around them, a few devotees were napping after lunch. A slight breeze whistled across the courtyard. Chotu was trying to climb Waris's back as Waris's hands protected him from falling. His eyes were fixed on Saraswati, while Saraswati's were glued on Chotu.

> It's a mystery deep and baffling:
> Worldly life—a hidden fire!

The qawwals had been singing the same verse for the past one hour. From the tree, a few birds were matching their rhythm.

Waris had spent the past two days around the mother and son, reducing his hours of sewa, playing with Chotu whenever he was next to them, while engaged in a conversation with Saraswati. He told her about his village, his childhood. He also told her about his father, no longer feeling the need to avoid thinking about him. With his words, the memories became more real, almost physical. He could see the drops of water on his father's beard after wuzu. He could smell his skin, could feel the tickle of his beard on his face. He could see his arms in his own arms, as he played with Chotu.

'And what about your mother?' Saraswati asked him.

'I don't remember anything about her. I wished my father had not done it but he buried all her clothes and her possessions after her death. There were no signs of her anywhere. We never talked about her. We knew never to ask our father about how she died or what she was like when she was alive. I don't know how as children we knew but somehow we just did. Do you ever talk to Chotu about . . .?'

'His father?' asked Saraswati. 'No, not yet.' A resigned sadness crept back into her tone. 'He too has no memory of his father. He has his grandfather and grandmother at home, so perhaps he might think that his grandfather is his . . . I don't know. We also don't talk about the death of his father. Maybe I will talk to him when he is older. Tell him stories about him. Give him memories he doesn't have.'

'I think he'll like that a lot.'

'What sort of a man was your husband?' Waris asked after a few moments of silence.

'Better than husbands usually are. He was sensitive. Sometimes when his mother would get on my nerves and I would lose my cool, he would listen patiently and tell me to ignore her comments. He would say she is an old woman who will die soon. It will be just us after that. What a fool he was!' said Saraswati, laughing lightly, the sadness still embedded in the laughter.

'You know, Chotu reminds me of him. He has his features and his empathy. The other day, his grandmother was saying something to me, one of her usual rants, and he began hitting her.' Saraswati giggled, while narrating the story. 'She eventually had to stop speaking to keep him from hitting her.'

'What did his grandmother say to you?'

'She called me the cursed one. That is her name for me ever since his death.'

Saraswati was quiet now, her eyes on her hands, her thumb scratching the skin next to the nail on her other thumb. 'Do you think it's true, Mian Waris,' she asked in a hesitant tone. 'That some people are cursed?'

'Not at all. Never,' Waris said, emphatically. He turned towards her, as if to hold her, but didn't.

'We all have our fates, our own individual destinies,' he spoke, passionately. 'Sometimes sadness is our fate but that doesn't mean we are cursed. It doesn't mean we have brought this fate upon us or others. It is all written up there,' he said, pointing towards the blue sky with thick white clouds, a few eagles appearing and disappearing into them. 'It is not in our control. We are mere puppets in His hands. This whole drama of cursed and blessed is us humans trying to find justifications to explain our destinies. Please don't think that about yourself. You can't.' Waris was pleading.

'You know, it doesn't bother me that much, this title of cursed,' said Saraswati with a slight smile, her eyes still on her hands, her tone betraying her words. 'It just reminds me of my mother-in-law's helplessness. She has lost a son. I can't imagine . . . She used to bother me when he was alive. I feel like I have more patience for her now.'

'I feel for my in-laws,' she continued, each word taking its time to fall, like the leaves of an autumn tree. Her eyes allowed a few tears to escape. 'My husband was their only son, the only one healthy enough to earn for the family. Dark days have fallen upon us since his death. My father-in-law spends his entire day at moneylenders', getting loans at exorbitant rates of interest.'

Waris shook his head in disgust.

'How will we ever return that money? Chotu will be indebted for life even before he is old enough to understand what money is. I want him to get away. Away from all the pain that awaits him in this household.' The words now appeared swiftly. 'I want him to become a learned man like you. I want him to travel the world. I want him to go to Lahore or Delhi and find employment in the Mughal court. I want him to leave all of us behind.' Saraswati could not speak any more as if she had just realized what she had said, wished for her son, and herself. She was silent, thinking about her comment, wondering if she actually meant what she said.

'That's a harsh fate you want for him.' Waris could feel a rising lump in his throat. He knew if he didn't finish his thought, he might not be able to very soon. 'Being swept away like cotton in a storm, one minute in this direction, and another at another moment, I wouldn't wish this even for my worst enemies.' His face was red. He spoke as if from a distant place, removed from this conversation, removed from his body. His eyes were on the ground. 'If you want him to find employment in the Mughal court, he would need to learn Arabic and Persian. It's better if he starts early. Languages can be difficult to learn when one is an adult. Perhaps you can talk to your village imam at Malka Hans and he would be able to take Chotu as his student?'

Saraswati laughed sarcastically, shaking her head. 'Oh Waris, what do you think Malka Hans is? It's a poor village filled with peasants. There is a village mosque but there is no imam. The villagers don't have the money to spare for that kind of luxury.'

Waris felt himself being drawn back into the conversation, his eyes wide in anticipation, looking at Saraswati in front of him. 'I can teach him these languages,' he said. 'Why not? Yeah, I could do that. I could move to Malka Hans and become the village imam.' Saraswati looked back at Waris, surprised at this sudden suggestion, still trying to comprehend what Waris had just said, unsure how to respond.

'Would you like that, Chotu?' Waris said to Chotu, as he turned around and dropped Chotu on his lap. 'Yes. I'll teach him these languages. He will be a learned man. He will be an important man. People will call him Mian sahib wherever he goes. Chotu Mian sahib.' Chotu chuckled, as a dimple formed on his chubby cheek.

8

The Jogi

I come from a long lineage of wise men, from Abraham, Jacob, Moses and Amos to Bhagwan Krishna, Guru Nanak and our own Ranjha, the buffalo herder. While others are more particular about these distinctions—shepherd, cowherd and buffalo herder, I see all of us as being part of the same tradition. Divinity speaks through us, or we speak on behalf of the divine. There is a massive theological gulf between these two statements, some have argued. I think it's all the same.

But while I do participate in the sacred line of these holy men, there is one major difference. Whereas these men have found God, the internal rhythm of life, in the wilderness, away from our cities and villages, I have only discovered chaos and uncertainty. While they were the harbingers of truth, of certainty, I am the messenger of doubt.

Before you roll your eyes in frustration, eagerly skimming through the page, trying to see how much longer you'll have to put up with me, a lowly shepherd from Ranganpur, I want you to consider this. Can any human ever resist their fate? Can we challenge the mould we are created in? Can we ever evade our

destiny? So, I have proudly embraced it, my role in this qissa, of
which you'll be informed shortly.

Now that I have your attention, allow me to say a few more
words. How often is a shepherd like me accorded the attention
of an esteemed reader like you? I ask you—are doubt and faith
two contrasting states, as they are made out to be, or is there
a greater affinity between them than we realize? Could they
be two sides of the same coin? For isn't doubt the necessary
precondition for confirmation, the establishing of faith? Wasn't
this the methodological approach of the learned Islamic scholar,
Imam Ghazali?

How is a lowly shepherd like me aware of the great Islamic
philosophical traditions, you might wonder. Of course, I am
not. But then I don't really exist, do I? I am an extension of
my creator, the writer, the poet, Waris Shah, who indeed is
well versed in this literature. I am a conduit of his wisdom, an
extension of his thought. It is not I who speak, but Waris. It is
not I who exist, but Waris.

So why has Waris created me? Why have I been allotted
such an important space at such a crucial point in the story?
I exist to doubt, a doubt that paves way for enlightenment. I
reconcile these two contrasting thoughts.

Doubt is the first thing I do when the jogi appears on the
outskirts of Ranganpur, wearing a saffron cloth around his partially
covered body, ash smeared on his torso, a begging bowl and a staff
in his hands, and two stone rings in his ears. He has the right attire,
but something doesn't quite fit. Perhaps it is the radiance of his face,
his beautifully defined features, his searching eyes. 'What is that
place?' he asks, pointing to the silhouette of Ranganpur behind me.

'That is Ranganpur, the town ruled by the Kheras, headed
by Ajju and his son, Saida. They are a vengeful people, especially
when their pride is hurt,' I tell him.

'Why do you offer that advice when I asked for none? What do I know about pride and honour? I see them for what they really are. They are nothing but an illusion, as is the rest of the world. Can't you tell I am a jogi who has trampled all sense of self? They have nothing to fear from me and there is no reason they should bring me harm.'

His reply flames the spark of doubt in my mind, and I wonder if this jogi is actually Ranjha, dressed in a different garb. We have all heard tales of the buffalo herder, the family servant who fell in love with Heer. Everyone knew of the recalcitrance of the new bride and her longing for her true love. Every day when Saida walks the streets of the town, trying to cover his bruises, we all laugh behind his back.

'The Kheras were a proud people once. They used to march with their shoulders broadened, their heads raised but all that has changed now,' I say to the jogi. I notice a sparkle in his eyes as he is drawn into the story. 'It changed with the arrival of the new bride. She has brought shame to them, rubbed mud on their faces.' I see a faint smile appear on the edge of his lips.

'All day long, she yearns for her beloved, her Ranjha. She doesn't eat, drink or sleep. She doesn't allow Saida to enter her room and beats him whenever he tries to force himself on her. She has made a spectacle of the Kheras. They have lost the strut in their stride since her arrival.'

'The bride, I have heard, is in love with her family servant, the buffalo herder. Ranjha is his name. Bards have described his features in every possible detail—his long, sharp nose, his symmetrical face, the dimples in his cheeks, his long, curly hair, and a bow-like mustache,' I continue. 'If you had not shaved off your hair and cut your mustache, I would have sworn upon God that it was you, her beloved, her Ranjha, who has come to Ranganpur to reclaim what is rightfully his.'

'What kind of absurd talk is this? Have you been chewing bhang?' says the jogi, stuttering, his face reddening. 'Can't you see that I am a jogi, who has renounced all family life? I have no relationships, no bonds. I come from a long line of jogis, beginning from Dhanvantri himself. My name is Dukh Bhajan Nath. My grandfather was Dhanantar Vaid, the most powerful nath of his generation. My guru Hira Nath was a disciple of Muni Agastya and it is to his shrine I am heading. I spent the past twelve years on the banks of the Ganga, lost in meditation. Now I will spend the next twelve years in wandering for that is the cycle we jogis follow. I carry in my potli herbs, medicines and spells of all kinds. Like Luqman, I can cure all ailments. I know nothing of Heer or the Sials but I will pray that she finds some peace, that she is reconnected with her Ranjha.'

'Jogi, you claim a prestigious lineage and you overwhelm me with all the names, but I can hear how your tone softens when you utter Heer's name. Even if I had any doubts, I am now completely convinced. You are Ranjha, dressed as a jogi, to reunite with your Heer.'

The jogi drops his potli on the ground and moves towards me threateningly. He grabs me by my collar and gives me a jerk. 'If you don't end this bullshit right now, I am going to bury you in the ground. Do you even know who you are dealing with? I am a powerful jogi, the most powerful there has been in generations. Even demons quiver when they hear my name. What chance do you have, you stupid shepherd?'

Even before I can gather my thoughts and form a reply, I notice the fearful bleating of my sheep. We both look in their direction and see them all, motionless, their heads turned towards the denser part of the jungle. Two bright eyes emerge from the darkness, and then a furry face forms around it. It is a wolf, its teeth gleaming, saliva dripping down the side. It walks slowly, at a regal pace. The sheep, paralysed with fear, are rooted to their spot.

I feel the loosening of the grip around my collar, as the jogi takes his staff and throws it in the direction of the wolf. It pierces the air, as if it is the spear of Indra, the staff of Moses, and rips through the body of the wolf. The wolf falls immediately and dies a painless death. The sheep, relieved of the immediate threat, go back to grazing.

'Thank you so much. You have saved my life,' I say to the jogi, as I fall to his feet. He holds me by the shoulders and makes me stand.

'You have no reason to thank me, for I understand your pain. I too was a buffalo herder. You were right all along. I am indeed Ranjha who has come back to claim his Heer.'

Tears of joy well up in my eyes, as a lump develops in my throat. 'I thank God that you have come to rescue the poor soul. All day long, she cries in her bed. There is only one word in her vocabulary and that is your name. You will be doing her and the Kheras a favour by taking her away. I will do all I can to help you.'

'Tell me about Saida's immediate family, my friend. Tell me everything you can,' he pleads.

'I have already told you about Ajju. Then there is his mother. But it is Sahiti, Saida's sister, you need to be wary of. Nothing is hidden from her, for she has a cunning mind. At first glance she will know that you are Ranjha and that you have come for Heer. Once your secret is out, there is no turning back. She will make sure that you never achieve your goal and that the two of you are never united. But there is one way you can make that enemy your friend. Rumour has it that she is in love with a camel driver. Murad is his name. Secretly she yearns for his

love. If you can help her achieve her goal, she will ensure that
you reach yours.'

The steady tuk-tuk of the wooden wheels acted as a lullaby.
Waris's body moved with the rhythm of the cart, slowly
traversing the half-baked road that connected Pakpattan with
Malka Hans and beyond. Occasionally the driver would goad
the bull to keep moving.

Chotu, sitting on Waris's lap, was sleeping, while Saraswati,
next to him was also drifting away. There were around ten
people on the congested cart, their bodies packed tightly
together. Waris struggled to keep his eyes open with the warm
spring sun shining down on him.

He had dozed off when he felt Saraswati's head on his bony
shoulder. His body tensed up and his heart began racing. Waris
could feel the echo of his heartbeats resonate in his chest. He was
afraid that Saraswati might feel the tremors as well. He looked in
her direction but her face was covered by the *pallu* of her sari.
Her body was still moving unconsciously to the rhythm of the
cart. She was fast asleep. Waris felt as if he were holding a secret
that was being betrayed by his face, his eyes and his body. He
looked around to see if anyone had caught on but most of the
passengers were asleep. A couple, who were awake, were staring
into the dusty jungle that surrounded them.

Waris sat quietly, unable to sleep, looking into the forest in
front of him. His heart continued to beat rapidly, creating ripples
in his body that transformed into little caterpillars in his veins and
then bloomed into butterflies as they tickled him all over with the
flapping of their wings. He wanted to move, wanted to press his
hand on his heart, to slow down its pace and stop this uncomfortable

sensation but he was afraid of waking Saraswati. Her head bobbed back and forth, precariously balanced on his shoulder.

She finally woke up when the cart stopped next to another mud road leading to Malka Hans. The passengers were expected to walk the last few kilometres to the village. She woke up suddenly, conscious of herself, shifting uneasily. Waris mirrored her response as he felt the butterflies in his stomach grow claws, hold his intestines and turn them. He was uncomfortable but kept a straight face.

Saraswati got off the cart first and Waris handed Chotu to her, their fingers touching once again, but this time less self-consciously. Chotu wriggled a little before placing his head on his mother's shoulder and going back to sleep. The cart, with the rest of the passengers, moved on.

'I don't think we should enter the village together,' said Saraswati, her eyes on the ground, as if in search of a lost object. 'It might raise uncomfortable questions. Can you wait here for a couple of hours before you begin walking towards the village? You will reach before sunset. You will see the mosque right at the edge. I am sure you will not have any problems finding accommodation there.' She spoke as if she were a stranger, as if they had not spent the past few days sharing secrets with each other, secrets that they had kept even from themselves. The grip of the claws on his intestines became stronger.

Saraswati gave Waris a cursory look to which he could only manage a nod. With Chotu in her arms, she began walking towards the village. Waris continued watching her, little clouds of dust rising from her feet, her figure slowly melting into the road, the road slowly disappearing into shrubs flanking it.

A jogi's begging bowl is more precious than all the rubies in the world. Perhaps it's the epithet 'begging' that tends to confuse people. Yes, it is true that a jogi begs for food, with me, his begging bowl, in hand. But this is no ordinary kind of begging. This is not the begging that people are reduced to due to their extraneous circumstances. This is the begging of a king. It is a begging full of pride, honour and prestige. It is the kind of begging made august and majestic by Buddha, as he roamed with his Sangha, from one settlement to another. Mahavira too blessed me by carrying me from one household to another, collecting food. Chandragupta Maurya, our splendid king, who expanded the boundaries of his empire, took up *sanyas* towards the end of his life and begged for food.

In this relationship between the beggar and the donor, it is not the beggar who receives the gift, but rather the donor who is blessed for their contribution. Here the very logic of the relationship is turned upside down, the meaning of the word begging redefined.

But like all good things, this too came to an end, with the advent of Kaliyuga. Lured by the power and the pride that comes with jog, many evil men took up the garb and held me with their filthy hands. They soiled our glorious tradition for their temporal greed. They entered the homes of unsuspecting people, who still remembered the good old days, and hiding behind the facade of sacredness, they eyed the treasures of the home and the womenfolk. They leapt towards these women when there was no one around, and came back for the treasures under the cover of darkness. They picked up a few magic tricks from here and there and performed them for a handful of coins, as if they were animals on a leash. They began mixing herbs and plants without understanding their true nature. Because of their shoddy knowledge, they caused people more damage than they had been brought to fix. They gave jogis all over the world a bad name, so much so that even the good ones were permanently tainted.

On which side of the spectrum does our Ranjha lie, you might ask. He is a deceiver in a jogi's attire, of that there is no doubt. He is in Ranganpur to fool the Kheras, to scatter the ash of illusion in their eyes and take away his Heer from under their noses. How is he then any better than a false jogi, who has made this sacred profession profane? He is, on the other hand, a true powerful jogi, one who has been blessed with all the boons, who can cure all evil spells, and find remedies for all who are ill. Of his capability, as a jogi, there is no doubt. He is, therefore, a bit of both, fake and real, true and false. By this time, I am sure you are quite comfortable with the contradictory nature of Ranjha—a bit of the human and the divine, a character as well as a symbol. Here then is one more paradox for you to chew over.

News spreads like wildfire as soon as Ranjha enters Ranganpur—that a handsome jogi, an oxymoron in itself, is in town. Young beautiful women, those who are married, and those who are not, flock around him, as peahens parade around a dancing peacock. They meet him next to the well, drag him to women's spinning gatherings. They find excuses to touch his face, to hold his hand. They stare into his ocean-like eyes and ask him if they are worthy of love. They pose all kinds of questions, ask him for all kinds of spells—to sweeten the sharp tongue of their mother-in-law, to find a suitable partner for their sisters-in-law, to find a cure for their husband's disinterest in them, to ensure his fidelity.

The jogi listens to them all. He offers advice where he can and prepares amulets where required. He chants mysterious mantras on food items and gives them to the wives of disloyal

husbands. The jogi comes to life in the company of these
women for he is a perennial lover, a prisoner of his nature. For a
brief moment, he is temporarily distracted when he is showered
with love. He forgets what he is here for. Forgets the unabated
devotion of his one true devotee. He is lured by the charm
of these new converts, their promises of commitment, their
enthusiastic adherence to the faith. In the company of these new
devotees, the divine rediscovers its own divinity, a divinity that
was initially rendered to him by the devotion of the primordial
devotee, now waiting for him.

He walks from one house to the next, with me, the begging
bowl, in his hand. Food is generously given to him wherever he
knocks, so much so that I overflow with abundance. He rejects
any stale food and curses the fate of those who dare to offer
him any. Even as a jogi, he walks with pride as if he were Raja
Vikramaditya.

In this state, one day, he came across the partly open door
of a house and realized it was the home of Saida Khera. This
chance encounter reminded him why he was in Ranganpur. He
stepped inside the open door. It was a vast, empty courtyard, with
several rooms spread around it. 'Is Heer here?' he asked loudly,
as if he was Hanuman threatening Ravana in his own Lanka.

'Who is it that makes noise? Who is it that dares enter our
house?' shouted Sahiti, as she heard Ranjha's call. The house was
empty except for Sahiti, Heer and a family servant, Rabel. Sahiti
had heard rumours of the jogi before this chance encounter.
She had seen how all the village womenfolk were fawning over
him. But she was not impressed, as her heart only had space for
her one true love—Murad, the Baloch. Besides she was a smart
woman, who understood the ways of the world. She knew all
about the mischievousness of the jogis in Kaliyuga. She knew
what happened behind closed doors when jogis insisted on

being left alone with a sick maiden and how their hands roamed around the unsuspecting bodies in search of the source of evil. This evil resided not in women's bodies but in the jogi's cursed heart, of that she was sure.

'How dare you enter our home, when you know well enough that us womenfolk are alone in the house? I know what form you hide behind your sacred face. All your charms will be useless here,' said Sahiti.

'My dear woman, why do you speak so harshly to a jogi? I come in peace. I come in search of some food,' said Ranjha, as he extended me towards her.

'It is not food that you come in search of but something else. I can see how your eyes roam around our house, trying to see what lies behind closed doors and windows. I heard loud and clear your initial call, asking for Heer. Aren't you Ranjha, disguised as a jogi, now in Ranganpur to fulfil your evil desires? Heer is ours now. She belongs to us. We will not let you bring shame to the Kheras, the way you once stomped on the Sials' pride.'

'What ridiculousness you speak! Have your parents not taught you any manners? Is this how maiden Khera women behave? Do they not respect sacred men? You misheard what I said and now you make a mountain out of a molehill. Perhaps you are hard of hearing. Maybe there is something wrong with your ear. I could prepare a dose of herbs for you, and all will be cured. For what you heard as Heer was actually pir. I didn't ask for Heer, but rather announced my entry to your house. All I said was, "Pir is here."'

'Should I fall at your feet, clean its dust with my eyelids?' said Sahiti, sarcastically. 'Should I count my blessings that you have blessed us with your presence? You are not welcome here. I command you to leave immediately. I know you are not a pir and neither are you a jogi. You are nothing but a pompous charlatan and there is nothing in this house for you.'

'What material are you made of, for you are not a daughter of Eve? I have never heard such bile being spewed out of a human mouth, let alone that of a woman. When a woman speaks, spring should leave her beautiful lips and spread happiness everywhere. Little rainbows should form around her words and birds should begin to sing. Butterflies should dance around those sentences and flowers should bloom where they fall. Instead, lava flows out of your mouth and destroys everything on its path. Life would cease to exist where your words scatter.'

Sahiti laughed, 'If that is the kind of women you are in search of, I am afraid you are in the wrong place. Perhaps you should jump into a well and find your way to heaven. There, you might find some of those species that you just mentioned.'

'It is not that paradise I am in search of, but heaven on earth. It is right here, in our midst, heaven and hell, and all that we pray for,' said the jogi.

'Oh, you jogi, what a hypocrite you are! You who pretend to renounce the world, who claim to abandon all his relationships, will tell us, women, about this world? We are the creators of the world. We bear it in our womb for nine months. We look after it, protect it and ensure its survival, before it turns out and tells us how to live. We are the source of its existence, of all its truth. We don't need the advice of a pretentious jogi like you to tell us about the philosophy of life. We are all born with that knowledge. It is imprinted on our souls.'

'What life do you speak of, you stupid woman, when you have no experience of it at all? Like a frog stuck in a well, you assume that your surroundings are reflective of the world. I am a jogi who has travelled the world. I have seen it with my own eyes and participated in all its experiences. It is I who can teach you a thing or two about the world, not the other way round.'

'You callous man, while you claim to explore the world and partake in everything it has to offer, who takes care of your ageing parents, who looks after the kids? Who makes sure that their world doesn't come crumbling down while you are away on your adventures? Where do you think life resides? Where do you think the world exists? Does it exist in your aloofness, or does it stay alive in our daily chores?'

'You foolish woman, look how arrogantly you speak. Your lack of knowledge shines through your comments, I don't know why I am even wasting my time arguing with you. Don't you know that jogis never marry and that they don't have any such burdens?'

'How then can you claim to be an expert on life, when you reside outside its orbit?' she replied.

'Oh, you manipulate your words, and go around and around in circles. Women could outwit Satan if they put their minds to it. Aren't you the reason we were cast out of heaven, the angels of Harut and Marut were trapped in a well, the reason why Puran Bhagat lost his limbs and Raja Rasalu never found his way home?'

'It is not the manipulation of women, but the greed of men that is the cause of our curse. Women are the reason beauty exists in the world; we are the ultimate specimen of divine creation. To reject us, to diminish us, is to reject divinity. Have you forgotten how even Lord Shiva bowed in front of Parvati, one who had descended from heaven?'

Sahiti was still mid-sentence when one of the doors surrounding the courtyard opened. There she was. Heer herself, dark circles under her eyes, her hair dishevelled. She had lost a lot of weight, and she could barely stand on her two feet. Her face was partially covered by a dupatta.

'What is this noise I hear?' she inquired.

'Welcome. Look who is here. You alone were missing from this scene.' Sahiti dripped sarcasm.

'Oh, dear Sahiti, why are you always so unkind to me? What has made you so bitter? Why does my presence in this house bother you like a thorn in your side? Is there some unrequited love that resides in your heart? Is it the thought of an absent beloved that gnaws at your existence? Does my married status threaten your position as the maiden of the house, a reminder to you that this is not your house? Or is there just bile in you?'

'Don't you dare gang up with this jogi and attack me in this manner,' Sahiti replied. 'Why should I not speak the truth? Why should I not express my desires?'

The jogi was in a state of shock at the sudden appearance of Heer. He had lost all interest in Sahiti. I could feel his grip loosening over me as if life was slowly being drained out of him. He stared at her with unblinking eyes for some time and then said, 'Why do you have that treacherous dupatta on your face? That hideous thing should burn in the fire of hell. There are no secrets hidden from a jogi. I know what resides in your heart. I know what sickness has overtaken you and I have the cure.'

Heer caught a glimpse of the jogi from behind her dupatta. Her heart fluttered. Could it be true? Could this jogi be her Ranjha? She needed to be sure. 'If you can find a cure for me, I will present you with the entire world. I haven't had a day of peace since I entered this house.'

'Don't you worry. Your jogi is here now.' Saying this, he took out a couple of dice from his bag and threw them on the floor. 'I see it all here. I see what is wrong with you. Your soul was ripped apart from you and you were thrown to the wolves. You are lost without your shepherd. You are lost without your buffalo herder. But I see clearly on the floor. You are destined to meet again. Your goal is near now. What you search for is close to you. Just search within.'

'The problem started for you when you were married to an ass,' continued the jogi. 'A swan was married to a monkey. A rose was presented to a toad.'

His words reassured her, but traces of doubt cast their shadow on her existence. How could she suddenly discover happiness in her courtyard after all she had been through? She threw her dupatta on the ground to get a better view, to remove all doubts, to be sure. There he was, without a doubt, her Ranjha, her buffalo herder, her jogi. Their eyes met, and they lost each other in them. Levees that had kept their tears in check all this while threatened to break, threatened to drown them, to submerge the house, Sahiti, Rabel, Ranganpur, the entire country of Punjab. But before these tears could manifest themselves, Sahiti spoke. 'Why are you still in this house? Have you no shame? Do you think I will let you stay here after you hurl abuses at my brother?'

'Sahiti, you need to show this jogi some kindness, for you don't know the power he has.' Her eyes were still fixed on Ranjha, while his were on hers. In this moment, there wasn't one, but two Heers—one who was lost in the eyes of her lover, unaware of anything else that existed around her including this other version of herself, who knew pretences still had to kept (another paradox). 'He is a blessed soul, and we are lucky to have him in our midst. Even if you hate him, I don't think we should turn him away without offering him some food. He is a poor fakir who needs our mercy to survive.' She looked around after finishing the sentence, the two versions of Heer becoming one once again. She wanted to rush to the hearth herself, prepare churi and feed her Ranjha, her jogi, with her own hands.

'If that is what it will take to get rid of him, so be it,' said
Sahiti. 'Rabel, fetch me some food, so that we can finally see the
back of this devil.' The jogi had not heard what Sahiti had said, his
attention solely on his Heer. He did not see Rabel returning with
some stale flour and unhusked rice. He was still lost in her, when
Rabel put the food in me, firmly pushing it down. The jogi, no
longer in his body, lost his grip on me and I fell to the ground. In
an instant, I was shattered into several pieces.

The sound brought him back to life. He realized where he
was, and what had happened. The realization brought with itself
an uncontrollable fury, a fury that had been pent up for years,
decades. The fury overpowered the jogi and he slapped Rabel
across her face. She fell to the ground, a red handprint appearing
on her cheek. 'You stupid woman, look at what you've done.
This was my old companion, a special boon that was gifted to
me by my Guru. Don't you know the right way to present food
to a jogi? What is this food you are giving me?'

'How dare you attack my maid in my house?' shouted
Sahiti, as Ranjha's fury found its way to her, multiplying as it
transferred from one body to another. They both fell to the
ground, Ranjha and Sahiti, slapping, punching and kicking each
other, as Rabel joined them.

'Please, Sahiti, have mercy on the jogi,' said Heer, tears
forming in her eyes, cracks appearing in the levee, the world on
the brink of destruction. 'He is a gentle soul.'

Bruises appeared on all the bodies as the two women
overwhelmed him. Sahiti held him by the head and dragged
him to the ground, as Rabel continued kicking him. The jogi
was thrown out of the house, his clothes torn, blood oozing
from the cuts on his face. My scattered pieces were thrown on
his face as the door was closed with a loud bang.

Saraswati fidgeted uncomfortably, adjusting her pallu over and over again, unable to shed the feeling that her chest was uncovered. She ran her hands over her back, trying to ensure that it was not bare. She felt as if the clothes on her body were not enough to cover herself.

His eyes followed her from the vantage point of a stool, at the centre of the courtyard, under a kikar tree. Dina, her father-in-law, never moved from there when he was at home, neither to drink nor to eat. He watched her walk towards him with a plate, his hands grabbing the plate from the top of her hands, as an unfamiliar, uncomfortable smile appeared over his face.

'Oh, you cursed one, why are you standing here, pretending to be a goddess! Go and get my food, you imbecile,' said her mother-in-law, Nanda, sitting on a different stool, next to her husband, fanning herself with a hand fan, sweat glistening on her neck.

Back in the kitchen, as she prepared the plate for her mother-in-law, she could still feel Dina's hands over hers. She tried shaking them off. Washed them. But the touch of his coarse, dry skin continued to linger.

After they had finished, she dragged two charpoys, standing at the edge of the wall, and placed them under the tree for Dina and Nanda's afternoon nap. Saraswati was back in the kitchen again, packing lunch for Waris.

As she walked towards the mosque, she wondered if Dina had always made her feel this way. What had he been like when her husband was alive? She couldn't remember. Dina was a vague, blurry image from that distant memory. Everything about Dina's existence had become clearer after her husband's death—the cloudy, foggy face had formed into an old, wrinkled one, with a thick, white mustache. The invisible eyes had transformed into large, black eyes that never stopped staring. The contour of his body had been replaced by a feeble, bony figure, that seemed as if it was shrinking every day.

To Saraswati, it felt as if the palpability of Dina's existence was becoming more real, with each passing moment. His peripheral presence was gradually taking centre stage, threatening to overshadow all other characters. Everybody disappeared when he was around, even Saraswati, and what remained were his eyes and Saraswati's image in those eyes.

She felt the little arms of Chotu around her legs. She was caught by surprise. She picked him up and hugged him tightly. Waris was standing outside the mosque, in a white chola and dhoti, a white turban on his head, his long black hair falling on his shoulders, and his thick, black beard, with a few grey hair, packed around his chin. He was smiling.

'He is a bright kid, this little one,' said Waris, as Saraswati passed him the utensil with food, and took back the empty utensil from the previous day. 'He will be speaking Arabic and Persian in no time.'

'But then how will I understand him?' said Saraswati, as she placed Chotu on the ground.

'Learning new languages will not make him forget other languages,' Waris replied earnestly.

Saraswati smiled politely, realizing he hadn't understood her joke. 'So how are you liking our village? Have you adjusted well?'

'What is there not to like? I am getting home-cooked meals. I spend my entire day in the company of these children, telling them my childhood stories. And then in the evening, I spend some time writing. I cannot imagine a more fulfilling life.'

Saraswati noticed a plea in his eyes. They were saying something more, perhaps asking a question that his lips wouldn't let escape. The question felt like a prick on her heart.

'Writing?' she asked, distractedly.

'Yes.' Waris was happy she had asked him about it. 'I started recently. The evenings can be unbearably lonely sometimes.

There is nothing to do, no one to talk to. So, I started writing to keep busy.'

'What do you write?'

'My thoughts. Things that I want to express . . . things I have observed. Stories from my childhood. Memories . . . reflections. Spirituality, religion, philosophy.'

Saraswati noticed a twinkle in his eye as his lips moved passionately. They were no longer pleading, now lost in a different world. Happy wherever they were. 'Thoughts on our past, present, future.'

'I wish to hear your writing some day, but I don't think I'll be able to understand it.' Waris's lost plea had found its way into her tone. 'You are such an intelligent philosopher who has seen the world, and I am an unlettered woman, whose life is measured in these daily steps, from the house to the temple, and now this mosque.' She finished the sentence abruptly, eager to not exhibit her sadness. 'Maybe Chotu will be able to understand it when he is older. I hope he becomes as knowledgeable as you are.'

'It's not difficult at all.' Waris was still lost in that world away from Malka Hans, Saraswati and the pain in her tone. 'In fact, that is the most important thing I want to do. Present complex ideas, thoughts, in a story, in a simple way, so that many more people can engage with these concepts that are usually just discussed in madrasahs. I think you will like it. You had a huge role in it.'

'Me?' Saraswati was surprised. She was now part of this elusive world.

'Yes. Of course.' Waris spoke uncomfortably. 'Of course, you did . . . Well in a way . . . That you became the reason I am here . . . Or Chotu. Chotu is the reason . . . And now I am here. And there is so much time. And all these thoughts. Things

that I am thinking about. That I never thought before. Difficult
to say. But easy to write. And . . . yes, time. I have so much
time. So I get to write.' Waris was rambling and blushing as he
spoke. 'I will narrate parts of it to you, one of these days. I think
you'll like it.'

Saraswati enjoyed Waris's rambling. 'Yes, one of these days,'
she spoke in a teasing manner, before a slight disappointment
entered her tone. 'Not today, or tomorrow. Or even the day
after. How will that be? Where would that be? Inside the
mosque?' She waited for an answer. 'Or out here? In the open?
Perhaps never. But that's alright. I am happy in the knowledge
that it exists, as a possibility, sometime in the future. One of
these days.'

'Don't be disheartened, my Bhagbhari,' said Waris in a
loving manner, in a manner that he had never spoken before,
that seemed so foreign to him, yet familiar. 'We'll find a way,' he
said, now more comfortable in this newly discovered expression.

'What is that you called me?' Saraswati spoke in the same
language. She had been lured into it, without even realizing it.
'Bhagbhari? The lucky one? Are you mocking me, Mian sahib?'

'Not at all.' Waris sounded offended. 'That can never be.
May the angel of death snap life out of me before that day
arrives. But you are lucky for me, the luckiest thing that has
ever happened to me and I cannot be grateful enough.'

Lying on her charpoy, in the night, Saraswati was still
thinking about her conversation with Waris. She had enjoyed
being called Bhagbhari, the lucky one, the blessed one. She
repeated the name in her head, a wave of happiness washing over
her body every time she did so. She felt a tinge of excitement
emerging from within. Its sudden arrival frightened her. She was
afraid of losing it. She tried holding onto that sensation, but it
began slipping away as she had feared.

She felt a light touch on her shoulder. It woke her up from a sleep she didn't realize she had fallen into. It took her a moment to realize it was real; it was happening. Dina was standing next to her charpoy. They were all in the courtyard of the house. Chotu was on her cot with her, while Nanda was sleeping on her charpoy, next to them, with the empty charpoy of Dina beyond that. His other hand was in his dhoti, moving up and down. Her first emotion was that of relief; relieved that she could not see his penis, relief followed by a false hope, perhaps he wasn't stroking it but just scratching it.

His hand began moving from her shoulder towards her breast. Her body froze, in shock, in fear. There was no doubt any more. Then with a suddenness that surprised even her, she pinched Chotu's back forcefully. He woke up immediately, crying loudly. Nanda woke up as well, and Saraswati could also finally move. She sat up on her charpoy and began consoling Chotu.

'I was just going out to take a piss,' said Dina, as he moved hurriedly.

'Make sure Chotu is quiet before he comes back. I do not want your father-in-law being woken up in the middle of the night again,' said Nanda, eyeing Saraswati suspiciously before going back to sleep.

Saraswati was still sitting up on her charpoy, consoling Chotu when Dina came back. He walked straight to his charpoy and lay down. Chotu went back to sleep after a little while, but sleep had been swept away for Saraswati. Nor was she feeling lucky any more.

I am the source of humanity's greatest pleasure; I am the source of its gravest pain. I am celebrated as divine union by some,

vilified by others as the devil's game. I can be represented only
in symbols, for my existence doesn't do justice to all that I am.
Each new emblem conjoined with me enhances my essence. It
brings forth to light an unknown aspect of mine. It celebrates
a hidden quality, completes me, fulfils me, makes me more of
what I truly am.

You can refer to me as sex, sexual intercourse or even
sexual desire, but I am more than each of these epithets. I flow
between these definitions, these limitations imposed on me. I
am an amalgamation of all of these together and still so much
more. How about we add love, lust and friendship into the mix?
Perhaps a pinch of admiration. I represent the brute bestiality in
humanity, an overpowering of their physical state. I represent
the highest pinnacle of human art, the apogee of human intellect.

Like gold dust, I am scattered on the pages of this beautiful
book. I am the reason for its beauty. I add a shine to the story,
to all the characters and their relationships. In the course of this
qissa, novel, whatever you want to call this writing, sometimes I
exert my presence in full force, and sometimes I recede behind
innuendos and implications. From behind this shield, I express
myself in jokes, in humour and other kinds of tacit insinuations.
In this way, I am acknowledged without being acknowledged
and my uncomfortable presence is provided a comfortable
language. I could give you a few examples, such as Ranjha's
relationship with Sahiba, his encounter with Sahiti, but that
will defeat the purpose. It will lay bare my mechanisms that are
meant to be discreet. For once the lure of my magic is described,
it will render my spell charmless. Some things are better left
unacknowledged, better left unsaid.

But I also know I am the source of the ugliness of the
story. I am behind its violence, the reason why it is a tragedy.
For when you link me with other abominable characteristics,

you see a side of me that is gruesome. Coalesced with pride, property, possession, patriarchy and power, you experience an aspect of me that you should rather not. In these incarnations, I become a demon, a boisterous monster whose thirst can never be quenched.

It is my unconsummated desire that gnaws at the heart of Sahiti, if we are to believe the poet. Like a mould, I grow within her; like a parasite, I take over her existence. I then become the master of her actions. I, the source of all her frustrations. Her opposition to Ranjha, her revulsion for Heer, are meant to be understood through this lens. Please forgive me, dear reader, for I understand your irritation. I too see how a complex character is reduced to such a basic instinct. If it were up to me, I would have added more but please do understand. I am bound by the limitations imposed on me by the plot of the story, the trap that is set by the poet. If I am meant to be the motivator of all her actions, so be it.

Like a little flame, I am also lit in the heart of Heer, a flame that transforms into a raging fire at the sight of the jogi. It is a fire that threatens to consume her, a fire that needs to be quelled. It is in this state that she approaches Sahiti. She sits next to her as Sahiti is lost in her thoughts. Holding her hand, she caresses it gently as if she is soothing a burn on her skin. 'Oh Bhagbhari, why do we fight when we can be the best of friends?' she suggests.

Sahiti, shocked out of her thoughts, looks at Heer surprised, slowly comprehending what Heer has suggested. She recognizes the fire in her eyes, her existence. She holds Heer's hand firmly and says, 'That is what I have always wanted. For us to live like sisters, as friends. But you repulsed all my efforts.'

'Oh, blessed one, now you know what fire threatened to consume me all this while. Now you understand why I couldn't

be your brother's wife. I have been married to Ranjha since I
laid my eyes upon him. My soul, my body is only for him.' A
teardrop falls from Heer's eyes on to her cheek that Sahiti cleans
with her finger.

'Heer, my sister, my friend, I can understand what you are
going through, for I too am experiencing a similar hell. I too am
in search of this heavenly river that can quench my thirst. My
beloved, my Murad, is away from my eyes, from my arms, and
every part of my body yearns to be with him, like a body yearns
to be with the soul. Here, feel my heart,' she says, as she places
Heer's hand on her heart. 'Can you feel its impatience? Can you
hear his name? That is all I desire at all times.'

'How did you meet him?' Heer asks.

'We have been in love since time immemorial. He came
with his caravan to our humble abode, our Ranganpur, and
here in the market our eyes met. I haven't been the same
person since that day and I am convinced that a similar blaze
burns in his heart as well. All day long, I crave to see him and
be seen by him. I long for his touch, for his kiss that will bring
me to life. Oh Heer, if you can find a way for me to be one
with my Murad, than I will do everything I can to get you to
your Ranjha. Together we'll be in the arms of our lovers, our
desires fulfilled.'

'Oh, Sahiti, your words sound like the songs of Kabir to my
ears,' says Heer, as she hugs Sahiti and gives her several kisses.
'My jogi will unite you with your Murad for he is a powerful
mystic. But before I can assure you of his support, you need to
apologize to him. You were very unkind to him the other day
when he came to our abode. You humiliated him and threw
him out of the house. In anger, he has gone to the mountains
of Kala Bagh, where he waits for the world to end. Please go
to him. Go to him now. Fall at his feet. Hold his hands and

convince him of your loyalty. Tell him his Heer waits for him like a fish out of water. Assure him of my commitment to him, testify to my purity. Tell him how Saida was refused my bed. Tell him how he was thrown out of the room with a bruised body when he tried to force himself upon me. Tell him that the Panj Peer looked after me and they are a witness to my sanctity. Tell him I am willing to walk through fire if that is a test he wants.'

So Sahiti, with an offering in her hand, as is the custom when one approaches a holy man, climbed the mountain of Kala Bagh. There on the top of the mound was Ranjha, the jogi, meditating with his eyes closed in front of a fire, slowly and gradually shedding away all his thoughts about me and other connections with the world. 'My jogi, my lord, forgive me, for I was too blind to see. But I see now. I recognize your superiority. Please accept me as your jogan and forgive all my sins,' she says, as she places the arti with the offering in front of him and starts massaging his feet, gently moving from his sole to his calf. The offering was covered with a cloth so Ranjha could not see what the offering was.

'Take away this pity offering of yours. These coins, worth five rupees, that you have brought for me. They are no good to me, nor are your pleas,' says Ranjha, as he pulls his feet away from Sahiti and kicks the offering, its contents scattering on the floor.

'Maharaj, if there was any doubt in my heart about your spiritual prowess, be assured, it is all gone away now. I see how you saw my offering without even lifting the veil. Don't reject me now for, like Heer, I too am committed to you. I will be your servant till the end of life and beyond, if only you'll take me.' She tried grabbing his feet again, but Ranjha didn't allow her, looking away from her in anger.

'Don't waste your breath on me; don't spare so many words. How can I ever trust you? For God has made womankind untrustworthy. Once you get what you want, you move on to your next prey. It is due to you that Indra was robbed by the demon Vritra, the Pharoah was humiliated, Croesus lost his empire, Nebuchadnezzar lost his pride, Alexander was rendered homeless, and Solomon was punished by God. You are the source of evil in this world. You bring wickedness wherever you place your deceiving feet.'

'Oh, Ranjha, what a powerful jogi you have become, but still there is so little about women you seem to know. You blame us as the source of evil in the world, but not the creator who created women? You call us deceiving, wicked and forget our loyalty. While men wander from house to house, like stray dogs, even after marriage, we remain committed to them, no matter what. You doubt us women, but have you forgotten your own Heer? Have you forgotten how she promised to abandon all her honour, her pride, for your love, how she continued to resist even as a bride? She locked herself in her room and beat Saida with sticks. She refused to partake of even a morsel of food, for she remains tied to your memory. Who then is dishonest? Who lacks commitment? The jogi who doubts his Heer, or the devotee who never wavers? Even now she lies in bed, lost in your thoughts. She has sent me with her message, to remind you of her fidelity.'

On hearing Heer's name, Ranjha moves close to Sahiti and holds both of her hands. 'Oh Sahiti, you are indeed the blessed one, Bhagbhari, for you bring such good tidings. Oh, please help me meet Heer, just once, and I will make all your wishes come true.'

So, with Sahiti's help, the two lovers are united again. They meet on the top of this mountain. They rush towards each other like two armies waiting for war. They ravage each other like two wolves fighting for meat. They consume each other like alcoholics thirsting for wine. They crash into each other as the river crashes on its banks. They fall on each other like rain falls to the ground. They embrace each other like the flowers welcome spring. They dance together as the birds sing.

They emerged from this union as new beings. Heer was no longer Heer on the brink of death. In my glory, she shone like the morning sky, like the north star, like a glowing moon. She had to lose herself in the arms of her lover to be acquainted with herself once again. She rediscovered the redness of her cheeks, the thickness of her hair, the depth in her eyes and the seductiveness of her lips. She walked back to the village with a new kind of gait, my gold dust sprinkled all over her. She glittered like desert sand under the sun's glare. Her sheen blinded all around her, as silent whispers followed her— something has changed.

His voice surrounded them. It covered them, like a warm chaddar on a winter's night. They were all bound to each other in its embrace. It scaled the walls of the mosque and spread through the village, like a thicket of fog emerging from the depths of the night. It quietened all other sounds, overpowered them and wrestled them to the ground. It then rose to capture the sky, spreading its wings on its black canvas covering every part, inch by inch, like Gabriel's wings.

And then at the culmination, his voice cracked, a minor rupture in a long, sustained note. It was the minutest of sounds, heard by all and sundry, clear and loud. They were all breathing with him, tears welling up in their eyes. In the middle of the crowd was Saraswati, Chotu sleeping on her lap, Nanda and Dina sitting next to her, with more than half the village around them. Waris was sitting at the other end of the mosque, facing the crowd and singing.

The news spread slowly, that the mosque's imam was writing Heer. But soon it spread everywhere. Wherever Waris went, whoever he met requested to hear a few verses. Waris tried avoiding these requests, feeling unsure about the quality of his work. How could he ever compare to the legendary rendition of Damodar? His Heer was still widely recited all over Punjab. It was with Damodar's version that his work would be compared. Waris was not ready. He needed more time. He needed more revisions, but the requests kept on coming. They made him uncomfortable, more so than the discomfort he was going to put himself in if he acceded to the requests. Saraswati too, on her daily visits, in their brief encounters on the threshold, with Chotu by her side, made the request frequently. Finally succumbing to all the pressure, Waris asked the people to gather one night in the mosque after *isha*.

If Waris was nervous about his performance, it didn't show. He took to singing Heer as if he had been doing this forever. Waris sang as if no one was listening, as if he was the only one present in this mosque on this lonely night. With his eyes shut, the veins in his neck protruding, Waris sang about Ranjha's exile from his village. Standing at the edge of Takht Hazara, with his potli on his shoulder, he cast one last look at his home, the entire village gathered to dissuade him, his brothers pleaded with him to stay. Waris was there as well. He wanted Ranjha to stay. He could see his reluctance. But Ranjha would not listen. He left.

Many in the crowd had heard different versions of Heer but never before had they lamented for Ranjha's loss. *Heer* had always begun from Heer, but Waris had started from Ranjha. His departure from Takht Hazara had been swift earlier. Ranjha had never exhibited such hesitancy. Waris was not singing but crying and the crowd mourned along with him. They cried for all the sons who had left their homes never to return; they cried for their wedded daughters, gone to faraway villages. They cried for themselves, for all they had left behind. With her hands on Chotu's forehead, Saraswati too cried softly. She cried for Waris, as she noticed a glistening tear fall down his cheek, but she also cried for herself, her home, her family. She cried for her husband. She cried for his parents. She cried for Chotu. Around her could be heard loud sounds of sobbing and the beating of chests. They cried as if it was Sham-e-Ghariban.

Having brought his audience to this state, Waris stopped. Ranjha had left his village. The familial, ancestral bond had been broken. Would he ever return? Would he ever see his home again? Sweat dripped from Waris's temple, as he gasped for breath. He looked straight ahead, beyond the crowd, beyond the walls of the mosque, beyond the limits of the village. He was looking at Jandiala, at the faces of his brothers.

No one in the audience asked for more. No one could handle more. They sat there, quietly, stunned, mourning silently for Ranjha's loss, for Waris's loss.

Then one man, Achu, a farmer from the village, said, 'Mian Waris . . .' His voice brought Waris back from Jandiala. 'Mian Waris, do you think God has abandoned Punjab?' he asked, unsure of the words that came from him. They all knew what the symbol of Ranjha represented. It was not possible not to know. The symbol was all around them, in their language, in their expressions. Ranjha was Krishna, Ranjha was the divine. And now he had left Takht Hazara, his home. Who would look after them now? 'He has to be angry with us,' he said, confirming his own doubts. 'For why else would He leave us at the mercy of the Durrani army on the one hand and the Sikh guerrillas on the other?'

Waris listened quietly, hanging somewhere in the middle of the two worlds, between the reality of the qissa and his.

'Some say, it's because we Muslims have abandoned the pious ways of our religion. This is why God is punishing us,' Achu said, looking around, expecting confirmation. Many in the audience nodded and agreed.

'Why then should Hindus, Sikhs, Jains and others suffer for our sins?' asked Waris, still far away from the confines of this mosque.

'No one here is following true religion, Mian Waris,' said Dina authoritatively. 'We have all lost piety. We have all lost our way. We have all strayed from our duties and from what is righteous. We are all in the same boat.'

'There is no denying the fact that we are living in the Kaliyuga,' said Waris, matching Dina's tone. 'But I don't think God has abandoned us or is angry with us. Remember what the Quran says? That God is closer to us than our jugular vein. How can someone who resides within us, is around us at all times, is part of each and every thing we see, experience and feel abandon us? I know poets like us sometimes describe God as a distant lover or a husband, who needs to be appeased by the devotee, a God who sometimes leaves humanity to its fate to recede somewhere else but that is not how it is. These are all literary devices we use. That doesn't mean God is actually like a jogi meditating on a mound, roaming in the wilderness, or upset at His people. The connection between humanity and divinity can never be broken.'

'But why will God continue loving us even if we don't follow His commands or obey His orders? What if we don't follow our duties or adhere to religious rituals?' asked Achu rhetorically, not expecting Waris to have an answer, but he did.

'Of course, He will. That is the nature of divinity—all-merciful, all-loving. You see these rituals, these duties are essential because they offer a pathway to divinity. I have never missed a namaz in my adult life and I pray to God to never miss one. But these rituals are only one way of reaching God. Many Sufis, dervishes, jogis have discovered other ways and they are equally effective. These rituals exist to guide us through the process, to help us navigate this extremely complicated journey, but the rituals are not the destination; they are not the end goal, and neither should they be seen as one. When these rituals become more important than the destination, you might as well abandon them, for they are no longer helping you reach God.'

'Mashallah!' 'Truer words have never been spoken,' said voices from the crowd.

'Coming back to the question of Punjab, let's not delude ourselves by blaming religiosity for the political upheaval in our home.' Waris was discovering a passion that surprised him. He spoke with his eyes focused on Achu. 'This is only a distraction that is sometimes put forth by those whose fault it is that we are in this situation. I have read the treatises of Shah Waliullah and thought much about the hypothesis he puts forward. What will this approach achieve?'

Many in the audience didn't know who Shah Waliullah was. They had no way of knowing. Shah Waliullah wrote in Arabic, a language that only the educated few could understand. His sentences, words were designed to be consumed only by intellectuals. If his words were songs, if they were sung by poets and bards, wandering from one village to another, like the words of Fareed, Shah Hussain and Bulleh Shah, then maybe he would have been known widely.

But just because many didn't know of his name didn't mean they were not familiar with his ideas. His thoughts had begun to seep into everyday conversations in different parts of Punjab. The richer Muslim landlords, who had read his work, expressed his ideas in their own words, to people in their surroundings. His arguments had begun to resonate with many people trying to make sense of the drastically changing political situation around them. Waris, too, had heard these conversations. The simplicity of the arguments annoyed him. He responded, though not to the people around him, but in his writing. The threads that Shah Waliullah wanted to disentangle and separate, Waris wanted to weave together to make a beautiful fabric, the fabric of Punjab, the novel of Punjab.

Many times, Waris had thought about responding to these comments that he had heard but he could never manage to engage with them. How should he even begin? The whole exercise seemed futile. But something had changed today. He did not want to hold back any more. He wanted to express his opinions. He wanted the entire world to hear them. He was no longer talking to the crowd in front of him, but to Umer, all those years ago, when Aftab and he had chosen to remain quiet. That memory had survived in his mind, gnawing at him occasionally. Over the years, he had realized the burden of that memory, of why Aftab hadn't responded, or how his identity held him back, but what did Waris have to lose? The memory had paved way for guilt, for not protecting his friend, Aftab, a guilt that Waris was trying to overcome today. He was not in the mosque any more, but in the library of his madrasah all those years ago.

'Our anger, that should be reserved for the political powers, is turned within. Instead of doing something, encouraging agency, this approach makes us even more passive, while those who have made decisions for us, who pushed us to the brink of this precipice, continue as before. Are they to go scot-free while we engage in self-immolation?'

Waris let the words linger in the air. No one had anything else to say.

9

The Escape

I have brought ruin to our great house. I went to its threshold, held its feet, begged disaster to enter. I took catastrophe by the hand and led it into my home, welcomed it as a guest, while it trampled upon my pagri, my honour. Oh, what a great house we were, before this disaster struck. The Kheras of Ranganpur, the proud descendants of Suryavansh Rajputs. We are the caretakers of this land and all the people that have been entrusted to us. We ensure its security; we ensure justice. Look at us now. Our faces rubbed in the dirt, the secrets of our inner chambers being used as comic relief by bards and jesters, our authority and pride compromised.

I don't blame that Sial girl, for who is not aware of the treacherous nature of the Sials? They were mere buffalo thieves till a few generations ago, even though they now pretend to be so esteemed. Their men are capable of selling whatever they can, only to increase their wealth, while their women have never known any scruples. Their recently earned wealth doesn't compare to the prestige that our great tribe has had for so many years. This match should never have been made. I should have known better. Never again will a Sial woman walk in our village. Never again will they be wedded to the Khera clan.

The Ranjhas are not even worthy of being mentioned in the same breath as the Kheras. They are lower than the lowliest, worse than the worst of them all. With a handful of buffaloes, they think they can be one of the great clans. Cursed be the land upon which they have established their villages. Cursed be the river that flows next to them. And cursed be the people who have to deal with them.

Lest I expend all my curses upon these two unholy tribes, how can I forget my own daughter, the devil's agent, the ungrateful soul, who, to satisfy her own illegitimate desires, soiled the family's honour. Imagine! This is the world we are living in. Kaliyuga. A father talking about his daughter's desires. Oh God, why didn't you lop off my tongue before these words left my mouth? Why didn't you put me in my grave before this day? If only. If only I could lay my hands upon her, I would extinguish her life myself. I would do so publicly, in front of all of Ranganpur, in the same way she has shamed us in front of everybody. Then I would throw a feast for our entire community so that they can all join us in cursing her, in making sure that her soul rots in hell for the rest of eternity. How much joy would that bring me? What satisfaction! I will have to spend the rest of my life deprived of this pleasure. If only.

Oh, what a beautiful, pure child she was, before she turned into a whore. Her demeanour changed the day that Sial temptress walked into our house. The bards had cautioned us for generations. They had recalled tales of Heer and her infidelity towards her family, but still we didn't listen. Never again will this name be recalled in Ranganpur. Never again will anyone recite Waris Shah's Heer.

How innocently Sahiti approached her mother that day, asking for permission to go out into the fields. 'The bride has been cooped up in the house ever since she has arrived. Some fresh air will bring her respite. It will cheer her up and she might finally warm up to Saida,' she said. Little did my wife know what plans the two harlots were cooking up.

A message was sent out to every woman to meet them in the fields the next morning. Kammoo, Sammi, Bakhtawar, Tajo, Nando, Daulati, all joined them. Not a single young woman was left behind. They all gathered outside, running through the ripe fields, setting up swings under giant trees, drinking water from the canal that flowed next to the village.

They were like the spring breeze running through the plains of Punjab. They were like the swirls of monsoon. They were the warmth of the sun on a winter's day. They were the smell of drops of rain after a long summer. They were fairies disguised as women. The birds sang with them; the trees danced along. The water played the drums, as flowers bloomed. If laughter took on a human form, if happiness was ever incarnated, if God's creative force walked among us, if heaven actually existed, it was here, on the outskirts of Ranganpur that day.

Little did we know that what we mistook for beauty was the charm of evil. Those we thought of as fairies were the sisters of Satan. Like Durrani's army, they came pretending to come in peace. Like the Sikh forces, they blindsided us and caught us off guard. A thorn from an acacia bush was found and used to prick Heer's feet. Next to the tiny hole that appeared on her foot, my devilish daughter took a bite. The foot was red with blood now; the pain that Heer feigned was excruciating. She rolled on the floor, like an animal fighting for its last breath, like a soldier about to face death.

In that state of hers, she was carried back home. 'It was a giant black snake that appeared from under a rock,' said Sahiti. 'It caught us all by surprise and attacked Heer's feet.'

A loud cry escaped Heer's mouth as Sahiti was done conjuring up this tale. 'I am dying! I am dying!' she cried without a break, pulling her hair, beating herself, kicking and pushing away anyone who came near. Life drained out of my face, while Saida's legs began to tremble. My wife too joined the ruckus, sure that Heer was going to die. We had brought her to our home with so much fanfare; we had taken along the greatest baraat there ever was. We had showered her family with the most expensive gifts. We had celebrated the creation of this bond for days. All of that was threatening to crumble, as our bride was on the verge of death. How would I face the Sials? What would I say to Chuchak? These were the thoughts that unsettled me.

Someone from the village suggested that milk be applied to the wound; others recommended curd. Some brought us herbal remedies, while some suggested magic spells. I was prepared to not spare any expense, but nothing seemed to work. We brought amulets from saints meditating far away in the jungles. We brought in fakirs who claimed they could cure all diseases. We sought the advice of every hakim and consulted Ayurveda experts. Despite all medicine, Heer writhed in pain. 'I am dying! I am dying!' she continued to cry.

'Oh father, we have tried everything we could, but all in vain,' said Sahiti. 'We mustn't lose hope. There is a jogi, I have heard, who sits on the mound of Kala Bagh. He is a powerful practitioner, I have heard, and makes all the snakes, scorpions and other creatures bow in front of him. If he were to help her, I am sure she would survive. In his blessed hands, Heer, no doubt, will be revived.'

So, without wasting a moment, I sent Saida to the holy man. He returned shortly after with empty hands, bruised face and torn clothes. 'That jogi is a fraud, a dacoit,' said Saida. 'He beat me up like a common thief and refused all my pleas. I approached him with folded hands. I even touched his feet. I told him all about Heer's condition, but he refused to listen. "It is your unfortunate fate that you cannot escape. Your wife is destined to die. There is nothing I, or anyone else, can do, for any woman who shares your bed is cursed and will relinquish life," he said. "But I haven't bedded her yet. Our marriage has still not been consummated. We might be legally married, but we are not wife and man."

'"A marriage that hasn't been consummated is not a marriage. Perhaps this woman might actually be saved," he said. And then when I thought he would help us, his eyes went towards my feet and he saw that my shoes were still on them even though I was inside his hut. In my desperation to save the life of my bride, I do acknowledge that is a minor error I committed. He lost his temper, as if I were a lowly Jatt claiming to be a king. He attacked me with all his might, while I was defenceless to his blows. Here I am now, in front of you in the condition that he left me.'

'How dare that jogi lay his hands on my beloved son!' I raged. 'Summon all my men immediately. We will deal with this menace right away. We will show him the true might of the Kheras. We will remind him of our warrior roots.'

'Oh, my dear father, what is the point of this anger?' said Sahiti. 'The poor jogi doesn't stand a chance against you, of that there is no doubt. But will that solve our problem? Will that save Heer? Maybe the jogi had some true grievance against Saida. Maybe Saida failed to approach him with the humility that should be accorded to religious men.' From the

corner of my eye, I could see Saida about to intercede, ready
to defend his position, but Sahiti continued speaking. 'All this
talk is wasting precious time. Look at Heer's condition. She
will not survive another night if something is not done. Why
don't you, yourself, go to the jogi, my dear father and beseech
him to come? Tell him he is our only hope and that we will
be ruined if he doesn't arrive. Ask him to come. Please ask
him to come.'

So with folded hands and a lowered head, I reached the
top of Kala Bagh. I approached the hut of the jogi, where he
was sitting next to a fire, his eyes closed in meditation, unaware
of any other existence but himself. 'Oh, powerful jogi, it is I,
Ajju Khera, the head of the Khera clan, the proud owner of a
thousand buffaloes, at your threshold. I am a beggar and you are
the king. All my wealth, my honour and my pride are useless in
your presence. Today, I have come to your humble abode, with
all my hopes pinned on you, I hope you will not turn me away.
Please come with me to Ranganpur to save our bride from an
imminent death.'

'Oh, you leader of men, you should have come to me first,
instead of sending your imbecile son. He doesn't deserve your
prestigious house, neither does he deserve Heer. If the future
of the Khera clan is in his hands, then I am genuinely sorry for
your lot. I will come with you for you truly understand how to
speak to a jogi, how to approach one. You understand our status
in the world and your lack of it, in front of us. Take me now to
your house. I will solve this problem that threatens you.'

So, with his hand in my hand, we walked towards Ranganpur.
There he was welcomed as a hero, as a soldier returning from
war, as an emperor marching into his capital, as Ram returning
to Ayodhya. He was showered with petals and rose water was
sprinkled over him. Garlands and wreaths of flowers were put

around his neck, as if he were a bridegroom entering the house of his in-laws.

He walked into the room where Heer was writhing in pain and immediately her demeanour changed. It seemed as if his magical presence had sucked the venom out of her feet. For the first time in a while, she stopped crying, and we were all relieved. 'Prepare an empty hut for me, outside the village. There I will take your bride and lock myself inside with her. I will spend the next twelve days and nights in prayer. No one shall be allowed to enter; none but a young maiden from your house. Even if the shadow of anyone else falls upon the hut, my magic will be rendered useless, and Heer will die.'

So as per the instructions of the jogi, the hut of a shepherd was identified and prepared for the bride and the jogi. Bedding was placed on the floor where Heer was laid while the jogi sat beside her along with Sahiti.

The story of their escape reached us early in the morning, before the arrival of dawn, before the first crowing of the rooster, before the sound of the azaan. The hut was discovered by the ploughmen who had to plough the soil before the onslaught of the sun. He noticed the door of the hut, swinging in the night breeze. He peeked inside and found it empty. The three of them had escaped—the jogi, Sahiti and Heer.

It was their little secret. They would stare into each other's eyes for a brief moment, the only two people in the crowd who knew who Bhagbhari was, every time she was mentioned in the poem.

The first time Saraswati heard the term, it had caught her by surprise. She had been sitting in the audience, in the courtyard of the mosque, staring at the floor, Chotu next to her, now too old to sit in her lap. She looked up immediately and saw Waris's eyes on her, a smile across his face, as he continued singing. She felt her heart jump at this sudden reference, the excitement frightening her more than it brought her joy. She felt her skin disappear leaving her insides bare, as a rain cloud appeared over her head, pouring only on her. Then as these initial emotions dissipated, she realized that the world had remained unchanged. There were still many people around her, packed together in this tiny mosque, listening to Waris's song.

But while everything was the same, something had changed. She was no longer one of the many listening to the story of Heer. She was no longer sharing an experience that was being experienced by several others. This wasn't Waris, the master poet, whom people loved, but her Waris, her poet. This wasn't just the story of Heer any more, but an ode to their relationship, an unnamed, unacknowledged relationship that came into existence only in discreet references, its reality expressed only through symbols, spoken of only through things unsaid. Slowly she rediscovered sensation in her body, the flow of blood to her cheeks, and a warm embrace in her chest that untied all knots. Her head tilted slightly as she looked at Waris with a twinkle in her eyes and a smile on her lips. Her eyes remained fixed on him, for the rest of the night and the nights that followed, whenever she joined everyone else in the mosque to listen to Waris.

Theirs was a relationship that blossomed in those few moments, scattered over several nights—the alluded references to Heer, the brief locking of eyes, the inadvertent smiles. Those daily moments on the threshold of the mosque, when they exchanged a few words, that the two looked forward to, were now lost. Chotu, while still studying with Waris, was old enough to walk to the mosque on his own. They would exchange glances sometimes when she would visit the temple next door, while Waris sat outside the mosque, with a group of people who seemed to surround him at all times now.

Perhaps they would have been able to exchange a few words if Waris were alone. But that was never the case. From that first night when Waris had reluctantly sung, his popularity had taken off. Tales of his performances, of his rendition of Heer, spread to neighbouring villages and beyond, and every night, a group of people travelled to Malka Hans to listen to him. Among his new fans were several young men, who started staying back at Malka Hans, eager to be in his company.

Saraswati continued sending Waris meals through Chotu. Waris would hold the utensil in his hands, searching for her invisible fingers, thinking about the few times their fingers touched. He would smell the food, searching for Saraswati's fragrance in it, as he remembered from that spring day sitting on the bullock cart next to her. He would have imaginary conversations with her with each bite, tell her tales about his past that now flooded his conscious mind. He enjoyed swimming in them. Enjoyed putting them down on paper every night, reading them over and over again, talking with his loved ones— his father, Maulvi sahib, his friends and now Saraswati.

He swam in his past and the present every time he began writing, the two merging into each other, becoming indistinguishable, as Ranjha was from Waris. But who were the other characters in the qissa? Where had they come from? Could each character be mapped to one person, or did they all borrow from people he knew? How much of Saraswati existed in Heer? What aspect of her personality manifested itself in Sahiti? How much of himself did he pour into all the characters? Were they all an extension of him, as all humans are an extension of the divine? Is this how God created the world? Are we all characters of a qissa, a story that is constantly unfolding?

But whereas God could not change the past, Waris could. He could revisit some of his earlier chapters and write them again, each new reading allowing him to discover a new version of reality that had hitherto evaded him. Even the creator was unaware of the magnificence of his creation. Perhaps the qissa is never meant to be finished. It is meant to be read and revised over and over again, till it got close to the state of perfection, of divinity. An unattainable state and yet the ultimate destination of everything. This revision would not end with Waris. This state of perfection will not be achieved in his lifetime. The story will continue after him, with some other writer picking up the qissa, re-reading it and taking it where it is destined to be—a state of perfection. Waris was doing his part. Taking a story that was bequeathed to him by writers before him and making it better. The qissa was their *amanat* to him. He did not own or possess it. It did not belong to him. It belonged to no one. It belonged to everyone.

Every time an unknown aspect of the qissa manifested itself as he read through it, his mind rushed back to Kasur, to the room of his teacher, Maulvi Ghulam Murtaza and his scrolls of Ibn-Arabi's writings. How often had Maulvi sahib told him about this phenomenon. And here it was now, in front of him. He wished he could speak with Maulvi sahib and tell him about his own writing. Maulvi sahib had mentioned to him in passing that he was translating Saadi's *Gulistan* but at that time, Waris's mind had been elsewhere. Now he wished he was back in that room. Wished he had asked him questions about it. Wished he could read it.

But then sometimes Waris felt as if Maulvi sahib was present. Waris would discover him in his tone, in his mannerisms, as he spoke to these young men who gravitated around him. He noticed how he would use the same inflections, the same punctuation of silence. He spoke in Maulvi sahib's voice, as if he was not Waris, but Maulvi Ghulam Murtaza. Where did Maulvi sahib end and Waris begin? Each new moment presented a new version of Waris that Waris himself was unaware of.

The young men who now surrounded Waris came from all kinds of backgrounds: gentry, landed elite, scholars and ordinary peasants. Some of them returned after a few days, to be replaced by new ones, while others stayed on permanently. They surrounded him at all times and bombarded him with incessant questions. It was only during mealtimes, and later in the evening when he would work on his manuscript, that he would get some time on his own. But they would still be around, busy with each other. Sometimes when Waris's thoughts were not consumed by his memories, by the non-stop revision of Heer, he would observe these men and spot the youthful images of Umer and Aftab in them. A heavy weight of pain would settle on his heart when he thought about them. But hidden within this pain were also moments of joy, joy that these memories existed, existed so that they could be missed. These young men treated him as their master, as a Sufi saint, and they were his devotees.

He would teach passionately, his passion settling upon his audience as a thick layer of mist pressing upon the ground on a winter morning. He would speak confidently, discovering a voice he didn't even know he had. He would be swayed by his words, warm sweat appearing on his body when he discovered his rhythm. He would hear the voice of Bulleh Shah in his own, and would remember how sometimes that dervish from Kasur would break into dhamaal, raptured by the sound of his words. The realization of the power of his words would bring him immense joy, but would also raise questions—questions such as where these thoughts and words were coming from. Who was he drawing from, when he was in this state? As soon as he found himself lost in these thoughts, searching for the origin of his words, words would begin to fail him. They would appear as recalcitrant animals that could not be tamed, could not be convinced to cooperate. Sometimes he would be in the middle of a sentence, a large group of people looking at him with interested eyes, their ears glued to him, sitting in front of him, when he would be drawn into these questions. These questions would give birth to more questions. What were they doing here? Why were they listening to him? Who was he to teach these people? Why did they all love him? He didn't deserve this. What was he pretending to be? Who was he?

The thought would bring back memories of Bulleh Shah's verse, 'What do I know who I am?' Waris didn't understand the question then. It haunted him now. 'What do I know who I am, Waris? What am I doing here, performing every night in front of hundreds of people. What kind of a Syed am I? Have I become like Bulleh Shah myself? How do these people see me? Do they see me as Kasur once saw Bulleh Shah? At least Bulleh Shah was at his home. Where am I? What am I doing here? I don't belong here. Why am I here? I should not be here. I should leave.' But then this question was always answered by an image of Saraswati. Her face would appear in front of him, the same face that he had spotted at the shrine of Baba Fareed all those years ago. It would calm him down, dissipate his spiralling set of questions.

His students were unaware of the turmoil that Waris would sometimes experience. To them, he appeared sorted, confident and knowledgeable at all times. He had answers to every question in metaphysics, philosophy, theology, religion, literature, history and politics. They asked him about his travels, about the cities of Kasur and Lahore, for many hadn't travelled beyond their immediate surroundings.

Sometimes others from around the village too joined this conversation, listening to the questions that were asked of Waris and his patient responses. Waris was more comfortable in these smaller groups, in intimate settings. He was at his charismatic best here, words, ideas, thoughts flowing from the depth of his intellectual well. He found comfort in these small groups. They provided him a sense of belonging, of being surrounded by friends and family. They brought him joy, happiness that Waris didn't know was possible. Perhaps these conversations, this community around him, were another reason he was here.

Often the students asked him about the state of the Mughal empire, about the Durrani king, and about the Sikh political groups. They asked him about his opinions, about his predictions for Punjab, and consumed his responses greedily. Waris spoke without reservation and was critical of all. He criticized the Mughal kings and princes for loving luxury; he blamed the Mughal aristocracy for being power hungry. He was dismissive of the Sikh political groups, for he did not think of them as being worthy of being rulers, and neither did he support the Afghan king, for he had seen and experienced the destruction caused by him. His views became the views of the group, views that were then disseminated in other villages and cities, when these men returned home.

On one of these afternoons, when Waris sat under the banyan tree, in the middle of the village, surrounded by these young men, and several others from the village, Rehmat joined the group. Rehmat was one of the elders of the village, respected by all. It was at his door that most of the villagers knocked when they needed dispute arbitration. He was the first person with whom people shared happy news, the first one to learn about tragedies. He was an old man in his seventies, yet quite active.

He liked walking around the village, interacting with people, learning about the latest news.

He appeared wearing a white kurta and dhoti, pagri on his head and a staff in his hand. His back was slightly bent. He wore a thick moustache on his lips that were always turned upright. Everyone stood up on seeing him, including Waris. 'Please come, Babaji,' said one of the young men in the group, as they made a place for him next to Waris.

'Mian Waris, what are you preaching today?' asked Rehmat as he placed a hand on Waris's knee.

'Babaji, who am I to preach anything? I just respond to my friends' questions. I am always at their disposal,' Waris replied softly.

'Very well, very well,' said Rehmat, his voice slowly fading. Soon the conversation picked up from where it had been disrupted on his arrival.

'So Mian Waris, if none of these rulers are worthy of ruling us, then how should we be governed?' asked Ahmad, a young man who had been living with Waris for the past several months. He belonged to a peasant family from a neighbouring village.

'We need a government of philosophers and scholars,' continued Waris. 'We need a government which is run by wisdom and knowledge, and by rules. We need some of that today in the chaos that has become of Punjab.' Everyone nodded and made affirmative sounds.

'But Mianji, if this is to happen, then compassion will be lost,' said Balinder, another young man who was a temporary part of Waris's entourage. He came after a month or so, stayed for a few days and then left. 'For scholars will rule according to laws, and laws are blind to human needs. They are fixed, rigid, to be followed under all conditions.'

'That is an excellent point, Bal,' said Waris, 'And I am going to respond to that point. But before I do that, I am going to talk a little about the philosophy behind laws.' Waris spoke slowly, pausing between each word and sentence as if he had all the time in the world to finish.

'See, laws are meant to reflect the condition of humans and the needs of our societies. In other words . . .'

Silence.

'. . . they are a reflection of our general needs. So inherently, laws are meant to be compassionate and empathetic. But as you've rightly pointed out, laws can also be rigid.'

Silence.

'Sometimes they can be oppressive if they don't address the specific needs of an individual. To counter this point, I will say that it is not laws that are tyrannous.'

Pause.

'But rather humans who interpret and implement these laws. By nature, laws are flexible, fluid, like the flow of water.'

He imitated a flowing river with his hand.

'It is we humans who channel them in whatever direction we want. When it suits the king, it is acceptable for Sunnis to marry Shias.'

Silence.

'And when it doesn't, it is equally acceptable to kill them both. Both of these actions have been justified by laws.'

The discussion continued until the evening azaan was heard from the mosque. As most of the men headed towards the mosque, Rehmat placed a hand on Waris's shoulder and said, 'Mian Waris, will you do me the honour of visiting my abode after prayers tonight? There is something urgent I need to discuss with you.'

They sat awkwardly for a long time, Waris and Rehmat, in Rehmat's courtyard later that night, Rehmat shuffling his feet,

with his eyes on the ground. His daughter-in-law appeared
after a little while with a tumbler of water and handed it to
Waris. 'Bless you, daughter,' said Rehmat, his hand in the air
in blessing, as she handed the tumbler and disappeared. Waris
didn't look up at her and neither did she look at him.

'Babaji, is something wrong?' asked Waris. 'You haven't
said much, since I have come.' His voice trembled a little. 'Can
I be of any assistance to you?'

'Mian Waris, we have been blessed by your presence in our
village. You've brought much pride to Malka Hans. All over
Punjab, folks are taking your name and calling you Waris of
Malka Hans. There could not be greater pride for us. We are so
blessed that you are here, among us.'

An uncomfortable, embarrassed look appeared on Waris's
face. 'Babaji, it is God's blessings that are over all of us. What is
the status of a lowly fakir like me, in front of His grandeur? But
I thank you immensely for your kind words. Malka Hans is my
heaven.' Waris looked at Rehmat pleadingly. 'I can't begin to
tell you what the village means to me. I am more at home here
than I have ever been anywhere else. It is closer to my heart
than Jandiala, the village of my birth, the home of my ancestors.'
Waris's eyes searched Rehmat's eyes to see if his words had any
impact on him.

'Kinder words have never been spoken about our village,
Mian Waris, and be assured that everyone in Malka Hans,
including myself, is grateful to you for deciding to live among us.
But I am afraid I have to be the bearer of bad news.' Rehmat's
tone changed to a sombre one. Waris's heart dropped. Of course,
there was bad news. There always is.

'What I am about to tell you is not my personal decision
and I hope you know that I protested as much as I could against
this decision that has been forced upon me. These aren't my

words, or my sentiments, that I am about to express to you. I have been told to convey to you that you should leave the village. The message has come directly from our jagirdar, Diwan Ghulam Baksh.'

'But why, Babaji?' blurted out Waris.

'Mian Waris, you are asking me a question for which I don't have a clear answer,' said Rehmat. 'You know the diwan doesn't consider people like you and me worthy of any explanations. It is his village, his kingdom, and we are subject to his whim. We are just meant to listen and follow commands.'

'But Babaji, you must have discerned some reason for this command.' Panic appeared in Waris's voice, as if finding the reason for this command would somehow help him change the decision.

'Waris, my puttar, I think it has to do with your growing popularity and influence. Dozens of people flock to you all the time. Hundreds listen to your words, to your opinions every night, and several more hear of them through your listeners. Do you think any jagirdar will tolerate that kind of influence for any individual but himself in his jagir?'

Nothing more was said.

Rehmat and Waris sat quietly opposite each other, with their heads bent, eyes on the ground, Rehmat finding it hard to speak after what he had said, while Waris dealt with the turmoil in his head—where should I go now? Is there any place in Punjab safe for me? Does Jandiala still exist? Are my brothers still alive? What about Kasur? What about Maulvi Ghulam Murtaza? Is permanent exile the fate of all his students? But why should I go? I should resist. I should stay put. But how can I fight the jagirdar? How can I stay at Malka Hans if he doesn't want me to stay? What about Saraswati?

How do I tell her what evil has befallen me? Can I take her with me? But would that be right? Would it be fair to expect her and Chotu to share my experience of homelessness, my exile? Why would she want to leave?

They met early in the morning, a couple of days later, next to the well, before the first signs of dawn ripped through the dark canvas of the night. Waris had sent a message through Chotu who had relayed it to his mother. It had been over a couple of years since they had talked directly. The message surprised her. She knew there was bad news. There always is.

She appeared, before the morning azaan, with a pot in her hand. 'Oh Bhagbhari, I have been asked to leave,' cried Waris, as soon as she appeared. 'I will have to leave the village.' Saraswati looked at Waris stunned, words failing her, her eyes scanning his face for an explanation.

'You are the first person I have told,' continued Waris. 'But I can't leave you. I can't bear the thought of not seeing you, of not speaking to you.' Even though they hadn't spoken in such a long time, Waris knew that there was a possibility and that was enough for him. Waris choked as he finished his sentence, while tears began to well up in Saraswati's eyes. She placed the pot on the ground and held Waris's hands. The first time they ever had.

'Oh Waris, you have appeared as a renewal of life for me. How will I go on living without you?' she said, acknowledging the relationship in words to Waris and herself. Now that it had been acknowledged, it also had to be acknowledged that it was on the brink of ending, an abrupt end to a relationship that had only begun.

'Come with me,' he said, desperately.

'Where?'

'I don't know, maybe Kasur or Jandiala. But come with me. Chotu and you.'

She was silent for a while, her eyes on the ground, his hands still in hers. And then she spoke. 'Oh Waris, I would want nothing more in life but to be in your presence for the rest of my days, but how can that be? How can I abandon everything and leave with you? What will people say about me? My Chotu will never be able to return to his ancestral village. I have no reason to hold on to it, but I cannot take Chotu's kin from him, his heritage, his lineage.' Warm tears from Saraswati's eyes fell on Waris's hands. 'And I cannot bear the thought of leaving him behind.'

'That's the last thing I would want. I will never be the reason a child is separated from . . .'

Waris felt a heavy rock on his chest. He felt his heart being pulled in two different directions. A numbing sound began to appear in his ears, as a darkness spread in front of his eyes, a darkness that he was all too familiar with, a darkness that hadn't raised its head in a long time. Saraswati noticed Waris sniffling but his eyes remained dry, the spark in them that she would often notice now behind a darkness. She gripped his hands stronger, afraid to let go. They stood like that for several minutes, unafraid, if only briefly, of their relationship being discovered.

The sound of the azaan rose from the minaret of the mosque. Saraswati left his hands, picked up the pot and began collecting water from the well. Waris stood there as she filled her pot and began to walk away, without saying goodbye, not knowing what to say. She turned around after a few steps, her eyes and nose red, a shadow of pain across her face. Their eyes met, one last time, before she headed back. Waris continued standing there, as the azaan finished.

In the mosque, devotees gathered in straight lines, preparing to offer namaz. Waris had never missed fajr since his childhood. This would be the first time.

I cannot be bought or sold. Or so the story goes. I am exchanged, quantified and traded as a commodity. I am owned, possessed, like the vast acres of land that the Sials control. I am sometimes situated in a location, a physical space, and even a human body. Like a parasite, I grow within it, so that the body's entire existence is on my account. I am displayed as a sign of pride, worn on the top of a head, a pagri. I am protected and hidden, from the eyes of others, wrapped in a chaddar and tucked away. If not well guarded, I can be lost in a moment, hard to regain. I am honour. *Ghairat, izzat,* as you might say.

But how can honour be parasitic? Isn't honour a matter of pride, the highest human attribute, the highest accolade a person aspires to? All of that is true. But as has been the theme for much of this novel, this qissa, everything here appears in pairs. These pairs can appear in human forms, as lovers, but also in dualities, contrasting qualities. Mind you, this is not the world of Manichaeism's dualism, a never-ending battle between evil and good, light and darkness, but rather the Sufi concept of dualism, which isn't dualism at all, but rather monism, where night lives with day, east with west, and evil with good. Here these aren't contesting attributes, but rather an extension of each other.

In my various hues, various incarnations, I am the central character of the final stage of this story. So without further ado, let me take you to the story and the characters. Let me take you to Ranganpur, where Heer, Ranjha and Sahiti are standing outside the hut that had been reserved for the jogi and Heer. It

is well before morning. A few fading stars are the only witness
to their escape. As jogans, Heer and Sahiti are standing around
Ranjha, as gopis around Krishna, as Sita around Ram, as Parvati
around Shiva, as Zulekha around Yousuf, as Luna around
Rasalu. Ranjha, true to his divine nature, recites a few magic
spells under his breath and out of thin air appears Murad on a
white camel, his eyes wide open in bewilderment. The camel,
more surprised than the rider, begins to cry. Murad's eyes fall
upon Sahiti, and he jumps off to give her a hug.

'I don't know how I got here,' he says, looking at Sahiti,
while still holding her in his arms. 'I was riding with my caravan
in the deserts of Thar, trying to cover as much distance as possible
in the night's embrace, guided by the stars, when I blinked and
the next thing I know, I was here.'

'This powerful jogi brought you here,' says Sahiti. 'He has
brought you here to unite you and me.' Murad looks at Ranjha
and acknowledges him with a slight bow of his head, joining
together the palms of his hands. Ranjha raises both of his hands
to bless the couple. In this way, the first couple takes off, heading
in the direction of Thar, on Murad's camel, Sahiti sitting behind
the rider, her arms around him, her face resting on his back,
with Murad guiding the camel expertly. Ranjha and Heer, hand
in hand, too set off, on foot, in a different direction, towards
their destiny, the fate that is waiting for them.

In the morning when their escape is discovered, the Kheras
form two parties to track down both the girls. These are two
parallel scenes, so let me take you first to the party that is chasing
Murad and Sahiti. They eventually catch up with the fugitive
couple, but by the time they do, the Baloch rider is already united
with his caravan, a caravan of countless camels, and numerous
men, all brave and strong, with their swords dangling by their
sides. What chance do the Kheras have against the might of

the Baloch? There is a small battle, an excuse for one, and the Kheras are easily defeated. Sahiti has now become their bride and the Baloch know how to protect their honour. The Kheras return to Ranganpur, wounded and humiliated, without Sahiti, with their honour scattered on the desert sands of the Thar.

You might have a few questions here. How did Murad and Sahiti catch up with their caravan so quickly? How did the Kheras know where to go? The Thar is, after all, a massive desert, and only one familiar with the landscape would know how to search for routes. If you are one of those sceptical readers, then might I suggest, as politely as I possibly can, and with utmost respect, that you've missed the central essence of the story—its magical rationality, its circular chronology. The questions you ask are valid but not necessarily suited for the kind of narrative I am trying to construct here. My apologies, not I, the writer Haroon, but I, the fictional character of Waris (who of course is an extension of the writer Haroon). This is a different model of storytelling where the linearity of the story is a peripheral aspect of the qissa.

Now that we have resolved that, let us move to the other parallel scene that unfolds at the same time as the one at Thar.

Our second couple is not as lucky. How can they be? Has anything ever been easy for them? Our Ranjha does not have his kinship to fall back on, as you know. He is not a warrior, he never was. If that had been the case, wouldn't he have fought his brothers for his rights? Wouldn't he have fought the Sials for Heer? Wouldn't he have confronted the Kheras, instead of escaping with Heer in the dead of the night? No, he is not a warrior. Like Waris, who can only sing, he can only tell the tales of his woes through his flute. He has been cast in a different mould. He is a symbol of a different kind of masculinity.

So, when the Kheras are eventually able to catch up with him, he can only plead for help as they take Heer back. It is a pitiful scene. Heer being dragged by the Kheras, resisting furiously, shouting and screaming, her hair dishevelled, her arms and legs flying all over. Ranjha is lying on the ground, bruised, lying on the ground helplessly, pleading. A true plea for help, a true call for justice, from the mouth of a jogi is heard by the King of Justice, Adl. It so happens that this entire scene is unfolding in his kingdom. His entire kingdom reverberates with this plea for help, as the animals quiver and all the subjects are shaken out of slumber. The King of Justice responds to this powerful plea. He orders his soldiers to bring him the source of this plea. Thus, Ranjha is presented to his court. 'Bandits have taken away my wife,' he said to the king, 'And that too in your kingdom, you who are a symbol of justice, like Akbar was before you and Vikramaditya before him.'

With his legacy questioned, the king ordered, 'Bring me the Kheras and Heer, this man's wife, as he claims.' His command was implemented immediately. His soldiers caught up with the party and forced them to turn around to return to the court of the King of Justice. Once everyone was in his presence, the King ordered his qazi to hear the case and pass the right decision. The Kheras presented their case passionately. They told the qazi about how they took a baraat to Jhang, the greatest baraat the world had ever seen. They recalled how there was a qazi who oversaw the marriage and there were two witnesses who saw the proceedings. They recalled how Heer was brought back to Ranganpur and presented to the entire town as their bride. There was absolutely no doubt that Heer was lawfully wedded to Saida, they argued.

Our Ranjha, of course, had no such witnesses. Could he summon the forest? Would the Chenab present its testimony for him? Could he ask the buffaloes to speak in his favour in front of the qazi? All he could manage to say was, 'Heer and I are lawfully married with the divine as our witness.'

This was a straightforward case as far as the qazi was concerned. So he did what qazis often do. 'All the rituals of marriage were properly followed and Heer is lawfully wedded to Saida,' he pronounced. 'She is his wife, his honour, and it is his right to claim property over her.' A man of books, a qazi, is incapable of reading the truth in the hearts of lovers. What significance do these rituals, these laws, have in matters of love?

As Heer is being taken away again, Ranjha lets out a wail, a true wail, a powerful wail that threatens to destroy the world like the trumpet of angel Israfil. The world comes to a screeching halt, stopped in its tracks, as if by the tandava of Shiva. There is only one sound that resonates throughout the court of the king, throughout his kingdom, throughout the world, as if it is the eternal sound, the only sound—Ranjha's wail! 'Let ruin fall upon this town. May all its humans perish in the fire of righteousness. May the only living creatures that survive this ordeal be the cattle.'

A fire descends from the sky and runs like a bull on heat through the kingdom. All the houses, the citizens, and farms are on the verge of destruction. It is as if divine wrath is falling upon the kingdom of Ramesses. Every creature of the kingdom turns its face towards the King, searching for answers, asking what injustice the king, a king whose name was Justice, has performed for this wrath to fall upon them. With his very survival and that of his subjects threatened, the King of Justice looks at Ranjha and understands his mistake, understands the travesty that has been committed on his watch. He understands that this is God testifying about the sacred bond that exists between Heer and Ranjha. For they may not be married in the court of law, but they are married nonetheless.

Before much damage can be wrought, the King of Justice orders his soldiers to chase the Kheras and bring back Heer, to be reunited with her lawful husband, her Ranjha. The soldiers do as ordered. The Kheras protest, give references to all legal laws but the king doesn't listen any more. His eyes have been opened by divine wrath. When Heer is united with Ranjha once again, the fire at the kingdom of the King of Justice, Adl, ends immediately. Justice has finally prevailed.

United once again, the unfortunate couple heads towards Jhang. I am not sure what drew them to that land. What were they expecting? Did they believe they had outmanoeuvred their fate? Were they delusional to think that the Sials would welcome them as husband and bride? Did they think that the Kheras were the only force keeping them apart? Unaware of the destiny that awaited them, they walked to the outskirts of the town.

'Look there,' said Heer, pointing towards the banks of the Chenab. 'That was where I first laid my eyes on you and was smitten.'

'And there is the forest, where we met every day. Where our love blossomed, away from the rules, regulations and restrictions of society. Where you brought me churi and fed me with your own hands,' said Ranjha.

'Ah yes. And there is that spot, where I caught up with Kaido and beat him up, when he threatened to tell the world about our secret,' said Heer. 'He cursed me and all our friends when we told the world about his real self. He threatened to seek revenge, that lame idiot, threatened to show me. Let him try. Let him try to lay his hands on me or you. I will show him. I will show him. I will break his legs and beat him with them. Let him try.'

'And there is that place where you broke your pearl necklace and I entered your palanquin. Oh, you saved me that day as well, from the vengeance of the Kheras.'

With their arms around each other, the couple walked in the memories of their youth, when the shepherds of Jhang spotted them. They approached them immediately. 'Welcome back to Jhang. Welcome to your home,' they said. 'The entire town has heard about how you rubbed mud on the faces of the Kheras and escaped. The Sials have been convinced about the veracity of your love. They want to welcome you. They want to marry you with all the pomp that a wedding between Chuchak's daughter and Mauja's son deserves. Come with us. They are waiting for you, prepared, ready to welcome you.' Thus, in this way, Heer and Ranjha were lured into Jhang.

They walked through the gate of the town, welcomed as a triumphant army, as the forces of Nadir Shah in Delhi. Standing atop the tall walls of Jhang, its residents showered flower petals upon the couple. Rose water was sprinkled over them to bless their arrival. Garlands were placed around their necks as they were taken by the hand and brought to the house of Chuchak.

Here the entire family was standing at the gate. Maliki rushed towards her daughter, wrapped herself around her, her eyes red with tears. Chuchak walked towards Ranjha and embraced him. Standing behind them was Sultan, Heer's brother, a broad smile across his face with Kaido next to him. He limped towards the couple with the support of his stick and placed his hands on their heads. 'May you be blessed for the rest of your lives,' he said. Heer felt annoyed at his blessing and shook her head in disgust. Kaido noticed but didn't respond, a smile pasted on his face.

With Chuchak's arm around Ranjha and Maliki's around her daughter, the couple was taken into the house. Here a special cot had been prepared for them with a clean white chaddar and fluffy pillows. 'Please sit here,' said Chuchak. The entire town had gathered in the vast courtyard to welcome Heer and Ranjha. It was a festive atmosphere, as if this was a wedding party. The women of the town had worn their newest clothes and were showing off their jewellery, while the men arrived with trimmed moustaches and beards. Servants of the Sial household distributed food and drinks to the guests. They all stood facing the couple, who sat at the centre of the courtyard. Heer and Ranjha were still in a daze, words failing them. The shepherds, it seems, were telling the truth. The Sials had truly changed.

'Oh, my daughter, how my eyes have yearned to see the sight of your face,' said Maliki. This was the first time she was seeing Heer after she had been married off to the Kheras. 'Now they can rest again. They lost sleep the day you left this house.'

'My daughter, my dearest daughter,' continued Maliki, with a seriousness in her tone. 'I know I am not worthy but please forgive me for what I have done.' Maliki couldn't look her daughter in the eye. 'We had been blinded by the majesty of the Khera name. We threw our precious daughter in front of swine. I know I am not worthy of forgiveness but please forgive me.' Maliki had her hands joined in front of Heer. She broke down as she finished the sentence. Tears welled up in the eyes of every onlooker, tears of remorse, tears of shame, for they were all participants in what had happened to Heer. They might not have been witness to the events that transpired behind closed doors that day, when the Maulvi got Heer's consent to this marriage, but they all knew. They were all culprits.

'Oh, mother, please don't embarrass me this way,' said Heer, with a tremor in her voice. Her mother had never expressed her love in this manner. Heer had craved this love all her life, and here it was in front of her. If only this love had surfaced earlier, how different would have been her fate. She felt sorry for her mother, but also angry, angry that it took so long. 'Do mothers ever ask for forgiveness?' said Heer. She stood next to her mother, tall and proud, as her mother seemed to shrink. Heer took her in her arms and engulfed her. She absorbed all

her embarrassment, all her guilt. She cried with her mother.
Cried for her. Cried for herself.

'My sweetest daughter,' said Chuchak. Tears now also
appeared in his eyes as his voice shook. 'Oh, my sweetest
daughter, how we wronged you.' His voice broke the more
he spoke. 'We heard how the Kheras treated you.' He couldn't
speak any longer. He had to pause to compose himself. He
could not let the entire town watch him cry. And then when he
swallowed his emotions, he said, 'You did not deserve that fool.
You did not deserve that fate. I am grateful to this jogi who has
rescued you and brought you here. How will I ever repay him?'
His voice was cracking again. 'Dhido, my son. We were wrong
to treat you the way we did. Our eyes had been shut by conceit.
We gave our daughter, our honour, to demons, when an angel
was present in our own house. Please forgive us for our mistakes
and accept us now, as your humble servants.'

Chuchak broke down, unlike he had ever done before,
unlike any other man had ever done in Jhang. He was weeping,
loudly, his shoulders slouched, his hands in front of him,
tears wetting his neatly ironed shirt. Ranjha could not take it
any more. He didn't see Chuchak in front of him but Mauja
Chaudary. Could he not forgive the sins of his father? Ranjha
embraced Chuchak in his arms and cried with him. Sounds of
loud wails now came from the guests. The wedding party had
been transformed into one of mourning and atonement.

'Oh, dear father, why do you embarrass me?' said Ranjha,
when some of his tears had receded and he could manage to
speak. 'I was an orphan, but you took me in. You welcomed
me as a son, fed me for twelve long years. How can I ever repay
what you've done?'

'My beloved father,' said Heer, her condition worsened,
her height no longer tall, her demeanour no longer proud. She

needed to be protected, protected from these emotions that took her father away from her and presented instead another man, a man she did not know, didn't want to know. She moved towards him and placed her head on his chest. 'Thank you for accepting us and taking us back. Today you've corrected all your wrongdoings.' Somehow, she managed to speak through all the tears. 'Today you've been forgiven all your sins. All my life you have been like a banyan tree, whose shade was temporarily removed when I was wed to the Kheras. Today I have rediscovered my shade. I have rediscovered my tree. This is the happiest day of my life.'

Chuchak broke down once again.

'Come now, my brother,' said Sultan to Ranjha after a little while, when it was safe to exchange a few words without crying. 'I have prepared a new set of clothes for you. The village barber will wash you, cut your hair and your beard. Come, prepare to become the groom of this house.' Ranjha was taken into a separate room, where he was washed and his beard and hair cut. He wore new clothes, and applied attar to his neck and wrists. He appeared transformed. The atmosphere in the courtyard changed once again. It was a wedding party once more. There were sounds of laughter, a joyous laughter that emerges after extreme sadness, carrying within itself its traces, laughter as the sun appearing after the onslaught of dark monsoon clouds, laughter like a rainbow across a humid sky.

Maliki appeared with a red chaddar with golden embroidery on it and placed it on Heer's head. She was now the bride once again, to be married to her beloved, lawfully this time, laws not made and imposed by humans, but eternal laws that were written by the divine, laws free of all corruption. Ranjha, the groom, sat next to her. Sweetmeats emerged from the Sial kitchen and were placed on a table in front of the couple. The father and the mother of the bride took a sweet and fed it to the couple. They were followed by other guests, only those that were married and had healthy children.

When everyone had completed the ritual, Chuchak sat next to his daughter. The clouds that had made way for the sun, for the rainbow, had reappeared once again. 'My dear daughter, please forgive me.' Chuchak spoke in the same shaky voice, his shoulders still bent, dark circles under his eyes which were glued to the ground. 'Please forgive me.'

The clouds now passed over to Heer as they covered her in their darkness. 'Father,' she said, scared, perhaps for the first time in her life. 'Father, what has got into you? I have already forgiven you. Look around. Look how happy everyone is.' She held the chin of her father, but he refused to look up. He melted with her touch, completely crumbled, folded into himself. 'Oh, dear father,' said Heer, as she took him in her arms and began to console him, as silent, uncontrollable tears poured from her eyes. Tears without sound for she didn't want her father to know.

'Please forgive me,' he kept on repeating.

'My dear son,' said Chuchak, as he finally lifted himself, cleaning his nose with the edge of his kameez, sniffling, his eyes swollen. 'My dear son, Heer is already yours. She is already wed to you, but we still have to follow the rules of the world.' Chuchak was beginning to compose himself. 'If we send her to Takht Hazara with you at this moment, then she will never get the honour she deserves. She will always be remembered as the girl who eloped and you will never be able to walk with your head held high. Your sisters-in-law, of whose atrocities you have already told me, will never treat her as an equal and she will always be ridiculed.' Ranjha nodded in affirmation, while Heer sat with her arms around Chuchak, patting his back, hearing but not really listening. 'Why don't you return to Takht Hazara and

come back with a baraat that our daughter deserves? Take her as
your wife in front of the entire world, so that no one can ever
again challenge the legality of your relationship.'

Maliki jumped into the conversation. 'Yes, yes, yes,' she
said. 'Yes. Go to Takht Hazara now and come back with a
massive baraat, a baraat more splendid than the one that was
brought by the Kheras. Then we will send our daughter with
you with honour. She will return with you to be the queen of
Takht Hazara.'

'Yes,' said Chuchak. 'Queen she deserves to be. Our
beloved daughter. Yes, go to Takht Hazara now and prepare for
her welcome. We'll take care of your Heer till then. She is yours
now. Your amanat to us.'

Eager to protect the honour of his bride and his own,
Ranjha decided to head back to Takht Hazara. He had still not
forgotten about the pain that his brothers and sisters-in-law had
caused him, but he was returning victorious. He had achieved
the challenge that had been set out for him. He was going to
marry the most beautiful woman in Punjab. He was going to
marry Heer. Yes, he would return to Takht Hazara to return
with the greatest baraat Punjab had ever seen. People would
forget all about Heer's previous baraat. His baraat would be
accompanied by dancers and musicians of all kinds. It would be
accompanied by all the birds, animals and beasts. It would have
an unending rain of coins for the beggars. This was not going to
be a wedding of two humans, but rather two divine beings. So
with these dreams of his baraat in his head, Ranjha headed off to
Takht Hazara with plans to return soon for his bride.

'My dear daughter,' said Maliki, as she approached her
daughter on the charpoy. 'Oh, how grateful I am now that you
are back. I prayed to God every day for this day. I promised
God that I would give up all my vices if he returned you to me

and here you are. Give your mother a hug before she loses you once again.' Tears from Maliki's eyes fell on Heer's back as the mother hugged the daughter, while Heer still held her father in her arms. Sultan too appeared from behind the crowd and put his head on the lap of his sister.

'My dear sister,' was all he could manage to say. Heer was now consoling all her family members, convincing them in vain that this was a happy occasion.

They were all in that position, Heer wiping the tears of her father, mother and brother, when Kaido arrived with a tumbler in his hand, sweat dripping down its body, the same smile that Heer had noticed at the threshold of her house pasted on his face. 'Here my child,' he said, passing the tumbler to Heer. Heer looked at her uncle suspiciously.

'Oh yes, I completely forgot,' said Maliki as she got up and took the tumbler from Kaido. 'I prepared this drink specially for you, to mark your arrival, and to also mark your departure which is going to happen soon.' She tried handing the drink to Heer, but she still wouldn't take it. 'Remember how as a child you loved this drink—milk with almond and honey.' Maliki laughed lightly as she said, 'As a child, you could survive on this for days. You would refuse to eat anything and only demand this drink. We eventually had to stop giving it to you. Here now, take this drink. You can have it as much as you want.' Heer turned her eyes away from her mother and the glass in her hand and looked at her father, who was still in her arms, his body ready to melt once more if Heer didn't hold him.

'Have the drink, my child,' he said, calmly. 'Your mother has prepared it especially for you. Have it, my child.' With her eyes still on her father, she took the glass from her mother and gulped down the drink, eager to finish it, eager to put an end to this conversation, eager to return to taking care of her father.

'Forgive me, my daughter. Forgive me,' said Chuchak, as he crumbled again. 'Pray for the forgiveness of your parents. Vouch for us in God's court. We know that we broke the law but tell Him that it had to be done. It had to be done. It had to be done, Heer. It had to be done.' Words were now coming as laments from Chuchak's mouth. 'Tell Him that we loved you, that we let no harm befall you. That we protected you. Did this for you. It had to be . . . Heer!'

'My father, why do you keep . . .' Heer felt a constraint in her throat. Nothing seemed to pass through it—no more words of pardon or consolation or even . . . oxygen! She pulled her hands back from her father and held her throat, trying to push past the lump, her eyes widening, popping out of their sockets. 'I can't . . . I can't . . .' was all she could manage to say, her voice appearing as a whisper from the depths of a deep cave. Sultan still lay on her lap. Chuchak, unsupported by Heer's arms, completely crumbled, as if he had no backbone to support him.

'Forgive us. Forgive us!' he kept repeating.

Maliki held her daughter in her arms, wiping away the sweat that was now appearing on her forehead with her dupatta, gently rocking her body. 'We had no choice. You left us no choice, Heer. I know you understand. I know you understand.' She spoke calmly as if she was putting a child to sleep, as if she were singing a lullaby. 'You left us no choice, Heer. I know you understand.' Heer tried speaking, perhaps to tell her mother that she understood, or to disagree, maybe to tell her father that she would vouch for them in divine court, or maybe to curse him for all eternity. But she couldn't speak. No words left her throat. Soon all oxygen also escaped.

Heer died in the arms of her family, in the arms of her loved ones, poisoned by those who had vowed to protect her, in front of hundreds of witnesses, guests who had come to celebrate this wedding, guests who would now be a part of this funeral as witnesses and participants. This was not Jhang, they were not guests. These were residents of Lahore and they had just witnessed and participated in the execution of Bhai Mani Singh.

With her death, I was born again in the house of the Sials, honour, ghairat, izzat, whatever you may choose to call me. Heer had taken me away, stolen me and eventually killed me, but now the Sials had resurrected me. I was once again the crown on their head. Chuchak could now once again walk proudly among his kin. The entire town was a witness to what he had to do to win me back. The entire town was a participant.

Heer's body was still lying in the courtyard of her father's house, when a messenger was sent to Takht Hazara. 'Don't bring the baraat any more,' the messenger said to Ranjha. 'Heer is no more. You must remember how she always remained sick. Well, that sickness has now claimed its victim. She passed away two nights ago, not long after you left, and the Sials have already buried their beloved daughter.'

Hearing the news, life slipped away from Ranjha's body. He died that very instant.

Epilogue

O Waris, why did you have to turn the qissa into a tragedy? Why couldn't you, like poets before you, unite the lovers, either in this world or the next? You could have sent them to Makkah, as Damodar did, where they lived happily ever after in an eternal life. Why did you have to show the brutal, ugly face of reality? Why did you ask us to suspend our disbelief, when this is how you were planning to repay our trust?

O Waris, you were the creator of this world. You could have taken us wherever you wanted. You made divinity intercede on behalf of the lovers, you made jogis and pirs pray for them, but then you rendered them so helpless? O Waris, what tragedy chased you to the pages of this book, a tragedy that even Ranjha's flute or Heer's beauty could not fix?

How else could the story have ended? How else is forbidden love treated in our land? Is this not the fate of women, of those who are brave enough to rebel? Yes, it is a true story, truer than its characters and its plot. This is a primordial tale, the unfortunate way of the world. How many Heers have been sacrificed on the altar of honour since the beginning of time? How many more will meet with the same fate? How many Heers have died in the arms of their families since I penned this story? This is not the story of one Heer, but of countless Heers. She is not one person, one character, but all of these women.

You ask me why I couldn't reunite Heer and Ranjha in the afterlife but why would I do that? Has anyone ever seen heaven? Has anyone ever come back to describe hell? Can we even say with certainty that they exist? Why should I speak of something of which I have no experience? If Heer and Ranjha were destined for heaven, they would have discovered it on this earth. They would have experienced eternity in their short lifespan. They would have found eternal bliss. Heaven is an easy escape, of which we'll talk about some other day. Let us right now focus on this moment, this world, these rules and these norms. What good would have come from uniting the lovers in heaven when their love was not good enough for this world?

Acknowledgements

This book could have not been completed without the help, support and feedback of my spouse, my partner in crime, Anam Zakaria. It was to Anam I turned every time I was happy or unsure about something I had written. On our daily walks during the COVID-19 lockdowns, I would read to her and she would tell me what was working and what needed more fleshing out. Anam, of course, is a fantastic and acclaimed author and a mentor to young writers. She is the kindest of critics, the best there is, and understands how to provide feedback to a writer, without breaking their soul.

Anam is also a counsellor and has a deep understanding of human psychology. I know that I understand myself much better and have been able to handle some of my mental health challenges due to her insight and support. Her insight was pivotal to understanding some of the psychological themes I wanted to explore through the characters in this book. More importantly, being married and living with Anam for almost a decade has provided me with gender sensitivity, which is such an integral component of this book. Sahiti's character, her discourse with the jogi, would not have been possible without that crucial understanding of gender relations, gender violence, emotional work undertaken by women, double burden and triple shift. Thank you, Anam, for your patience and for providing me the space to grow. I am a better person because of you.

During the course of this book, Anam and I were blessed with a beautiful daughter, Lina, who is our world. Thank you, Lina, for giving us the greatest pleasure in life!

I was an educator and teacher for eight years, having taught multiple subjects such as history, sociology, philosophy to hundreds of students across several institutions. These brilliant students, whom I have had the privilege to teach, have expanded my understanding of these subjects. It is these experiences, these shared moments in classrooms with my students, that I was able to tap into for many parts of the book. I have immensely enjoyed the process of teaching and love my students who have given me such amazing memories and helped me in my intellectual growth. I want to thank all my students, including Mohsin, Ezza, Hamza, Manaal, Alizeh, Aliza, Imaan, Huda, Ali Humza, Zainab, Ali Samoo, Salma, Arbaz and many more. This list is not exhaustive, not even close.

Iqbal Qaiser, my eternal guru, my murshad, my teacher, has had an incredible influence on my life, my world view and my writing. Thank you, Iqbal sahib, for opening the world of Punjab for me, for introducing me to Waris Shah's Heer, for travelling the length and breadth of Punjab with me, and allowing me to see it, feel it, through your perspective.

My parents, Nyla Khalid and Khalid Manzoor, are my anchor. My day doesn't begin until I have spoken to them. They are my strength and I know I have their unconditional love and support. Thank you. My sisters, Nida and Sana, and all my beautiful nieces and nephews, the joy of my life. My parents-in-law, Eraj Zakaria and Neelofur Zakaria for their kindness, their pride and their love. My aunts and uncles who have always encouraged me and highlighted my work on every platform—Javed Manzoor, Lubna Javed, Tahir Manzoor and Robeena Tahir. Robeena Tahir was also my English language teacher and I often find myself back in her classroom, beginning to love the process of creative writing. I would also like to thank my aunt Tehmeena Malik, who was also my English teacher for many years. Her guidance forms the foundation of my writing.

I would like to thank all scholars working on Punjab's history, literature, religion, etc. whose work has been immensely helpful in understanding the world of Waris Shah and *Heer–Ranjha*. I am particularly grateful to Ishwar Dayal Gaur, whose book *Society, Religion and Patriarchy: Exploring Medieval Punjab through Hir Waris* was pivotal to my research. I would also recommend his book *Martyr as Bridegroom: A Folk Representation of Bhagat Singh*, a wonderful work of scholarship that explores 'folk' in the context of Punjab. Ishwarji was also incredibly supportive in a personal capacity, agreeing to talk to me over the phone about Waris Shah and Punjabi Sufi poetry. He also shared with me his paper, *Forgotten Makers of Panjab: Discovering Indigenous Paradigm of History*, which helped me understand the significance of using folk literature as a framework for understanding history.

A History of Punjabi Literature by Mohan Singh is an incredible resource to understand the evolution of Punjabi literature and so is *A History of Punjabi Literature* by Sant Singh Sekhon and Kartar Singh Duggal. Sant Singh Sekhon's translation of *Hir–Ranjha,* in addition to Charles Frederick Usborne's translation of this love legend, made the qissa accessible to an unfortunate Punjabi like me, whose ancestral language was robbed from him by the violence of colonialism. *Waris Shah: Zindagi aur Zamana* by Sharif Kunjahi, Sajjad Haider and Muhammad Asif Khan was also a great resource to learn about Waris Shah's life and his time. *Punjab: A History from Aurangzeb to Mountbatten* by Rajmohan Gandhi was extremely helpful to understand the political context of Waris Shah.

A few other scholars whose papers and works have informed my understanding of Punjab, spirituality and the qissa literary tradition are Nosheen Ali, Tanvir Anjum, Jürgen Wasim Frembgen, Ranajit Guha, M. Irfan Habib, Tahir Kamran, Akshaya Kumar, Farina Mir, Anne Murphy, Nikky-Guninder Kaur Singh, R.C. Temple and Romila Thapar. Any interested reader should explore the amazing work of these incredible scholars.

One remarkable thing to emerge out of the COVID-19 lockdown was a profusion of online seminars, talks and webinars. One such platform was the Lyallpur Young Historians Club, run by historians Tohid Ahmad Chatta and Khola Cheema. The platform invited a wide range of scholars, writers and academics working on Punjab. Lyallpur Young Historians Club has hosted many fascinating talks but the talks that were most useful to me for the course of this book were *History, Memory & Practice of Nathpanth in Punjab* by Yogesh Snehi and *Deconstructing Punjabi Sufi Poetry* by Zubair Ahmad. I would highly recommend visiting and subscribing to Lyallpur Young Historians Club's YouTube page to everyone with a scholarly interest in Punjab. A couple of other online talks that I found extremely useful were *Understanding Heer Kahani and Waris Shah: Dr Manzur Ejaz with Wajid Ali Syed* and *3 Heeran, 3 Ranjhey, 1 Qissa: Dr Manzur Ejaz with Wajid Ali Syed*, hosted by Wichaar webcast.

I would like to thank my literary agent, Kanishka Gupta. Kanishka and I have been working together for almost a decade now. He signed my first book, a few hours after I sent him a proposal. This happened when there was stark silence from all the other agencies and publishers I was reaching out to. Along with being my agent, Kanishka is also a dear friend and I am so glad to have him in my life.

Karthik Venkatesh, the editor of this book, is also the first editor I worked with. I was also lucky to have him as editor for *Walking with Nanak*. Even when I was in the research and conceptual stages of this book, I was clear that Karthik was the only person I want to work with for this project. I know that he feels as passionately about Waris Shah and Punjab, as I do, and I knew that this work could be trusted in his hands. Karthik has a scholarly interest in contemporary and historical Punjab and there couldn't be a better person for this job.

I would like to thank my publisher, Milee Ashwarya, and Penguin Random House India. I am absolutely thrilled that four of my books have found a home at Penguin Random House India, and I am extremely grateful for this opportunity.

Scan QR code to access the
Penguin Random House India website